Mysteries

To Xenia 19.11.93.
From Gran + Aunt Jean

Stories by Enid Blyton
The Rockingdown Mystery
The Rilloby Fair Mystery
The Ring O'Bells Mystery
The Rubadub Mystery
The Rat-A-Tat Mystery
The Ragamuffin Mystery
The Secret Island
The Secret of Spiggy Holes
The Secret Mountain
The Secret of Killimooin
The Secret of Moon Castle
Mystery Stories
Adventure Stories
The Mystery That Never Was
The Treasure Hunters
The Boy Next Door
The Children at Green Meadows
More Adventures on Willow Farm
Shadow the Sheepdog
Six Cousins at Mistletoe Farm
Six Cousins Again

Enid Blyton

The Rat-A-Tat Mystery
The Ragamuffin Mystery

MULBERRY EDITIONS

This edition published exclusively for Mulberry Editions
by HarperCollins Children's Books 1992

A division of HarperCollins Publishers Ltd,
77–85 Fulham Palace Road, Hammersmith,
London W6 8JB

Printed in England by Clays Ltd, St Ives plc

Contents

The Rat-A-Tat Mystery   7

The Ragamuffin Mystery   161

The Rat-A-Tat Mystery

First published in a single volume in hardback in 1951 by
William Collins Sons & Co Ltd.
First published in paperback in 1970 in Armada

Chapter One

Christmas Holidays

'How long do these Christmas holidays last?' said Mr Lynton, putting his newspaper down as a loud crash came from upstairs. 'I sometimes think I'm living in a madhouse – what *are* those children doing upstairs? Are they practising high jumps or something?'

'I expect it's Snubby as usual,' said Mrs Lynton. 'He's supposed to be making his bed. Oh, dear – there he goes again!'

She went to the door and called up the stairs. 'Snubby – what in the world are you doing? You are making your uncle very angry.'

'Oh – sorry!' shouted back Snubby. 'I was only moving things round a bit – and the dressing table fell over. I forgot you were underneath. Hey, look out – Loony's coming down the stairs, and he's a bit mad this morning.'

A black spaniel came hurtling down the stairs at top speed and Mrs Lynton hurriedly got out of the way. Loony slid all the way along the hall and in at the sitting-room door almost to Mr Lynton's feet. He was most surprised to receive a smart slap on the head from Mr Lynton's folded newspaper. He shot out of the door almost as fast as he had come in.

'What a house!' groaned Mr Lynton, as his wife came back. 'As soon as Snubby arrives peace and quiet vanish. He makes Diana and Roger three times as bad, too – as for that dog Loony, he's even more of a lunatic than usual.'

9

'Never mind, dear – after all, Christmas only comes once a year,' said Mrs Lynton. 'And poor old Snubby must have *some*where to go in the holidays – you forget he has no father or mother.'

'Well, I wish he wasn't my nephew,' said Mr Lynton. 'And WHY must we have his dog Loony every time we have Snubby?'

'Oh, Richard – you know Snubby wouldn't come here if we didn't have Loony – he *adores* Loony,' said his wife.

'Ha!' said Mr Lynton, opening his newspaper again. 'So Snubby won't go anywhere without Loony – well, tell him next holidays we won't have that dog here – then perhaps Snubby won't inflict himself on us!'

'Oh, you don't really mean that, dear,' said Mrs Lynton. 'Snubby just gets on your nerves when you're home for a few days. You'll be back at the office soon.'

Upstairs Snubby was sitting on his unmade bed, talking to his cousins, Diana and Roger, and fondling Loony's long silky ears. They had come to see what the terrific crashes were.

'You'll get into a row with Dad,' said Roger. 'You never *will* remember that your room is over the sitting-room. Whatever do you want to go and lug the furniture about for?'

'Well, I didn't really *mean* to move it,' said Snubby. 'But a sixpence went under the chest of drawers, and when I moved it out I thought it would look better where the dressing table is, but the beastly thing went over with a crash.'

'You're going to get a whacking from Dad pretty soon,' said Diana. 'I heard him say you were working up for one. You really are an ass, Snubby. Dad goes back to the office soon. Why can't you behave till then?'

'I *do* behave!' said Snubby indignantly. 'Anyway, who

spilt the coffee all over the breakfast table this morning? Not me!'

Roger and Diana stared at their red haired freckle-faced cousin, and he stared back at them out of his green eyes. They were both fond of the irrepressible Snubby, but, really, he could be very irritating at times. Diana gave an impatient exclamation.

'Well, I don't wonder Dad gets tired of you, Snubby! You and Loony rush about the house like a hurricane – and WHY can't you teach Loony to stop taking shoes and brushes from people's bedrooms? Did you know he's taken Dad's clothes brush this morning? Goodness knows how he got it off the dressing table.'

'Oh, golly! Has he really?' said Snubby, getting off the bed in a hurry. 'There'll be another explosion from Uncle Richard when he discovers that. I'll go and find it.'

Christmas had been a mad and merry time in the Lyntons' house. All the children had come home from school in high spirits, looking forward to plenty of good food, presents and jollifications. Snubby had been a little subdued at first, because he was afraid that his school report might be even worse than usual, and his uncle and aunt had been pleasantly surprised to find him most polite and helpful.

But this wore off after a few days, and Snubby had now become his usual riotous, ridiculous self, aided in every way by his black spaniel, Loony. His uncle had quickly become very tired of him, especially since Snubby had forgotten to turn off the tap in the bathroom and flooded the floor. If it hadn't been Christmas time Snubby would certainly have got a first-class whacking!

All the same, everyone had enjoyed Christmas, though the children wished there had been snow.

'It doesn't *seem* like Christmas without snow,' complained Snubby.

'Oh, we'll get plenty as soon as Christmas is gone,' said Mrs Lynton. 'We always do. Then you can go out the whole day long, and snowball and toboggan and skate – and I shall be rid of you for a little while!'

But there had been no snow yet, only a drizzling rain that kept the children indoors for most of the time, much to Mr Lynton's annoyance. 'Why must they *always* talk at the tops of their voices?' he said, in exasperation. 'And is there any need to have the radio on so loudly? And will *someone* tell that dog Loony that if I fall over him again he can go and live out of doors in the shed?'

Bit it wasn't really any good telling Loony things like that. If he wanted to sit down and scratch himself, he *sat* down, no matter whether someone was coming along to trip over him or not. Even Snubby couldn't make him stop. Loony just looked up with his melting spaniel eyes, thumped his little tail, and then went on scratching.

'I don't know *why* you scratch!' said Snubby, in exasperation. 'Pretending you've got fleas! You know you haven't, Loony. Oh, get up, do!'

One rainy morning Diana was mooning about, getting in her busy mother's way. 'Oh, Diana, dear – *do* get something to do!' said Mrs Lynton. 'Have you done all your morning jobs – made your bed, dusted your room, done the – '

'Yes, Mother – *everything*,' said Diana. 'I really have. Do you want me to help you?'

'Well, will you take down all the Christmas cards?' said her mother. 'It's time they were down. Stack them neatly in a big cardboard box, so that we can send them to Aunt Lucy – she makes scrapbooks of them for children in hospital.'

'Right!' said Diana. 'Oh, there's Snubby with his mouth-organ. Mother, doesn't he play it well?'

'No, he doesn't,' said her mother. 'He makes a simply horrible noise with it. Let him do the cards with you, then perhaps he'll put it down and forget it. I really do believe your father will go mad if Snubby wanders round the house playing his mouth-organ.'

'Snubby, come and help with the Christmas cards,' called Diana. 'Look out, Mother – Loony's coming down the stairs.'

'Christmas cards? What do you mean?' said Snubby, coming into the room. 'Oh – take them down? Right oh! It's always fun to look at them again. Let's put all the funny ones into a pile.'

He and Diana were soon happily taking down the gay cards. They read each one and laughed at the funny ones, stacking them all neatly into a box.

'Oh, here's the one Barney sent us!' said Diana. 'Look – isn't it marvellous! Just like old Barney too.'

She held up a big card, on the front of which was a picture of a fair ground. Drawn neatly in one corner was a boy with a monkey on his shoulder.

'Barney's drawn himself and Miranda on the card,' said Diana. 'Snubby, I wonder how he enjoyed Christmas-time with his family for the very first time in his life!'

Roger came into the room just then, and took up Barney's card too. 'Good old Barney!' he said. 'I wish we could see him these hols. I say – wasn't it MARVELLOUS how he found his father – and discovered that he had a whole family of his own?'

'Yes,' said Diana, remembering. 'He spent all his life in a circus with his mother, and thought his father was dead. And when his mother died, she told him his father was still alive, and he must find him . . .'

'And he went out to seek for his father, and hunted everywhere,' said Roger. 'And do you remember how at last he met him – last hols, it was, at Rubadub, that dear little seaside place where we were holidaying – and what an awfully nice man he was, *exactly* like Barney . . .'

'Oh, *yes*,' said Diana, remembering it all clearly. 'And then dear old Barney discovered that he hadn't only a father, but a grandfather and grandmother and an uncle and aunts . . .'

'And cousins!' finished Snubby. 'Gosh, what a wonderful Christmas Barney must have had. I bet he's forgotten all about us now!'

'I bet he *hasn't*!' said Diana at once. 'I say – I've got a smashing idea! Let's ask Mother if we can have Barney to stay for a few days! Then we'll hear all his news.'

'And we'll see Miranda, his pet monkey, again,' said Snubby thrilled. 'Do you hear that, Loony? We'll see Miranda!'

'Come on – let's go and ask Mother this very minute!' said Diana, and flew out of the room. 'Mother! Mother! Where are you?'

Chapter Two

Barney

The three children raced upstairs to find Mrs Lynton. Loony went with them, almost tripping them up, he was so anxious to get to the top of the stairs first. He barked as he went, sensing the children's excitement and wanting to join in.

Mr Lynton, trying to write letters in his room, groaned loudly. 'That dog! I really *will* have him kept out of doors if he goes on like this!'

'Mother! We've got such a good idea!' said Diana, finding her mother putting clean towels into the bathroom.

'Have you, dear?' said her mother. 'Snubby, could you tell me HOW you get your towel as black as this? You haven't been climbing chimneys by any chance, have you?'

'Ha-ha! Funny joke!' said Snubby, politely.

'Oh, Mother, do listen. We've got a *splendid* idea!' said Diana again.

'Yes! Can we have Barney to stay for a few days, Mother?' said Roger, going straight to the point. 'Do say yes! You like Barney, don't you?'

'And we haven't seen him since the summer holidays,' said Diana. 'Not since he found his father and all his new family, and went to live with them.'

'And we simply MUST see him,' said Snubby, snatching the bathmat away from Loony, who was shaking it as if were a rat.

'Well, dears,' began Mrs Lynton, looking most uncertain. 'Well . . . I really don't know *what* to say.'

'Oh, why? *Why* can't we ask Barney – and Miranda too, of course?' said Diana, astonished. 'You always liked him, Mother, you know you did.'

'Yes, dear, and I do still,' said her mother. 'But I don't feel that Daddy will welcome anyone else here while you are all three turning the house upside-down, and – '

'Oh, we *don't* turn it upside-down!' cried Diana. 'Haven't I been tidying things all the morning? Oh, Mother, we'll be as quiet and tidy as anything if you'll let Barney come. We simply *must* hear his news before we go back to school again.'

'Well, you must ask Daddy, Diana,' said her mother. 'If he says yes, Barney shall certainly come. I'll leave it entirely to him.'

'Oh,' said Diana, looking gloomy. 'Can't *you* ask him, Mother?'

'No,' said her mother, 'Stop turning on the taps, Snubby. I said *stop*. And take Loony out of the bathroom please. He'll have that sponge next, out of the bath rack.'

'Come on, Loony,' said Snubby, in a sorrowful voice. 'We're not wanted here. We'll go and have a game together in the garage.'

'No, you won't,' said Roger firmly. 'You'll come and back us up when we ask Daddy if we can have Barney.'

'I can't,' said Snubby. 'Uncle said he didn't want to set eyes on me again this morning. Or Loony either.'

'Oh, well – you come, Di, and we'll tackle Dad together,' said Roger. 'And for goodness' sake, Snubby, don't start playing your mouth organ outside the study door just when we're inside.'

Loony shot down the stairs at top speed as usual, followed by Snubby three steps at a time. Mrs Lynton shook her head and smiled to herself – nobody, NOBODY would ever teach Snubby and Loony not to hurl themselves downstairs.

Mr Lynton heard a discreet knock on his study door and raised his head from his letters. 'Come in!' he said, and in came Diana and Roger.

'What is it?' asked their father. 'Surely you don't want any pocket money yet, after all the money you had given to you at Christmas?'

'No, Dad, no,' said Roger hurriedly. 'We shouldn't *dream* of asking you for any yet. Er – we just wondered if – er – well, we thought it would be nice if – '

'Nice, and *kind* too,' said Diana. 'If we – er – if Barney could – '

'What *is* all this?' said her father impatiently. 'Can't you ask a straight question?'

'Well, we wondered if Barney could come to stay for a few days,' said Diana, bringing it all out in a rush. 'You remember Barney don't you, Dad? The circus-boy we got to know so well.'

'Yes, I remember him,' said Mr Lynton. 'Nice boy – very blue eyes – and didn't he have a monkey?'

'Yes, Dad!' said Roger eagerly. 'Miranda – a perfect darling. Could we have them to stay?'

'Ask your mother,' said her father.

'We have,' said Roger, 'and she says we're to ask *you*.'

'Then I say No,' said Mr Lynton firmly. 'And I'm pretty certain your mother really wants to say No as well – you're all wearing her out these holidays! Also, I've got your Great-Uncle Robert coming for three days, and I've really been wondering if I can't send Snubby and Loony off to Aunt Agatha while Great-Uncle is here – I don't feel that the old gentleman will be able to cope with the three of you – and that mad dog Loony too.'

'Oh, Dad! You didn't ask Great-Uncle in the Christmas holidays, surely!' cried Diana. 'He talks and talks and talks, and we daren't say a word, and – '

'Perhaps that's why I asked him!' said her father, a sudden twinkle in his eye. 'No – actually the old fellow asked himself. He hasn't been well – which is why I'm sure he can't cope with Snubby and Loony – and the mouth-organ.'

'Oh,' said Diana sadly. 'Well, it's no good asking Barney then – there wouldn't be room, for one thing. Oh, and I *did* so want to see him these hols – and now we shan't see him for ages. Couldn't you *possibly* put Great-Uncle off, Dad?'

'No, I couldn't,' said her father. 'And even if I did, I wouldn't have Barney here – one more to add to the madhouse! And you might warn Snubby he may have to go to his Aunt Agatha's soon.'

Snubby was horrified at this news. 'But I don't *like* being there!' he said. 'Loony has to live in a kennel – and I have to wash at least twenty times a day! I say, I won't play my mouth-organ any more. And I'll stop whistling. And I'll tiptoe down the stairs, and – '

'Ass!' said Roger. 'That would only make Mother think you were ill, or sickening for something! Blow! All our plans made for nothing!'

'And we shan't see Barney now,' said Diana. '*Or* that darling little Miranda.'

'I say,' said Snubby suddenly. 'Look – it's snowing!'

They ran to the window and looked out. Yes, big snow-flakes were falling steadily down. Diana looked up at the sky, but the snowflakes were already so thick that they hid it completely.

'If it goes on like this, we'll have some fun,' said Roger, feeling more cheerful. 'And when Great-Uncle comes to stay we can keep out of his way all day long – we'll be out in the snow, tobogganing!'

'And skating, if there's any ice,' said Diana, thrilled.

'But *I* shan't be here!' said Snubby, in such a desperate voice that the others laughed. 'I shall be with my Aunt Agatha and Uncle Horace, with poor old Loony howling by himself out in his kennel.'

'Poor Snubby. Never mind. Perhaps Great-Uncle won't come,' said Diana.

But the next day there was a letter from Great-Uncle announcing that he was arriving in two days' time. Snubby looked at his aunt in despair. Would he be sent away? He was ready to promise anything rather than that. Especially as the snow was now beautifully thick and deep, and the ponds had begun to freeze. There would be no tobogganing or skating at his Aunt Agatha's, he knew that.

But Mrs Lynton was quite firm. If Great-Uncle Robert was not very well, then the worst thing in the world for him would be a dose of Snubby and Loony. He might even have a heart-attack at some of the things Loony did.

'I must telephone to your Aunt Agatha at once,' she said. 'Don't look like that, Snubby – the world isn't coming to an end.'

She went into the hall to telephone – and almost as she touched the receiver, the shrill bell rang out. Ring-ring! Ring-ring! Ring-ring!'

'I hope it's to say Great-Uncle can't come!' cried Snubby. But it wasn't. Mrs Lynton turned round, smiling. 'Who do you think wants to speak to you?' she said. 'It's Barney!'

'Barney!' cried everyone, and they all rushed to the telephone. Roger grabbed the receiver first. 'Barney! Is it really you! Did you have a good Christmas?'

Then he listened to Barney's reply – and suddenly a look of utter delight came over his face. 'Oh, BARNEY! What a wonderful idea! Yes, I'll ask Mother – hold on. I'll ask her straight away!'

Snubby and Diana could hardly wait for him to ask his mother whatever is was that Barney wanted to know.

'Mother!' said Roger, 'Barney and one of his cousins are going to stay at a house his grandmother owns, by a little lake surrounded by hills – the lake is frozen and the hills are covered with snow – so there will be tobogganing and skating. And he says, can *we* go too?'

There were shrieks of delight from Diana and Snubby. 'Of course we'll go, of course!'

'Barney says, if you say yes, his grandmother will telephone all the arrangements to you,' said Roger, his eyes shining. 'Oh, Mother – it's all right, isn't it? We can go to stay with Barney, instead of him coming here – and Snubby won't have to go to his Aunt Agatha's – and Great-Uncle Robert can come here in peace, without any of us to worry him. Oh, Mother – we *can* go, can't we?'

Chapter Three

An Exciting Invitation

Mrs Lynton looked at the three eager children, and nodded her head, smiling round at them.

'Yes. I don't see why you shouldn't. In fact, I think it's an excellent way of solving all our difficulties. Oh, Snubby, dear, DON'T!'

Snubby caught hold of his aunt and was waltzing her round and round in delight, shouting, 'Hip-hip-hip, hurray, it's a hap-hap-happy day!'

Mr Lynton came out into the hall in surprise, and was told what the excitement was about. He listened with approval.

'Ha! That will give your Great-Uncle a little peace and quiet – and us too,' he said. 'I hope you're not going to leave Loony behind. I really should like to see the back of that dog for a little while.'

'You will, you will!' shouted Snubby, approaching his uncle to give him a waltz-round too, he was so very relieved. But fortunately he thought better of this – his uncle did not take kindly to such idiotic manners.

Roger was already telling Barney of his parents' consent, and getting a few more details. Diana snatched the receiver from him after a minute or two, longing to have a word with dear old Barney. A little chattering noise greeted her.

'Oh, is that you, Miranda!' she cried, enchanted to hear the familiar monkey-chatter once more. 'We'll be seeing you soon, Miranda, soon, soon, soon.'

'Woof, woof!' said Loony, not understanding what was going on at all, and quite amazed at all the excitement. He tried to tug the mat from Mr Lynton's feet and run off with it, but Snubby stopped him just in time.

Everyone was thrilled to hear from Barney. After Snubby had had a few words on the telephone with him too, the receiver was put down and they all trooped into the sitting-room to talk over the exciting news.

'Fancy – a house in the middle of the snowy hills – and by a frozen lake too – it couldn't be better!' said Roger exultantly. 'I must look out my skates. You're lucky, Snubby, you had new ones for Christmas.'

'What about our toboggan?' said Diana. 'I don't believe it's any good for us now – too small. We haven't used it for about three years. Blow!'

'I'll buy a new one with my Christmas money,' boasted Snubby. 'Oh, I say – I wish I could buy skates for Loony!'

Roger laughed. 'I wish you could. Loony would look priceless on skates – he wouldn't know which skate to use first!'

'Oh, it's too good to be true!' said Diana, sinking into a chair. 'Mother, you don't mind us going, do you? You won't be lonely, will you?'

'Dear me, no,' said her mother. 'I shall be glad to have time to devote to your Great-Uncle. Thank goodness Loony won't be here. When is Barney's grandmother going to telephone about the day and time and other arrangements, Roger? Did Barney say?'

'Yes. She'll phone tonight,' said Roger. He turned to the others. Barney sounded *exactly* the same, didn't he?' he said.

'Exactly,' agreed the others.

'But why shouldn't he?' said Mrs Lynton, surprised.

'Oh, I don't know,' said Roger. 'After being a circus-boy so long – with ragged clothes and often hardly enough to eat – and no schooling to speak of – and then finding a whole new family, and having to have lessons – and decent clothes and table meals instead of camping out – well, somehow I thought he might have changed.'

'Barney will never change,' said Snubby. 'Never. I say – think of tobogganing down steep hills – whoooooosh!' He slid at top speed over the polished floor, and stopped when he saw his aunt's face. 'And skating round and round – and in and out . . .'

He skated into a little table and Diana just caught it as it fell. 'Don't be more of an idiot than you can help!' she said. 'I bet you'll fall down a thousand times before you can skate even half a dozen steps. Ha – I'm looking forward to seeing you sitting down bump on the ice!'

Barney's grandmother telephoned to Mrs Lynton that evening. She had a kind, very soft voice, and Mrs Lynton thought how lucky Barney was to have a grandmother who sounded so nice. She told the waiting children what the old lady had arranged.

'She says that this house in the hills has been shut up for some time,' said Mrs Lynton. 'Her sons and daughters used to use it for winter sports when they were young. She is sending someone to clean it up and air it, and it should be ready for you to go in two days' time.'

'Is any grown-up going with them?' asked Mr Lynton. 'They must have someone *sensible* there.'

'Barney's *very* sensible,' said Snubby, at once.

'Mrs Martin – that's Barney's grandmother – says she is sending her cook's sister to look after them,' said Mrs Lynton. 'She will cook for them, and dry their clothes, and see that they don't do anything *too* idiotic. But I hope Roger will see to that, as well. He's quite old enough to take charge, with Barney.'

'We'll be all right,' said Roger. 'You needn't worry, Mother. My word – only two days and we'll be down at this little house!'

'It doesn't sound very little,' said his mother. 'There are five or six bedrooms, and a big old kitchen, and two or three other rooms. You'll have to help to keep it tidy, or the cook's sister will walk off and leave you!'

'I'll help her,' promised Diana. 'And we can all make our beds – though all Snubby does is simply to get out of his in the morning and pull the sheets and blankets up again.'

'Tell-tale,' said Snubby at once. 'It's *my* bed, isn't it?'

'I think tomorrow we'd better look into the question of skates and boots and clothes,' said Mrs Lynton. 'And you will all need good wellingtons, of course. I hope you've brought yours back from school, Snubby. You forgot them last term.'

'Yes, I brought them back. Anyhow, I quite well remember bringing *one* back,' said Snubby, helpfully.

'What's the house called?' asked Diana.

'Well – I think I must have heard it wrongly over the telephone,' said her mother, 'but it *sounded* like Rat-a-Tat House.'

Everyone laughed. 'How lovely!' said Diana. 'I hope that *is* its name. Rat-a-Tat House – why ever was it called that, I wonder?'

Next day was a busy one. Boots, socks, gloves, sweaters, skates – all were pulled out and carefully examined. The weather remained very cold and frosty, and snow fell again in the night. The forecast was cold weather, much snow, and hard frost – just right for winter sports, as Snubby kept announcing. He produced his mouth-organ once more, and nearly drove everyone mad by trying to learn a new tune. In the end Mrs Lynton took it away and packed it at the very bottom of one of the suitcases that were going with them.

But, not to be outdone, Snubby then went about pretending to strum on a banjo, and made a peculiar twanging noise with his mouth half-closed as he strummed an imaginary banjo with his fingers and thumb. This was really worse than the mouth-organ, and unfortunately, as the banjo was purely imaginary, it could not be taken away from him.

'Can't that boy be sent to Rat-a-Tat House today?' demanded Mr Lynton, hearing the banjo passing his door for the twentieth time that morning. 'My word, it's a good thing he won't be here when Great-Uncle Robert comes.'

At last the suitcases were all packed, the skates strung together, and clothes set out fresh for the next morning, when they were to join Barney. Loony rushed about eagerly all the time, trying to help, and making off with shoes and bundles of socks whenever they were put ready to pack. Even Snubby got a bit tired of him when he met Loony rushing *up* the stairs, just as he, Snubby, was rushing down, and both arrived in a bruised and tangled heap at the bottom.

'Ass of a dog!' said Snubby fiercely to the surprised Loony. 'I'll leave you behind if you do that again. I nearly broke my leg. Grrrrrrr! Bad dog!'

Loony put his tail down and crept under the hall chest. There was a smell of mouse there, and he had a wonderful time scrabbling round and round to find it, snuffling loudly all the time, much to Mr Lynton's amazement.

'We're to go to Barney's home first, and then go on with him and his cousin to Rat-a-Tat House,' said Roger to the others. 'I wish tomorrow would come. I say – I wonder what the cousin's like. Mother, how long can we stay away?'

'Till the snow's gone, I should think,' said his mother. 'That's what Barney's grandmother said. But, of course, if it lasts more than a week or so, you'll have to come back because of getting ready for school again.'

Roger groaned. 'Don't mention the word! Snubby, STOP that noise. Or play another instrument for a change. That imaginary banjo of yours is getting boring.'

Snubby obligingly changed over to a zither, which was certainly much pleasanter. He really was a marvel at imitating sounds. Mrs Lynton hoped he wouldn't start on a drum next!

The morning came at last – a brilliant morning, with a clear blue sky and pale yellow sun – and the snow underfoot as crisp as sugar. 'Heavenly!' said Diana. 'Just exactly right for us!'

Off they went in a taxi to catch the train to Barney's town, Loony too, so excited that he had to be put on the lead. Now for a good time – now for some sport – hurrah for the winter holidays!

Chapter Four

At Barney's Home

Barney's home was at Little Wendleman, and a car was at Wendleman station to meet them – a nice big utility van with plenty of room for luggage. Best of all, Barney was there to meet them, with Miranda sitting excitedly on his shoulder.

'Barney! Old Barney! And Miranda; hey, Miranda!' shouted Snubby, hanging out of the compartment window as the train drew in. He opened the door and he and Loony fell out together. Barney ran up in delight, his brilliant blue eyes shining as brightly as ever. Miranda, the little monkey, leapt up and down on his shoulder and chattered at the top of her voice. She knew everyone immediately.

'Barney! Dear old Barney!' said Diana, and gave him a hug. Roger clapped him on the back, and Snubby grinned all over his freckled, snub-nosed face. As for Loony, he went completely mad, lay on his back, and did one of his bicycling acts at top speed, barking loudly.

'Hallo!' said Barney, his brown face glowing with pleasure at seeing the children who had befriended him when he was a down-at-heel circus-boy. 'Gosh – it's grand to see you all again. Isn't it, Miranda?'

The little monkey leapt on to Diana's shoulder and whispered in her ear, holding the lobe in her paw the way she often did. Diana laughed. 'Darling Miranda – you haven't changed a bit, not a bit. And you do look smart in your little red coat and bonnet and skirt!'

Barney looked different. He was no taller and no fatter, and his face was as brown as ever. But now he was dressed well, his hair was cut properly, and he wore a tie, which he had rarely done when he had been a circus-boy. In fact, he looked extremely nice, and Diana gazed at him in admiration.

Barney laughed, as he saw the eyes of all three on him. 'Do I look different?' he said, in the voice they knew so well, with the slight American twang he had picked up in his circus travels. 'I'm not a circus-boy any more – I'm a gentleman – whew – think of that! Me, Barney the hoop-la boy, the boy who took any job he could, who never wore anything but canvas shoes, dirty old trousers, and a ragged shirt . . .'

He paused and twinkled round at the three listening children. 'Yes, I'm a gentleman now – but I'm still the same, see? I'm just Barney – aren't I, Miranda?'

Miranda leapt on to his shoulder again and jigged up and down, chattering in monkey-language. What did she care how Barney was dressed, or where he lived, or whether he was a circus-boy or a gentleman? It was all the same to her. He was just Barney.

'Yes, you're still just Barney,' said Diana, and gave a little sigh of relief. She had wondered just a little if having a family, and a fine house and money to spend would have changed Barney – but no, it hadn't.

'Come on,' said Barney. 'The car's here, see, and there's my father driving it.' He said the words 'my father' in a very proud voice. Diana felt touched. How very, very glad Barney must be to have a father of his own, and to have found him after so many years of thinking he was dead!

Barney's father, Mr Martin, was sitting at the wheel of the car. The children marvelled at the likeness between the two – bright blue, wide-set eyes, corn-coloured hair, a wide-mouth, ready to smile. Yes, they were certainly father and son. The only real difference between their faces was that Barney's was so much browner than his father's.

'Hallo, kids!' said Mr Martin, and smiled, looking more like Barney than ever. 'Nice of you to come all this way to see Barnabas – or Barney, as you call him. Hop in! We're to have lunch at his grandmother's, and then I'll take you to Rat-a-Tat House.'

'Thank you very much, sir,' said Roger politely. 'It's good of you to meet us like this – and jolly good of Barney's grandmother to invite us to stay with him at Rat-a-Tat House. We're thrilled.'

The boys piled the suitcases into the utility van. Loony clambered in, and sat up in a corner so that he could look out of the window. He loved hanging his head out of a car, his long ears flapping in the breeze. He was delighted to see Barney again, though he wasn't so sure about Miranda the monkey. He had suddenly remembered how she used to ride on his back, jigging up and down in a most aggravating manner. He looked at her out of the corner of his eye. Would she try that old trick again?

The car drew up in the drive of a pleasant looking house, timbered, with white walls, tall chimneys and wide casement windows. As they drew up, the front door flew open, and a little old lady stood there, as brown-eyed as the monkey that sat on her shoulder.

'Ah, here you are!' she cried. 'Welcome, welcome! I've longed to meet dear Barney's friends. Come along in, come along in!'

The children liked Barney's grandmother at once. She had curly white hair, a very pink, soft-cheeked face, brown eyes, and a lively smile. They smiled to see the monkey on her shoulder as they shook hands.

'Ah – you see I have a monkey just like Barnabas!' she said in a merry, bird-like voice. 'Monkeys run in our family – my mother kept two. Jinny, here are good friends!'

Jinny, the little monkey, was not dressed like Miranda. She wore a little yellow cape round her thin shoulders. She held out a tiny, wizened paw in a very solemn manner and shook hands with each of them. Loony stared in astonishment at her. What – *another* monkey – or was he seeing double?

Soon they were all sitting in a cosy room, with a blazing fire, gay curtains and a lovely meal laid ready on a round table. Snubby looked at it approvingly. Hot tomato soup to begin with – now that was just what he felt like! He took his place at once and beamed round. This was the kind of thing Snubby enjoyed.

'What comes next?' he asked Barney, in a loud whisper.

'Ah – Barnabas has told me what you like,' said the old lady, who had very sharp ears. 'Sausages – plenty of them – and fried onions *and* tomatoes – and potatoes and peas. Barnabas has had many a meal with you, I know – and now I am proud you should have a meal with him.'

Snubby thought this sounded fine. What a nice old lady. Barney was certainly lucky to have such a splendid family belonging to him. For a second Snubby was just a little jealous when he looked at Barney's handsome, smiling father. *He* would have liked a father like that – but he had no parents at all, worse luck. Snubby simply couldn't understand children who grumbled at their parents – they didn't know how lucky they were to have them!

It was a very pleasant meal. Barney told them about the lessons he had had during the last term. He had never

30

been to school, and his father had thought he must have plenty of private coaching before he sent him anywhere. The boy was very intelligent, and enjoyed his lessons immensely.

'He's as good at them as he is at walking the tight-rope or turning cart wheels!' said his father, with a laugh.

'How marvellous!' said Snubby, enviously. 'I'm no good at either! Barney – do you ever miss the circuses and fairs and shows you used to belong to?'

'Sometimes,' said Barney. 'Not often. But just at times I think of what fun it was sleeping out under the stars – or having a tasty meal out of some cook-pot in a fair when I was very hungry – and I miss the show people a bit.'

'You can always go off for a taste of that life again, whenever you want to, Barney,' said his father, smiling at him.

'I know,' said Barney. 'But I shall always come back home – come back here to you and Granny. I like the freedom of the show-life – but I like putting out roots too, as I can here. That feeling of *belonging* somewhere – to a place or a family – that's what I've missed all my life, and now I've got it, I'm going to keep it.'

The talk went on during the meal, happy, jolly talk, friendly and intimate. Loony lay beneath the table, amazed at the variety of titbits that came down to him from Snubby, Roger and Barney. Miranda, curious to see why Loony was so peaceful, slid down a table leg to investigate, and joined in Loony's little feast, much to his annoyance. Jinny, the other monkey seldom left her mistress's shoulder, and gravely took little titbits in her tiny paw. Sometimes she patted the soft old cheek near to her, and often did what Miranda did to Barney – slid

31

a small paw down her mistress's neck to warm her tiny fingers.

'Now, after lunch, the car will take you all to Rat-a-Tat House,' said Barney's grandmother. 'Mrs Tickle, the cook's sister, is already there.'

'Mrs Tickle – is that *really* her name?' asked Snubby. 'Is she ticklish?'

'I have no idea,' said Mrs Martin. 'And if I were you I wouldn't try to find out.'

'I thought a cousin of Barney's was coming too,' said Roger. 'Where is he? Are we going to pick him up somewhere?'

'No. He has started a cold,' said Mrs Martin. 'He may be along in a day or two, but not today. You'll have to settle in without him.'

This pleased everyone very much. They badly wanted to have a long, friendly talk with old Barney, and a strange cousin would have embarrassed them.

They piled into the utility van, and waved goodbye to Barney's grandmother and little Jinny, the monkey. Then away they drove over the snowy roads towards the white-clad hills.

'Wake me up at Rat-a-Tat House,' said Snubby, suddenly feeling sleepy after his enormous lunch. 'What fun we're going to have there!'

You're right, Snubby – you just wait and see!

Chapter Five

Rat-a-Tat House

The car had to go slowly along some of the roads because they were already slippery. It took about an hour to reach the little village of Boffame, which was two or three miles from Rat-a-Tat House.

'Now we shall soon be there,' said Barney's father, who was at the wheel. 'My word, we had some fun at Rat-a-Tat House when I was a boy, and played there with my brother and sisters and cousins. You'll have fun too, Barnabas, with your friends.'

They went through the little village, and then up a small, very steep hill. The car stopped halfway up, and would not go on. Its wheels slid round and round in the same slippery place.

'Get the sacks out and the spade, children,' said Mr Martin. 'I thought this might happen, so we've come prepared!'

They got the spade and dug away the snow under the wheels, slipping the sacks beneath them instead. Then Mr. Martin started up the car again, the wheels gripped the sacks instead of the slippery snow, and the car slowly reached the top of the hill. It stopped and Mr Martin waited for the children to come along to the car with the sacks and spade.

'It's a good thing I took all the goods yesterday that you'll need at Rat-a-Tat House,' he said. 'I doubt if a car will be able to get through if we have any more snow.'

'Perhaps we shall be cut off from everywhere!' said

Snubby in delight. 'Lost in the snowy hills. Marooned in Rat-a-Tat House. We shan't be able to go back to school. Hurrah!'

Loony barked joyfully. If anyone said 'hurrah' it meant they were happy, so *he* had to join in too. Miranda leaned across the car and tweaked one of his long ears, and there was a scrimmage immediately. Mr Martin looked round for a moment. 'I don't know what's happening at the back, but it's most disturbing to the driver,' he remarked, and Loony at once got a smack from Snubby, and yelped in surprise.

The car went slowly on. They came to another hill – would the car stick halfway up this time? No, it went up steadily and everyone gave a sigh of relief.

The countryside looked enchanting in its thick blanket of dazzling white snow. Every little twig was outlined in white, and every sharp outline of fence or roof was softened by the snow. Diana looked out of the window and thought how beautiful it was.

'We'll have marvellous tobogganing,' said Roger. 'Best we've ever had. And plenty of skating if the frost holds.'

'It's sure to,' said Barney's father, driving the car down into a little valley surrounded by snow-clad hills on every side. 'Now we're nearly there – you'll see Rat-a-Tat House in a minute – it's round this corner. Ah, there's the frozen lake, look.'

'Oh, it's quite a *big* lake!' said Diana, surprised. 'What a pity we can't go boating and swimming, as well as skating.'

Everyone laughed. 'Rather impossible,' said Barney's father. 'Perhaps you can come again in the summer and have some fun here with Barney and his cousins then.'

'So this is the house,' said Snubby, in approval, as they swung in at a small drive. 'Ha – I like it! It's – it's rather *odd* looking, isn't it? All those turrets and towers and tucked-in windows and things.'

'It's old,' said Mr Martin; 'but was so very sturdily built that it had lasted well for a great many years. It's seen a bit of history too. Oliver Cromwell once stayed here, and it is said that a celebrated Spaniard, who was taken prisoner, was brought here and hidden – and what is more, was never heard of again.'

'Gosh!' said Snubby, thrilled. 'I hope he isn't still there. I can't speak a *word* of Spanish. I like the look of Rat-a-Tat House. I feel as if plenty of exciting things have happened here.'

As they swung slowly slowly up the drive, the front door opened, and someone stood there smiling at them – a very small woman with plaits of dark hair wound round her head, and merry dark eyes. She wore a flowered overall, and over it a spotless white apron. The children liked her at once.

'Is that Mrs Tickle?' asked Snubby, leaping out of the car before anyone else.

'Yes,' said Barney. 'But *don't* ask her if she's ticklish, because hundreds of people have asked that already and she's tired of it. Hallo, Mrs Tickle! I hope you haven't been lonely.'

'Not a bit, I've been too busy!' said the little woman, coming to help with the suitcases. 'Are you cold? Come away in, then, I've a fine fire for you. Good afternoon, Mr Martin, sir – I'm right down glad to see you all, I was afraid you'd not get through the snow.'

'We were only stuck once,' said Mr Martin. 'I'll just see the children in safely, Mrs Tickle, and then I must go, because I want to get away before more snow falls. It looks as if the sky is full of it again.'

'That's right, sir, you get home before it's dark,' said little Mrs Tickle. 'Oh, my word, who's this?'

It was Loony, prancing round in the snow, getting into everyone's way as usual.

'I didn't know you were bringing a dog,' said Mrs Tickle. 'I've got no dog biscuits for him.'

'Oh, he doesn't mind having what we have,' Snubby assured her. 'He loves a slice off the joint or a chop.'

Mrs Tickle looked quite horrified. 'He won't get anything like that while *I'm* in charge!' she said, leading them all indoors. 'I like dogs to be kept in their place. And monkeys too,' she said, with a look at Miranda sitting on Barney's shoulder. 'Well, here you are – sit down and warm yourselves!'

She led them into a big, panelled room, at one end of which was an enormous fireplace with a fire of logs, crackling and blazing.

'Oh, it's lovely!' said Diana, glancing all round. 'It's like a house in a story book. And how light the room is!'

'That's the reflection of the snow outside,' said Mrs Tickle. 'Bless us all, what's the matter with that dog?'

Loony was growling in a most peculiar manner, and backing away from the fireplace, towards which he had run for warmth. Barney gave a bellow of laughter.

'He's just seen the bearskin rug in front of the fire! It's got a bear's head at one end and he thinks it's real!'

Certainly poor Loony had had a terrible shock! He had run towards the fire, and had suddenly seen the bear's head at the end of the rug, its two glass eyes shining balefully at him. Loony imagined that the bear was crouching down ready to spring, and had backed away at once, producing his fiercest growls.

'Idiot,' said Snubby. 'Look at Miranda – she's braver than you are, Loony!'

Miranda had also seen the bear – but she had seen bearskin rugs before and was not at all worried. She leapt down and sat on the bear's head, chattering away at Loony, and jigging up and down.

'She's telling you not to be such a coward, Loony,' said Snubby, severely. 'Really, I'm ashamed of you!'

'Well, children, Mrs Tickle will take you all round the house and show you your rooms,' said Barney's father, looking at his watch. 'And no doubt she has a fine tea waiting. Help her all you can, please. Barney, you are in charge here, remember, and if anything goes wrong, let me know at once.'

'Yes, sir,' said Barney. 'I suppose Rat-a-Tat House is on the telephone?'

'Yes,' said his father. 'So you'll be quite all right. Mrs Tickle knows where the toboggans are, and your skates – we brought them here when we drove her over with all the food and bedclothes and so on. Well, have a good time. Mrs Tickle, keep them in order – and don't stand any nonsense.'

'I'll keep them in order all right, sir,' said little Mrs Tickle, looking quite fierce. Then she smiled. 'I'll enjoy having them round me,' she said. 'Mine are all grown up now, and it will be like old times to have them rampaging round. I hope you get back all right, sir.'

They all went to see Mr Martin off in the car. It was getting dark already, though the gleaming snow threw its white light everywhere. 'Goodbye!' shouted everyone, and waved till the car had crawled out of the gate.

They all went back into the fire-lit sitting-room, with its wide windowseats, its enormous fireplace, and gleaming old furniture. Snubby stood by the fire, rubbing his hands in glee.

'Isn't this smashing?' he said. 'I wish we could go out

into the snow now, and toboggan. Fancy sliding down those hills at top speed. Loony, do you think you'll like tobogganing?'

Loony had no idea what tobogganing was, but he was sure he would like anything that Snubby liked. He felt the general excitement and decided to show off. He rushed round the room at top speed, barking, then suddenly lost his footing on the highly polished floor, rolled over and finished by sliding along swiftly on his back. Everyone roared.

'Is *that* how you're going to slide over the snow?' said Snubby. 'You'll get along fine like that, Loony.'

'Would you like to come and unpack?' said Mrs Tickle's voice at the door. 'And by that time, you'll be ready for tea, I've no doubt!'

She was right – they certainly would!

Chapter Six

Settling In

A wide staircase led up to the first floor of Rat-a-Tat House, and many rooms opened off the upstairs landing. Everywhere there was panelling, and Snubby went along knocking at the walls, rat-a-tat-tat!

'Snubby, *must* you do that?' said Diana. 'What's the idea?'

'Ha – secret passages of course!' said Snubby at once. 'You never know! This place might be riddled with them!'

'Well, I hope you're not going to knock on the walls every time you pass them,' said Diana.

'It's *Rat-a-Tat* House, isn't it?' said Snubby, with a grin, and knocked again on some wooden panelling – rat-a-tat-tat! 'I say, I wonder why it's got such a peculiar name? Do you know, Barney?'

No,' said Barney. 'But maybe Mrs Tickle does. We'll ask her sometime.'

Mrs Tickle was away along the landing opening doors as she went. 'You can choose your own rooms!' she called. 'Barney has one to himself, and so has Diana, but you other two boys are to share. The dog can sleep down in the kitchen.'

'Well, he can't,' muttered Snubby under his breath. 'And what's more, he won't! He'll be sleeping on my bed as usual!'

The rooms were rather exciting. They all had panelled walls, which Snubby proceeded to knock on smartly with his knuckles, cushioned windowseats, old-fashioned wash-stands, and cupboards that opened out of the panelling.

'You can hardly tell they're cupboards!' said Diana, opening hers. 'They look just like part of the oak walls. I never had a room like this before. I feel as if I've slipped a few hundred years back in history!'

'Our room's smashing too,' announced Snubby. 'Where's Mrs Tickle? Oh, she's gone. Good. I just wanted to say something she's not to hear. I am *not* going to let her shut Loony up in the kitchen tonight, so I shall think of some way to prevent it – and then he can come on my bed as usual. He'd be miserable if he had to sleep in the kitchen.'

Diana opened her suitcase and unpacked and put her things away neatly, while the boys explored the other part of the house. Mrs Tickle called up the stairs. 'Tea will be ready in five minutes – and the scones are hot, so don't be too long.'

Diana shouted for the others. 'Roger – Barney – Snubby! Tea's ready, so buck up and unpack!'

Roger and Barney came along and put their things away in the great old chests and dark cupboards. Snubby rushed up with Loony at the very last minute, covered with dust and cobwebs.

'Where in the world have you been?' said Diana, looking at him in disgust. 'Don't come near me, *please*! You're so cobwebby that you've probably got spiders crawling all over you!'

'Am I?' said Snubby, surprised, and brushed himself down so vigorously that dust flew everywhere. 'I found a little attic place – rather exciting, with old boxes and trunks in it. Hey, what's that!'

It was the booming sound of the old gong in the hall. Mrs Tickle was tired of waiting for them to come down and had suddenly remembered the gong. How it made them jump! Miranda leapt to the top of the curtains at once, and Loony ran under the bed.

'That's calling us for tea, I expect,' said Diana. 'Snubby, you've *got* to undo your suitcase and put your things away before you come down. Go on, now – buck up!'

'All right, all right, teacher,' said Snubby. 'Don't start trying to boss *me*! It won't take me long to unpack.'

It didn't. He simply undid his suitcase, opened his cupboard door, and emptied everything into it, pell-mell. He shoved the suitcase in at the back and then shot downstairs at top speed, Loony just in front of him. The staircase ended in a wide, polished hall, and Loony was able to slide all the way to the front with the greatest ease.

'Jolly good, Loony,' said Snubby admiringly, and walked sedately into the sitting-room, where the others were just about to sit down. Diana stared at him accusingly.

'You haven't had time to unpack. You go back and do it!'

'Everything is safely in my cupboard,' said Snubby. '*And* the suitcase is empty, teacher!'

'Don't keep calling me that,' said Diana exasperated, but Snubby didn't even hear. His attention had been caught by the meal on the tea table. On a spotless white cloth were six different plates of food. Where Diana was sitting was a very large brown teapot, a large blue milk jug, and a large basin of sugar lumps. Two dishes of jam were on the table and one pot of fish-paste.

Snubby looked in awe at the six plates of food. 'Stacks of new bread and butter – hot buttered scones, at least three each – gingerbread squares, all brown and sticky – a giant of a chocolate cake – a jam sponge twice as large as usual – and home-made macaroons! *Macaroons* – my very favourite goody. Hey, Mrs Tickle, Mrs Tickle!'

And the delighted Snubby with Loony at his heels went rushing out into the kitchen to the surprised Mrs Tickle to tell her what he thought of the tea. He debated whether to give her a hug but decided that he didn't know her well enough yet.

Mrs Tickle was very pleased with his admiration of the first meal she had provided. 'Go along with you,' she said, beaming. 'You're a caution, you are! You'd better be careful that the others haven't eaten everything by the time you get back to the table!'

That made Snubby rush off in a panic, but to his relief there was still plenty left. He had to gobble to catch up with them, but Snubby never minded that.

'Your table manners haven't improved at all,' said Diana primly. She felt quite like her mother, sitting in state behind the big brown teapot.

'Sorry, teacher,' said Snubby, in such a humble voice that everyone laughed. 'I'll stay in and write out "I must please dear Diana, I must please dear Diana" one hundred times!'

'I shall throw something at you in a minute,' said Diana. 'Probably the teapot.'

'Right,' said Snubby. 'But wait till it's empty. I may want another cup of tea. I say, look at Miranda, Barney – she's dipping her fingers into the strawberry jam and then licking them.'

'Miranda – how *can* you?' said Barney, reprovingly, and the little monkey hid her face in his neck as if she was ashamed – but the next minute, down went her little paw into the jam dish again!

It was a happy, merry tea, and Barney enjoyed it more than any of them. He had been a lonely boy for so many years, longing for the companionship, the teasing, the family talk that he had never had. Now he was quite at home in the fun, and entered into all the teasing with delight. But nobody ever had a readier answer than the cheeky, irrepressible Snubby – he was never at a loss as to what to say or do!

They all helped to clear away tea. By this time, of course, Mrs Tickle had had to light the lamps. These were old-fashioned oil-lamps, because there was no electricity in Rat-a-Tat House.

'You be careful of these lamps,' she warned them. 'And if you want to rush about with that mad dog of yours, Snubby, don't knock them over or you'll have the place afire.'

'I'll be careful,' promised Snubby.

'There are candles upstairs on the landing,' went on Mrs Tickle, 'and candles waiting in the hall for when you all go up to bed. And if you want wood for the fire, it's in that cupboard there, by the fireplace. I'll bring you more from outside if you want it.'

'No, you won't,' said Roger at once. '*I'll* do that – and just tell us whatever jobs you want done, Mrs Tickle, and we'll do them straight away.'

'That's what I like to hear!' said the little woman, pleased, and went out smiling.

Soon they were all sitting round the fire. 'Let's have a game,' said Snubby. 'I brought some cards. I'll go and fetch them.' He went off upstairs, knocking on the panelling all the way – knock-knock-knock – rat-a-tat-tat, rat-a-tat-tat!

'I wish he wouldn't,' said Diana. 'Why does Snubby always have to make *some* kind of noise?'

Snubby came back with the cards, and the children heard his knock-knock-knock on the panelling again.

43

Loony listened with his head on one side and so did Miranda. It was rather an eerie sound, hollow and irritating.

'Let's put some more wood on the fire before we begin,' said Roger, and opened the door of the little cupboard beside the fireplace, where the logs were kept. He hauled one out, threw it on the fire and shut the cupboard door. Then he went with the others to the table and they all sat down to play cards.

But they hadn't dealt more than one hand when something made them jump. It was a hollow, knocking sound – knock-knock-knock – rat-a-tat-tat! Knock-knock-knock – rat-a-tat-tat!

Loony growled, and that made them all jump, too. It wasn't Snubby knocking this time – he was there at the table with them, listening, half-scared.

'Pooh – it must be Mrs Tickle knocking or hammering something in the kitchen!' said Roger, seeing that Diana looked frightened.

'It isn't,' said his sister in a low voice. 'It's in this room. But there's nobody here but us!'

Knock-knock-knock – rat-a-tat-tat! It was exactly the same knocking as Snubby had drummed on the panelling when he went up and down the stairs.

'It *is* in this room,' said Barney, starting up. 'Whatever can it be? Who is it? I don't like it.'

'Let's get Mrs Tickle,' said Roger, and shouted for her. 'Mrs Tickle! We want you. Quickly!'

In came Mrs Tickle, most surprised. 'Whatever is the matter?' she said, seeing their startled faces.

'Listen,' said Roger, as the soft knock-knock-knock came again. 'That knocking, Mrs Tickle . . . what can it be?'

Chapter Seven

Knock-Knock-Knock!

Mrs Tickle stood in the middle of the room, listening. she looked alarmed. 'The knocking!' she said. 'The knocking! It's come again after all these years!'

'Whatever do you mean, Mrs Tickle?' said Barney. 'My father didn't tell me about any knocking – and he knows all about this house.'

'Maybe he doesn't know about the knocking, though,' said Mrs Tickle, looking relieved as the noise stopped. 'I heard the tale in the village of Boffame yesterday. It's because of the knocking that this house got its name.'

'Sit down, Mrs Tickle, and tell us,' said Barney, and the little woman sat down at once, on the very edge of a chair. She began to speak again in a low voice.

'I'm only telling you what's said,' she said. 'A tale that's handed down through the years, you understand. I heard it from old John Hurdie, in the post office, and he got it from his great-granny, so he said.'

'Go on, go on,' said Roger, as she stopped for breath. A piece of wood broke in the flames of the fire and the burning log fell to the bottom of the hearth, making them all jump.

'Well,' said Mrs Tickle, 'it's said that the house was called Boffame House after the lake and the village – but soon after people came to live here, there were strange knockings on the front door. . . .'

'On the front door?' said Roger. 'Do you mean someone hammered there with their fists?'

'No. They used the great knocker there,' said Mrs Tickle. 'Didn't you see it when you came in this afternoon?'

'The door was wide open, so we didn't notice,' said Diana, trying to remember. 'Is it a very *big* knocker?'

'Enormous,' said Mrs Tickle. 'And you wouldn't *believe* the sound it makes – thunderous, Mr Hurdie at the post office told me. But when the footman went to answer the door all those years ago and see who was there – there was nobody.'

'The one who knocked might have run away,' said Snubby, hopefully. 'Lots of people *do* knock at doors or ring bells, and then run away. They think it's funny.'

'Well, it isn't, it's stupid,' said Mrs Tickle. 'We've got a boy in our village who does that – but he did it once too often to me. Aha – I put glue all round the knocker – and what a mess he was in!'

Everyone laughed. 'But why didn't the person who knocked all those years ago stay till the door was opened?' asked Snubby. 'And who was he?'

'Nobody ever saw him, though often he came knocking day or night,' said Mrs Tickle, enjoying the telling of such a dramatic story. 'And what was more, that knocking went on for a hundred and fifty years, so the old story goes!'

'Ha – then it couldn't have been the *same* person knocking all that time,' said Snubby. 'But what did the knocking mean – anything at all?'

'Yes, it was said to give warning that there was a traitor in the house!' said Mrs Tickle. 'So there must have been a good many traitors then, it seems to me! And old Mr Hurdie, he says that when the knocking came, there was always a searching of the old place to see if anyone was hiding there – and the servants were always questioned to find out if one of them was untrustworthy. Oh, there were some goings-on in those old days, you mark my words.'

'How long ago did the knocking stop?' asked Barney. 'You said it only lasted a hundred and fifty years – but this house is much older than that.'

'It's no more than a hundred years ago now since Mr No-One hammered at the door with that knocker!' said Mrs Tickle. 'It's so old now that I reckon it would fall off the door if anyone touched it!'

Mrs Tickle's story was so very interesting that the children had quite forgotten about the mysterious knocking they themselves had heard a little while back – but they soon remembered it when it suddenly came again!

Knock-knock-knock . . . rat-a-tat-tat! There it was again, soft and hollow and mysterious – *and somewhere* in the room! There wasn't a doubt of it.

Barney sprang up at once. 'We've got to find what it is!' he said.

'Oh, dear!' said Mrs Tickle, beginning to tremble at the knees. 'Oh, dear – I've gone and scared myself with that old story. I'm all of a shake. It's the knocker back again – Mr No-One after all these years. But what's he knocking for? There's no traitor here!'

'Cheer up!' said Roger. 'He's not knocking at the *front* door, Mrs Tickle. Come on, Barney – let's trace where the knocking is!'

They waited for it to come again – and it did, as soon as they were quite silent. Knock-knock-knock . . . rat-a-tat-tat!

'It's over there – in that corner of the room!' said Barney, and ran towards the corner. The knocking stopped and then began again. Knock-knock-knock.

'It's coming from the wood cupboard!' cried Mrs Tickle.

'Bless us all, that's where it's coming from. But there's only logs there, that I do know.'

'We'll soon see,' said Barney grimly, and flung open the little door of the wood cupboard.

And out sprang a very indignant and rather frightened Miranda! The little monkey ran chattering to Barney and leapt straight to his shoulder, burying her little furry head in his neck.

'Miranda! MIRANDA! Why – it was only *you* in the cupboard after all,' said Barney. 'You little pest – you gave us such a fright! But why did you knock like that?'

'She was imitating Snubby!' cried Diana. 'She heard him keep on knocking on the panelling as he went up and downstairs – and you know how she loves to copy what we do – so when she got shut in the cupboard, she did what Snubby did – and knocked on the wooden door in exactly the same way – knock-knock-knock . . . rat-a-tat-tat!'

'That's it,' said Roger, most relieved. 'Phew – I didn't like it much. When did Miranda get shut in?'

'When you opened the wood cupboard door to put more logs on the fire,' said Barney. 'She must have slipped in without your noticing it, and you shut the door on her. Funny little thing – knocking like that!'

'Well, I hope she doesn't do anything else to give us such a scare,' said Mrs Tickle, getting up, and looking herself again. 'Right down feared I was! And don't you start thinking about that big old knocker on the front door – Mr No-One hasn't been at it for a hundred years, and it's not likely he'll start now.'

'Anyway – there are no traitors in this house now,' said Barney. 'Only four kids, you, Mrs Tickle, and a monkey and a dog. Miranda, don't do such an idiotic thing again.

I'm surprised we didn't miss you, but I quite thought you were asleep in that rug on the sofa.'

'Why didn't Loony go to the cupboard and scratch at it as he usually does when he hears a noise coming from somewhere?' wondered Diana.

'Easy,' said Snubby, with a grin. 'He's not awfully keen on getting Miranda out of trouble! I bet he thought she could jolly well stay there as long as possible!'

'Yes. I believe you're right,' said Barney, looking at Loony, who was busy scratching himself. 'Bad dog, Loony – to let poor little Miranda stay in the dark cupboard without lifting a paw to help her.'

'Wuff,' said Loony politely, and went on scratching. Snubby poked him with his foot.

'Stop it!' he said. 'Sit up and listen when you're spoken to.'

Loony wagged his tail, and it thumped on the floor – knock-knock-knock!

'Oh, my goodness – don't *you* start rat-a-tatting now!' said Snubby, and Diana giggled. She was very relieved to find that their scare had been groundless – and she half-wished that Mrs Tickle hadn't told them that queer old story.

'Let's get on with our game,' said Snubby. 'Let me see – we'd better deal again. Come on!'

They dealt again and Snubby looked at his cards. 'Ha!' he said. 'Couldn't be better! I can tell you this – even if Mr No-One comes and hammers at that knocker now, I shall go on with this game – I've got a smashing hand!'

Fortunately for him, there was no hammering at the front door, and he won the game easily, looking very pleased with himself.

It was cosy and warm in the sitting-room, with the log fire blazing away. The children felt very happy, thinking of the next day and all the fun they would have. Diana drew the curtains after a while, shutting out the starry night and the white snow.

Later on Mrs Tickle came in with a tray. 'Supper!' she said, beaming. 'Will you lay it for me, Diana, while I go and see to the poached eggs?'

'Poached eggs! Mrs Tickle, how did you know I was simply longing for one?' said Snubby at once.

'Well, I had a feeling you were longing for *two*, not one,' said Mrs Tickle, who had taken quite a liking to the snub-nosed, freckle-faced 'imp' as she called him to herself. Snubby grinned in delight.

'Two! How well you know me already!' he said. 'Loony – salute Mrs Tickle, please – your very *best* salute!'

And Loony, proud to show off his very newest trick, sat up and saluted quite smartly, much to Miranda's interest.

'There now – he's as sharp as his master!' said Mrs Tickle, putting down her tray and laughing. 'You're cautions, both of you. I'll be back with the poached eggs in a minute.' And off she went, chuckling over Snubby and Loony. Really – what a pair!

Chapter Eight

What Fun!

Supper was a very pleasant meal, a simple one of poached eggs, hot cocoa, and biscuits and butter. Diana began to yawn before she was half-way through it. Miranda immediately copied her, yawning delicately, showing her tiny white teeth, and patting her mouth as she did so, just like Diana.

Both Miranda and Loony were enjoying a buttered biscuit. Each of them licked off the butter first, Loony with his large pink tongue and Miranda very daintily with her tiny, curling one.

'*Not* very good manners,' said Roger, lazily. 'My word, I'm sleepy. It's this big fire, I suppose. Snubby, how are you going to prevent Loony having to sleep down in the kitchen? I bet Mrs Tickle will insist on it.

She did, of course. She appeared at nine o'clock, carrying her candle to go up to bed.

'Time for you all to go up,' she announced firmly. 'And I'll take that dog to the kitchen now, Snubby.'

'You won't mind if he chews up the rug there, and the cushion on the chair, and any slippers or towels you've left out, will you, Mrs Tickle?' said Snubby solemnly. 'I'll pay for them all, of course, if he does much damage – but it's very, very hard on my pocket.'

Mrs Tickle was taken aback. She looked at Loony who stared back at her unwinkingly.

'He can't *help* being a nibbly, chewy dog,' said Snubby

51

earnestly. 'It's his *nature*, you see. The funny thing is, he NEVER chews anything when he sleeps with me. Never.'

Mrs Tickle made up her mind at once. 'Well, you let him sleep with you then,' she said, 'if you can abide a smelly dog in your bedroom. I won't have him chewing up my kitchen, and that's flat.'

'I'll do *anything* to please you,' said Snubby, rather overdoing it now. 'Anything. I'll even have a smelly dog in my bedroom. Won't I, Loony?'

Loony thumped his tail on the floor and Miranda at once pounced on it. Loony swung round at her and she leapt on to his back, hanging on to his silky fur for all she was worth.

Loony raced round the room with her on his back, trying hard to remember how to unseat her. 'Roll on the floor, ass!' cried Snubby. 'Roll on the floor!'

But, as soon as Loony rolled over, Miranda was off like a bird, springing here and there till she came back to Barney's shoulder.

'Good as a play they are!' said Mrs Tickle, laughing. 'Now – are you all coming up or not? I'm not leaving you down here – not with an oil-lamp to upset and cause a fire! Mr Martin did leave strict instructions about that.'

'Right,' said Barney, getting up. 'Come on, everyone. Light your candles!'

He waited till they were all in the hall, lighting their candles, then put out the oil-lamp in the sitting-room. Miranda was annoying everyone by blowing out their candles as soon as they lighted them.

'Hey, Barney!' called Snubby indignantly. Come and stop this fat-headed monkey from blowing out our candles! She must be dotty!'

Barney gave on of his uproaring laughs. 'Oh, Miranda!'

52

he said. Do you *still* remember Grandmother's birthday cake? He turned to the others and explained.

'You see, my grandmother had her seventieth birthday a little while ago, and our cook actually put seventy little candles on it and Miranda helped Granny to blow them all out. She loved it!'

'So I suppose she'll blow out any candle she see's now.' groaned Roger. 'Stop it, Miranda. Gosh, she's blown mine out *again*! Barney, get hold of her. We'll never get to bed.'

Miranda was safely captured, and then the little procession made its way up the wide staircase, Loony tearing on ahead as usual, and Miranda firmly tucked in Barney's right arm, well away from his candle.

'Good night!' he said. 'Sleep well. We're all near one another, so if anyone's scared in the night, give a yell!'

But they were all far too sleepy to be scared by anything. The beds were very comfortable, and there were plenty of blankets to keep out the cold, for the rooms were none too warm. Snubby decided that the water in his jug was really far too cold to wash in – he would tackle that in the morning. He decided too, that he would tidy his belongings in the morning; it would take him so long now to sort them out from the heap he had thrown on the floor of his cupboard!

Loony was already asleep on the middle of the bed. Snubby pushed him firmly down to the end and then got into bed himself, quite pleased at the warm patch Loony had made in the middle. He lay for half a minute, wondering at the utter quiet and stillness of the old house – not a sound to be heard, not one!

How awful if the great old knocker began to knock as in the olden days! Snubby was giving himself quite a pleasant thrill about this when he suddenly fell sound asleep – so sound that he didn't even feel Loony creeping up the bed and lying heavily on his middle.

The morning was bright and clear and the sun shone so brilliantly that the snow on the pond began to melt fast. 'That's good,' said Roger, looking out of his window as he dressed. 'If the snow melts on the pond and we get no more, it will freeze again tonight and we can skate tomorrow, because the ice will be free of snow. Today we'll go tobogganing.'

After what Snubby called a 'super-smashing' breakfast of porridge, bacon, eggs and toast, they went to see what jobs they could do for Mrs Tickle. Her kitchen was enormous, and had a pump at one end to pump water for her sink. At the other was a large old kitchen range, but beside it was a new oil-cooker on which she managed to cook everything.

She had the fire going in the range to heat the kitchen, and it all looked very cheerful. She looked up as the children came in carrying the breakfast things and smiled all over her pleasant face.

'What else can we do for you?' asked Diana. 'I'll help you with the washing-up.'

'Well, you don't need to do that,' said Mrs Tickle. 'But if you could see that you each make your bed – and get some wood in for me – and clean the lamps – that would be fine. I'll be able to get on well then.'

'Upstairs everyone,' ordered Diana, taking charge. 'Roger, you get Snubby to help you with your bed, then you help him with his – or he'll just leave it as it is. Do you hear, Snubby?'

'No, teacher,' said Snubby, and skipped out of the way of a slap from Diana.

Everything was soon done, and well done too. Snubby's

bed was as well made as the others – the lamps were cleaned and ready for the night – and so much wood was got in that Mrs Tickle said she had almost enough for a week! She was very pleased. Snubby decided that he now knew her well enough to give her a hug.

'Now then, get away with you,' she said, surprised. 'Squeezing all the breath out of me like that. You're a caution, that's what you are. Oh, bless us all, there's that dog got my brush again. I'll give him such a larruping if I catch him.'

But she never could catch the artful Loony. He enjoyed himself running off with her brush, her duster, and her mop – till she took to keeping a big broom at hand and chasing him every time he appeared.

'Let's go and get our things on now,' said Roger, when all the jobs were done. 'I'm longing to get out into the snow. Let's toboggan first of all, before we have a snow-ball fight or anything.'

It wasn't long before they were all in their outdoor things – wellington boots, scarves, gloves, thick jerseys. It was bitterly cold out of the sun, but they soon got warm.

They had two toboggans – each big enough to take two or three of them at once. They set off up the nearest hill, draging the toboggans behind them. Loony tried to gallop off at a furious speed as usual, but to his dismay found that his legs sank right into this soft white stuff that so mysteriously covered the ground – and for once in a way he had to get along very slowly indeed.

Miranda wouldn't leave Barney's shoulder. She didn't like the snow, though it did occur to her that it would be fun to put some down Barney's neck. She kept her little paws under his collar to warm them. Barney liked feeling them there.

The hill was steep enough to give the children a very thrilling run down to the bottom. There they all tumbled off into the snow, roaring with laughter. Loony soon learnt to sit on the toboggan with Roger and Snubby, his long ears flying backwards in the wind. He loved it, and barked all the way down.

Miranda went with Barney and Diana. She was a bit scared of the sudden rush down the hill and cuddled under Barney's coat, her tiny head just peeping out. 'You're scared, Miranda!' said Barney. But when he tried to make her stay behind on the top of the hill, she wouldn't. No, she wanted to be with Barney every minute of the time.

They had races on their toboggans – two on each toboggan, and then one on each. Barney won easily. His brilliant blue eyes were bluer than ever on this dazzling snowy day, and he looked very happy. In fact, they were all very happy. It was Snubby, as usual, who was the first to feel the pangs of hunger.

'You *can't* be hungry already,' said Roger. 'Not after that colossal breakfast, Snubby. Why, you had six pieces of toast on top of everything else. It can't possibly be lunchtime yet.' He undid his glove to look at his watch.

But at that moment a bell sounded clearly through the frosted air – Mrs Tickle ringing to tell them lunch was ready.

'What did I tell you?' said Snubby, triumphantly. '*I* don't need to look at the time to know when a meal's due. Come on, Loony – race you to Rat-a-Tat House!'

Chapter Nine

A Happy Day

'What a lovely smell,' said Snubby as soon as he reached Rat-a-Tat House. 'What is it?'

'Stew!' said Roger, sniffing. And stew it was, full of carrots and onions and turnips and parsnips. Loony almost pulled everything off the table in his anxiety to see what it was that smelt so good.

'Now you stop that!' ordered Mrs Tickle, pushing him away just in time. 'If you come out to the kitchen with me you'll see I've got some delicious stew-bones for you. Paws off the tablecloth, please.'

'I'm quite tired,' said Diana, sitting down with a flop. 'Aren't you, Barney?'

'No, not really,' said Barney. 'But I'm used to a strenuous sort of life and you're not. I remember the days when I was a hoop-la boy and got up at half-past five to help to get the fair ready – worked all the morning – took charge of the hoop-la stall in the afternoon, and after that worked as gate-boy, taking the money – and then helped the fellow on the swing-boats.'

'Oh, Barney – your life must seem so different now,' said Diana, beginning to eat her stew. 'Barney, didn't you feel queer when your father first found you and took you home to a family you didn't know?'

'Yes, I did,' said Barney. 'I was shy for the first time in my life, I reckon. I couldn't seem to shake hands properly, or say how-do-you-do, or even look them in the face – except my grandmother. I wasn't shy of her. But

I guess that was partly because she had a monkey on her shoulder like me – and the two monkeys took to one another from the first. They even shook paws.'

'Are your cousins nice?' asked Snubby, holding out his plate for a second helping of stew.

'Yes. Very,' said Barney. 'You know – it was strange I've never been ashamed of being a circus-boy, or of any of the jobs I've ever done in my life, but when I met my clean and tidy cousins – they even had clean nails – and saw their fine manners – well, I sort of felt ashamed, and wished I could sink into the ground.'

'You didn't!' said Snubby, surprised. 'I bet you're worth six of any of your cousins. Why, you're even worth six of me and Roger. *I* think you're a marvel.'

'You may be a bit of an ass, Snubby, but you're a real sport,' said Barney, touched. 'But I'll tell you a peculiar thing – instead of my cousins looking down on me because I'd lived in caravans and tents, and done all kinds of odd circus jobs, they thought it was all marvellous – and they were *proud* of having me for their cousin. Think of that!'

'You deserve it,' said Diana. 'You had a jolly hard time, and you were all alone – but you never gave up. I *am* glad we met you that day – it seems so long ago now. We've had some exciting times together, haven't we, Barney?'

'Yes,' said Barney, getting up to take some things to the kitchen. 'But I'm afraid they're ended now. When things run smoothly and happily there don't seem to be so many adventures – or mysteries.'

Snubby forgot his manners and pointed his fork at him. 'How do *you* know? Saying things like that is enough to *make* things begin to happen at once. I smell something in the air.'

'Yes, you smell the remains of the stew,' said Barney,

laughing. 'Get up, you lazy fellow, and help me to take these things out and get the pudding.'

'Right,' said Snubby and stood up. 'Gosh!' he said in surprise. 'Something's happened to my legs – I can hardly stand on them.'

Roger and Diana found exactly the same thing. Their legs were stiff, and hurt when they walked. Barney laughed at them.

'It's all that trudging up the snowy hills,' he said. 'We must have walked up and tobogganed down fifty or sixty times. You'll be as stiff as anything for a day or two.'

'I can't possibly walk up even the smallest hill this afternoon,' groaned Snubby, in dismay. 'Honestly, I think I'll have to have crutches.'

'*I* can't go tobogganing any more today, that's certain,' said Diana, sinking into a chair. 'But, oh – I *don't* want to miss being out of doors on such a heavenly day.'

'Cheer up,' said Barney. 'We'll go out and build an enormous snowman – and we'll have a snowball fight – you'll find you can do that all right!'

Barney was right. Although they found that they could hardly walk when they left the table to stagger out with the dirty plates to Mrs Tickle, their legs gradually became less stiff – and by the time they went out into the snow again they could walk quite well – though none of them except Barney felt that they could possibly climb up a hill dragging a toboggan behind them.

'The snow's just right for snowballing!' called Diana, gathering some into her gloved hand. They all wore leather gloves, knowing from experience how woollen ones became soaked at once, and then the cold bit their fingers and chilled them through and through.

'I'll take Diana for my side, and you two can be together,' said Barney. 'Diana, you can make me snowball ammunition, and I'll do the throwing. Look – this is our little fort – if we are driven out of it the other side have won – but we'll stand firm!'

He made a big circle for himself and Diana, and Roger and Snubby made one for themselves too. Miranda was on Barney's side, of course, and Loony was on the other side.

Ammunition was soon made and the battle began. Snubby was a very wild thrower, but Roger was excellent, and most of his snowballs found their mark. Diana gasped and ducked and yelled, while Barney tried to protect her by sending a fast volley at Roger. Miranda was puzzled by the fight, and, finding herself in a dangerous place on Barney's shoulder, leapt off to a nearby tree.

She landed on a snowy branch, and watched the fight with great interest, sometimes jigging up and down on the branch and scattering snow from the tree.

Loony, of course, went completely mad as he always did when there was any kind of contest between the children. He floundered about, getting in everyone's way, and finally, for some reason of his own, dug an enormous hole in the snow, sending it flying out behind him as if he were a rabbit digging a burrow.

The fight went on until Barney became too strong for Roger, and leaving his own circle, advanced on the two panting boys, sending a stream of well-directed snowballs at them.

'Pax, pax!' yelled Snubby, as Diana also advanced, and snowballed him mercilessly as he slipped and rolled in the snow.

'All right – you win!' panted Roger, collapsing into the snow. 'Gosh, that was the best snowball fight I've ever had! Pax, Diana, pax – don't you dare to put that down my neck. Help, Loony, help!'

The funniest thing that happened that afternoon was when Miranda suddenly discovered the meaning of all this snowballing. She had sat on her tree, watching the others in astonishment as they rolled the snow into balls, and hurled them through the air – and all at once she understood the game.

Quickly she leap off the bough and gathered up some snow in her tiny paws, making a tight little snowball – and then, with a very good aim, she flung it straight at Loony, and hit him – biff, on the nose. He gasped and spluttered in surprise.

'Good shot, Miranda!' yelled Barney, and laughed his infectious laugh. 'Did you see that, you others? Miranda threw a snowball at Loony and hit him. Look out, Loony – she's made another.'

Miranda thought this was a wonderful way of teasing Loony – but soon her fingers began to feel very cold indeed, and, whimpering with the pain in them, she leapt up to Barney's shoulders, and stuffed her cold paws down his warm neck.

'Hey!' he said, startled. 'Are you putting snow down my neck, Miranda? You'd better not. Oh, they're your cold, cold paws – all right, warm them, then!'

The snow was exactly right for building a snowman too. Snubby had the ambitious idea of building a snow house as well, alongside the snowman.

'You build the snowman, Barney; you and Miranda and Diana,' said Snubby. 'Roger and I will build his house – a proper little snow house with a chimney and everything.'

Barney and Diana set to work on the snowman, and made a fat fellow, with a large round head and big feet sticking out at the bottom. 'His name is Mr Icy-Cold,' said Diana, with a giggle. 'Let's get him a hat.'

61

Roger and Snubby were hard at work on their snow house. They had borrowed two shovels from Mrs Tickle, which made the building a good deal quicker.

Soon they had built the rounded walls, as high as themselves, and somehow managed to make a roof that stayed on – a rounded one, like an Eskimo's igloo. They also added a little chimney.

'Now a window,' said Snubby, excited. 'Get *away*, Loony. Go and mess about with the snowman, not with us. You'll find yourself being built into the roof soon!'

They made a little round window, and left a round opening for an entrance. They were really quite proud of their work when they had finished.

'It's a proper snow house,' said Snubby, pleased. 'Big enough to sit in. Come on, Roger let's squeeze into it for a few minutes and see what it's like to live in a snow house.'

They got inside, and sat down. Snubby peered out of the little window. 'I can see our sitting-room window,' he said. 'And Mrs Tickle is inside, cleaning. Ooooh, I feel jolly cold! What about lighting a fire in our little house?'

That made Roger laugh. Loony came up to see what the joke was, and tried to squeeze himself in through the door and join them. He almost knocked down part of one wall and Snubby protested.

'You're so *rough*, Loony,' he complained, pushing him out. 'You *ruined* the snowman's feet by scrabbling for rabbits or something underneath them. I'll snowball you hard if you don't behave yourself.'

'Come on,' said Roger, 'I'm getting cold sitting here. I can't imagine how Eskimos can live and sleep in a snow house – I should freeze to death.'

He squeezed out carefully, followed by Snubby. Miranda came and watched them with interest. *Now* what were they doing? She hopped in through the window and then stared out cheekily. Loony made a rush at her, but Snubby caught his collar.

'No! If you and Miranda have a scrimmage in the snow house that will be the end of it. Roger – Barney – what about going in now? It must be nearly tea-time – or so the clock in my tummy tells me – and I could do with some scalding hot tea to drink.'

It was a very tired set of children who sat down to a late tea – tired but happy. Diana said she could really hardly lift the big brown teapot.

'We've forgotten to draw the curtains across the window,' groaned Roger. 'I meant to – and now I really feel I can't get out of my chair!'

The light from the big oil-lamp on the table streamed out of the window across the snow outside and just caught the outline of the snow house, and fell on the big snow-man too.

'He looks as if he's watching us longingly,' said Snubby. 'I bet he'd like to come in and join us. Poor old Mr Icy-Cold!'

Snubby was just lifting his cup to his mouth, gazing out of the window as he did so, when he suddenly put down his cup again, and stared fixedly.

'Hey!' he said, startled, 'Who's that out there – look, beyond my snow house? Somebody standing quite still. Look!'

Everyone looked, but no one could see anything or anyone. 'It's only the snowman, ass,' said Barney. 'Don't scare Diana. Who on earth would come and stare at our window at this time of night in this lonely district?'

'I don't know,' said Snubby, still gazing out. 'I can't see anyone now. I suppose I *must* have been mistaken.

63

But *honestly*, I thought there was someone standing quite still, watching us.'

Barney got up and drew the curtains so that they met. 'I tell you, it's only our snowman,' he said. 'Anyway, it can't be very nice for the poor thing to stand out in the cold and watch us eating a fine supper like this in the warm room. Goodnight, Mr Icy-Cold. See you in the morning.'

Chapter Ten

Whose Glove?

'It can't have been anyone,' said Diana. 'Loony would have barked.'

'Yes. So he would,' said Snubby, relieved. 'It was just my imagination.'

Both Barney and Roger forebore to say that Loony would probably not hear any footsteps on the snow, and certainly could not *see* anyone out of the window. They didn't want to scare Diana, and they both honestly thought that Snubby had made a mistake.

All the same, Barney resolved to go and have a look-round for footprints in the morning – if it was possible to make out any strange ones amid the marks made by their own feet. The talk soon went on to something else, and they all forgot about Snubby's fright. They enjoyed their supper immensely and, as usual, carried out the dirty things to Mrs Tickle. Miranda collected the forks and handed them over proudly in her little paw.

'There now!' said Mrs Tickle delighted. 'What a clever creature she is – but how you can wear her on your shoulder like that, Barney, I don't know – and her putting her hands down your neck too, to warm them!'

At half-past eight everyone was asleep – but not in bed. No, they were all asleep in their chairs by the fire, books on their knees or fallen to the rug below. Loony too, was asleep, making little excited grunts as he chased a rat in his dreams. Miranda had cuddled under Barney's jacket and could not be seen, but she, too, was asleep.

There Mrs Tickle found them when she came in to ask if anyone wanted hot milk before they went to bed, for the night was really very cold.

'Do any of you want . . .' she began, and then chuckled to herself. Well, well, well – all fast asleep! They ought to be in their beds, poor things, tired out like that!

She woke them all, and to their great astonishment they found that they were not comfortably in bed as they imagined, but slumped in their chairs by the fire. So that was what a morning of tobogganing could do! Groaning and yawning, they lighted their candles and crawled up to bed, with Mrs Tickle laughing at them and lighting the way. What a set of yawners!

They all slept late the next morning, and Mrs Tickle rang the gong in vain. In the end she had to go up and wake them all, and even pull Snubby out of bed and take all the clothes away!

However, they were bright and cheery after breakfast, though all but Barney were very stiff. They gazed out of the window at the lake as they ate fried sausages and fried bread. The surface was quite free from snow and the ice looked blue and inviting.

'What about skating this morning?' said Barney. 'Or are you all too stiff?'

'Well, I don't feel like using my aching muscles to climb up those hills in order to toboggan down them,' said Diana. 'But I'd like to try skating. I'll probably use a different set of muscles, and they won't hurt.'

They did their usual jobs, and helped Mrs Tickle willingly. When she heard they were going skating she gave them each a packet of biscuits.

'Skating's hungry work,' she said. 'You'll need a snack – and maybe if you have that you won't want to eat me out of house and home when you get in for your lunch.'

'I've got to stay behind and mend my sweater,' said Diana. 'I tore it yesterday and if I don't mend it before I go out it will all unravel. I'll catch you boys up later, down at the pond.'

The others left her to ask Mrs Tickle for a needle, and went off with their skates. On the way they passed the big snowman they had built the day before, and stopped to look at him.

'He's a real beauty,' said Barney. 'Quite the biggest I've seen. We ought to have given him a coat to wear to make him look real.'

'I say, just let's have a look and see if there are any strange footmarks about,' said Roger, remembering Snubby's scare the night before.'

'Oh, no!' said Snubby, quite ashamed now of the alarm he had raised. 'It was just that my eyes were tired with the glare of the snow, I expect. I saw things that weren't there!'

'We'll have a squint round, all the same,' said Barney. He walked round the snowman, but saw nothing unusual at all – merely a large number of jumbled footmarks made by their wellington boots the day before.

Then he looked at the snow house and round about. There was again a mass of footsteps and it was impossible to tell whether any of them belonged to a stranger – though Barney's sharp eyes showed him one or two that he thought were *not* made by rubber boots. But, no; it really *was* impossible to tell.

'Come on,' he said. 'Nothing here. Snubby *must* have been mistaken after all.'

Snubby went into his little snow house just for the fun of it. He sat down for a few moments, imagining that he was an Eskimo in an igloo. Then, hearing the others' voices getting faint in the distance, he stooped to go out again.

And then it was that he saw the glove. There it lay, half hidden by the snow, just at the side of the little entrance to the snow house. Snubby stared at it and picked it up, thinking for the moment that it must belong to Barney or Roger.

But it was a big glove – made of thick navy-blue wool. Not one of the children had hands large enough to fit the glove. Snubby turned it over, his heart beginning to beat fast. So there *might* have been someone out here last night after all – someone staring in through the lighted window, watching them. It wasn't at all a nice thought. He ran after the other two boys, shouting.

'Barney! Roger! Wait, I've got something to tell you.!'

They turned round, recognising something urgent in his voice. Loony, who had run on with them, turned back at once and floundered over the snow to Snubby.

'What is it?' said Roger.

'Look what I found in my snow house,' said Snubby, panting. 'This glove! I was just crawling out when I found it. Surely it isn't one of ours – it's so big.'

'No. It's not ours,' said Roger. 'We've all got leather gloves, Barney too. This is someone else's. I suppose Loony couldn't possibly have taken it from somewhere and dropped it there, could he?'

'No. Not possibly,' said Snubby. 'He didn't even *go* to the snow house with me. He ran on with you. I say, you know – I think there *was* someone out here last night after all. But why? Out in all this cold and snow.'

'Don't say a word to Diana or Mrs Tickle,' said Roger. 'You'll scare them stiff if you do. This may be just nothing. Anyway, we can't do anything about it now –

we'll just have to keep watch this evening and see if we can spot anything. I must say it's rather strange.'

'*Could* somebody have crouched in the snow house last night, and watched us?' said Snubby. 'I must have seen someone either getting in or getting out – I don't know which.'

They sat down at the edge of the shining pond to put on their skates. Barney had some fine new ones given to him for Christmas by his grandmother. He had never skated in his life, and he was much looking forward to it. He puzzled over the glove that Snubby had found, but soon forgot about it as he stood up, wobbling, on his skates.

Snubby and Roger had skated before. Snubby, oddly enough, was better than Roger, and he was soon off and away, calling to the others.

Loony was most excited to see his master apparently flying over the ice, he went so fast and so lightly. With an excited bark he rushed over the snow to the ice and tried to bound after him.

But to his surprise he found that all his four legs slid away beneath him, and there he was, sliding on his back, just as he sometime did in a slippery hall.

But it was much more difficult to find his feet again on the slippery pond than in a polished hall – each time he tried to stand he slipped over again, and at last he managed to sit down on his tail, looking very miserable.

'Bad luck, Loony!' shouted Snubby, circling round him. 'You can't manage your legs this morning, can you? You'll have to learn to walk slowly for once.'

But Loony leapt to his feet to follow Snubby, and again he found himself off his balance, his paws slithering away beneath him, and his nose bumping the ground. He somehow managed to sit down again and howled dismally.

'All right – I'll take you back to the bank,' said Snubby. 'And just be sensible and stay there.'

Roger was now on the ice, skating carefully, afraid of falling, but soon getting into the way of it. Barney stood and watched Snubby, and the ease with which he flew over the ice. It looked to be just a question of balance – and Barney knew all about that. Hadn't he walked the tight-rope a thousand times? Hadn't he stood on horses' backs when they galloped gracefully round a circus ring?

Without another thought Barney stepped on to the ice and set off smoothly and rhythmically. Immediately he felt at home, and his feet felt as if they had wings. He gave a shout.

'Ho! This is wonderful! Why didn't I ever skate before?'

Roger and Snubby watched him in amazement. They themselves a winter or two ago had had to go through the painfully slow process of learning skating the hard way – falling, slipping, bumping down on the ice, scrambling up only to fall again – before they could balance themselves and skate for more than a few yards.

And here was old Barney skating at thirty miles an hour as if he had done nothing but skate all his life long. Look at him now, going round in circles, then shooting off again, then spreading his legs wide and circling once more. What a boy!

'You *knew* how to skate, you fibber!' shouted Snubby.

'I did not! It's the first time!' called back Barney, his blue eyes gleaming brightly. 'It's heavenly – superb – best sport I've ever tried!'

Diana came on the ice just then, also full of astonishment to see Barney skating so easily. Miranda on his shoulder, enjoying this new game to the utmost. Diana was a graceful little skater, and went over to Barney, holding out her hand.

70

'Skate with me,' she said. 'That's right, hold my hands like that. Oh, Barney – you skate beautifully!'

It was grand fun to be on the ice that clear winter's morning. Roger fell over quite a lot and groaned, and rubbed himself, quite envious of the others, especially Snubby. Snubby did not skate as gracefully as either Barney or Diana but he was as usual, full of idiotic tricks, leaping in the air on his skates, twisting himself round in never-ending circles till he fell over in giddiness – and altogether behaving in what Diana called a 'very Snubby-ish way.'

They had a wonderful morning on the ice, and were glad of the packets of biscuits that Mrs Tickle had given them, which they shared generously with Loony and Miranda.

'Let's skate this afternoon too,' said Barney, who felt as if he could never have enough of flying through the frosty air so easily. So the whole day was spent on the pond. It was quite clear of snow now, except at the far end, where trees overhung it, and the surface was still snowbound.

They were very tired that evening – so tired that they dragged themselves upstairs very early indeed, immediately after supper. Mrs Tickle was amused – and pleased too, because now she also could get to bed early.

They all lighted their candles in the hall, and Barney held Miranda tightly so that she couldn't blow them out. Then up the stairs they went, yawning.

'I don't mind tell you that *nothing* will make me wake up tonight!' said Snubby, smothering a really enormous yawn.

'A thunderstorm would,' said Diana. 'It always wakes *me*.'

'No. A thunderstorm wouldn't wake me – nor an earthquake – nor even a bomb!' said Snubby.

But he was quite wrong – as wrong as ever he could be!

Chapter Eleven

Noise in the Night

Snubby was asleep almost before he had climbed into bed. He felt his eyes closing as he groped for the bedclothes, and then he knew nothing more. He didn't even dream.

The others were almost as sleepy. Even little Miranda was tired out with her day in the frosty air, and snuggled down at the foot of Barney's bed before he was in it. Mrs Tickle was the last of the household to go to sleep.

But she had not been skating for miles all day long. She undressed slowly, folded all her things as she always did, washed herself in the icy-cold water, and undid her plaited hair to brush it out.

She thought about the four children. Nice children, she said to herself, always willing to give a hand, and always jolly together. But that caution of a Snubby! He was the best of the lot, thought Mrs Tickle, deftly plaiting her long hair again.

'Him and his freckles and jokes! He reminds me of what my Tom used to be – always up to mischief and as artful as a monkey – yes, as artful as that little Miranda! I didn't take to her at first, but she's got such funny little ways. And that Loony! If ever a dog had the right name, it's him. Taking my clothes and brushes all day long and hiding them.'

She was in bed at last, having done all the things she did so meticulously every evening – said her prayers and read her Bible and rubbed cream on her rough hands.

She blew out her candle and settled down with her hot-water bottle, hugging it to her with pleasure – and then, like the others, she fell fast asleep.

The night was still and the frost was hard. There was not a sound to be heard, for even the owl was too cold to hoot, and flew sadly on his silent wings, looking for mice that he could not see. They were far under the snow, safe in their cosy holes.

And then a thunderous sound split the deep silence – a tremendous noise that echoed through the old house and awoke everyone immediately.

Nobody knew what it was. It had sounded in their dreams, and by the time they had awakened, only the echo of the noise was left in their minds.

Snubby leapt up in fright. Diana cowered under the bedclothes. Roger sat up and Barney sprang out of bed. Mrs Tickle covered her head with the bedclothes. 'A storm!' she said. 'Oh, my, what a crash!'

Loony barked madly without stopping partly with fright but mostly from anger. He had been so sound asleep – not even one ear open – and now this strange noise had awakened him without warning.

Roger, who shared a room with Snubby, called across to him: 'Snubby, did you hear that crashing noise? What do you suppose it was?'

'The end of the world I should think!' said Snubby, his heart still beating fast. 'It can't be a storm – look, you can see the stars in a clear sky.'

'I'm going to Diana, to see if she's scared,' said Roger, and he got out of bed and ran to Diana's room. He met Barney on the landing, holding a lighted candle.

'Hallo. Did you hear that row?' said Roger. 'Whatever was it? An explosion of some sort?'

'No. I don't know *what* it was,' said Barney. 'I was fast asleep. It sounded pretty near, anyway.'

They went into Diana's room. 'Diana! Are you all right?' called Roger to his sister. She was still under the bedclothes. She put her head out and looked at him in the light of the wavering candle-flame.

'Oh, Roger – Barney. Whatever *was* that?' she said, in a shaky voice.

'Can't imagine – perhaps a crash of thunder,' said Roger, speaking cheerfully. He hated Diana to be frightened.

'You needn't worry,' said Barney. 'The sky isn't stormy – the crash won't come again.'

But even as he finished speaking, it did come again. And this time they heard it clearly, not muddled as in a dream.

RAT-A-TAT-TAT! RAT-A-TAT-TAT!

The noise echoed all through the house, and then slowly died away. Diana disappeared under the bedclothes with a cry of fright. Roger clutched at Barney.

'The knocker!' he said. 'It's someone hammering at the front door with that enormous knocker. Good gracious – who is it coming here in the middle of the night?'

'Perhaps – perhaps it's my father,' said Barney. 'No, he would have telephoned. Gosh! I really don't feel as if I want to go down and open the door.'

The light of another candle flickered outside Diana's door. It was Mrs Tickle, who, although really too scared to get out of bed, had felt obliged to come and see if the children were all right. She shook so much that she could hardly hold her candlestick level.

'What was that?' she said. 'Someone knocking at the door? But – it's midnight! I'll not open the door. I daren't go down the stairs!'

'I tell you what,' said Barney, speaking as cheerfully as he could, 'we'll lean out of the window over the front door and ask who it is. It may be someone who is lost and needing help.'

Snubby had now joined them with a very frightened Loony, who produced a string of growls but no barks.

'WHY did you say that nothing in the world would wake you tonight, Snubby?' said Diana. 'Something *always* happens when you say silly things like that.'

'Come on,' said Barney. 'Let's go and shout out of the window. Or would you rather stay here with Diana, Mrs Tickle?'

'I'll stay here,' said Mrs Tickle. 'I'll look after Diana – and she can look after me. And mind, if it's someone lost, don't let them in till you've told me. Waking us all up like this at midnight! It's disgraceful!'

The three boys, with Loony and Miranda, went along the landing to the big window that overlooked the front door. They opened it with difficulty, for it was very stiff.

Outside lay the thick snow, and the snowman and snow house loomed up dimly in the bright starlight. Barney leaned out of the window, trying to see down to the front door.

'Who's there?' he shouted. 'Who's there?'

They all held their breath to listen for the answer. But none came. There was not a sound from below. Barney shouted again.

'Who knocked on the door? Answer, please!'

But still there was no answer. The night was silent and still. Barney shut the window, for the air was bitterly cold. He shivered.

'Nobody there,' he said. 'Not a sound to be heard.'

'Do your think we'd better go down and open the door – just in case?' said Roger.

76

'In case of *what*?' said Barney, fastening the window.

'Well, in case there's somebody ill there – or exhausted with being lost,' said Roger.

'Anyone who can hammer at that knocker with such fury can't be ill or faint,' said Barney grimly. 'And we *don't* go down! That's quite certain.'

They went back to Mrs Tickle and Diana. 'Nobody's there,' said Barney briefly.

Mrs Tickle began to shiver again, partly with fright and partly with cold. 'It's that Mr No-One,' she said. 'The one that used to come all those years ago – and hammer on the door to warn the family that there was a traitor inside.'

'Stuff!' said Roger. 'Rubbish! Fiddlesticks! That's a silly old legend. Anyway, there *isn't* a traitor of any sort or kind in this house, Mrs Tickle. *I* think it's someone playing a fat-headed joke on us.'

'Well, if that's so, we're not going to fall for it,' said Barney firmly, though he felt very doubtful indeed that it was a joke. 'We're going to go back to bed and get warm and go to sleep – and in the morning we'll do a little exploring for footprints up to the front door. Our Mr No-One had to go up those steps, and we'll at least see what his feet are like – big – small – middle-size.'

'Yes. That's a good idea,' said Snubby. 'Come on then – let's go to bed.'

'I'm going to sleep on the couch in your room, Diana,' said Mrs Tickle. 'We'll be company for each other. You'd like that, wouldn't you?'

'Oh, *yes*,' said Diana, and kind Mrs Tickle went off to collect her bedclothes and hot-water bottle, and then made her bed up on the little couch at the other side of Diana's room. Diana felt very comforted to know that she was there – and Mrs Tickle was also glad to have

Diana's company. That Mr No-One – what a fright he had given them all!

Snubby and Roger talked things over for a few minutes and then Snubby fell fast asleep again. Barney, in the next room, puzzled over the knocking for sometime, and over the curious fact that nobody was at the door. He didn't for one moment believe in the old legend.

'We'll find out a few things tomorrow morning,' he thought, turning over comfortably. 'Oh, sorry, Miranda – did I squash you?'

The little monkey had been so frightened by the noise that she had crept right to the bottom of Barney's bed and had cuddled by his feet.

The clock down the hall chimed the half hour – half-past midnight, thought Barney. Well, look out, Mr Knocker, whoever you are – we'll all be on your trail tomorrow morning!

Chapter Twelve

The Footprints

Everyone but Mrs Tickle slept soundly for the rest of the night. Mrs Tickle, who had not tired herself out with vigorous skating, as the children had, was not as sleepy as they were, and she lay and worried about the strange knocking for a long time.

At a quarter to seven she slid off the couch in Diana's room, put on her dressing-gown, and opened the door quietly to go to her own room. It was time to get dressed and go down and see to the lighting of the fires.

Later on, Barney went into Roger's room to dress with him and Snubby and to talk about the night's alarm. They none of them felt scared now; they felt brave and rather scornful of last night's fears. Outside was the brilliant sunshine and the dazzling snow, and the thought of skating and tobogganing drove away the alarms of the night.

Diana came knocking at the door. 'Are you ready to go down to breakfast? I'm dressed.'

'Yes, we're ready,' said Roger, opening the door. 'I vote we go and have a squint at the knocker that was used so vigorously last night.'

So, with Loony streaking ahead of them, the first thing they did was to race down the wide stairs, and go straight to the front door.

'We've not used this door since we first came,' said Barney. 'We came in this way when we arrived, but ever since then we've used the side door to go in and out.'

'We haven't had any fall of snow since we came,' said

Roger, considering. 'So let's think now – about footprints. We drove up in the car to the stone steps that run up to the door. . . .'

'So there should only be the marks of the car tyres in the drive – and *our* footmarks going up the steps to the door,' said Barney. 'And that means, there should now be *another* set of footprints – Mr No-One's – coming up the drive right to these steps, where they will unfortunately be muddled with ours. My word, isn't the door difficult to open!'

It certainly was. It had two great bolts, one at the top and one at the bottom – two locks – and a heavy chain. The locks were stiff to turn, but at last they clicked and the children were able to open the great door.

'We've never even *seen* the knocker yet!' said Diana, and she looked to see what it was like.

It was magnificent. It was in the shape of a great lion's head, and to use it one iron lock of its mane had to be grasped in order to lift the knocker. Diana and the others marvelled at it. They had never seen such a knocker in their lives – no wonder it made so much noise!

'I'll just feel it to see how heavy it is,' said Snubby, and took hold of the handle made by the lock of the lion's mane. He raised the knocker, but it was so heavy that it fell back again immediately.

CRASH!

Loony fell down the steps in fright, and Miranda shot under Barney's coat. Diana jumped violently and turned on Snubby at once. 'DON'T! I can't bear being made to jump like that. WHY must you be so silly?'

'Sorry,' said Snubby, very much startled himself. 'I'd no idea it was so heavy.'

Mrs Tickle came running into the hall, looking as scared as could be. 'What . . .' she began, and then saw the children standing there. 'Oh, bless us all, I thought it was that Mr No-One again. I was just coming to give him a piece of my mind.'

'It was only me,' said Snubby. 'Sorry! My word, isn't it an ENORMOUS knocker, Mrs Tickle. No wonder it gave us all a fright last night. Whoever knocked must have been a strong fellow, to crash it on the door like that.'

'Well, don't *you* do that again, or the breakfast will be spoilt,' said Mrs Tickle, still rather cross. 'I dropped an egg I was holding and it splashed all over my shoe – look!'

'Loony, lick it!' ordered Snubby, but before the dog could get to the shoe, Miranda was there, licking the egg yolk with much enjoyment.

'How *can* you, Miranda!' said Diana, in disgust.

'Let's look for footprints,' said Roger, and he went to the top of the steps and looked down.

There was not much help to be got from the mass of footprints there, nor from those just in front of the door, under the porch. A jumble of footmarks flattened the thick snow, and it was difficult to tell one from another.

'We all stood here together when we arrived,' said Diana. 'Your father, Barney – and we four – and Loony of course leaping about everywhere – but we shan't find Miranda's tiny paw-marks because she was on your shoulder.'

'There'll be the marks of the suitcases too,' said Barney. 'Yes, you can see them here and there.'

They all went down the steps, trying to keep to the sides, so that they did not make any further prints to confuse those already there. It was when they came to the bottom of the steps and into the drive that they really discovered something.

The marks of the car tyres were there, of course,

coming up the drive, and stopping by the door – then swinging round and back when Mr Martin drove off again. But there was a strange line of footprints, all by itself, coming right across the drive, from the snow-clad lawn nearby. The children followed them to where they themselves had made hundreds of prints when they snowballed one another.

'Look at these!' said Barney, in excitement. 'These prints aren't made by us – they're enormous! They are made by someone wearing really big boots – they look like wellington boots, many sizes larger than ours.'

The children looked down at them earnestly. Yes, these prints were not theirs. What a pity they were lost in the jumble of footmarks they themselves had made, and could not be followed any farther. They thought they could make them out here and there, but it was very uncertain.

'Let's follow them back to the front door,' said Roger. 'Everyone's got to be jolly carefull NOT to tread on them or spoil them.'

They followed them across the lawn and over the drive to the bottom of the steps, where, of course, they were then lost in a jumble of others.

Mrs Tickle came to the front door, looking rather impatient. 'Aren't you *ever* coming for breakfast?' she said. 'And do you want to catch your death of cold, messing about outside without even a coat on?'

'Mrs Tickle, come and look; we've found Mr No-One's footprints!' called Snubby. 'Do come!'

Mrs Tickle pricked up her ears at once. She went cautiously down the front-entrance steps, afraid of slipping, and was proudly shown the set of prints leading up to the bottom step.

'Follow us and we'll show you where they come from,' said Roger, and took her to where they had had their snowball fight. 'See, they are lost here – but Mr No-One went over the lawn from here, right across the drive, and then he must have gone up the steps to knock on the door.'

'Yes,' said Mrs Tickle, looking extremely puzzled. 'Yes, but why is there only *one* set of prints?'

'Because he was by himself!' said Snubby, thinking that Mrs Tickle was not very clever.

'Yes, I know that. But why isn't there a set of prints leading *back* from the front-door steps?' said Mrs Tickle. 'I mean – he'd got to walk *back*, hadn't he? And there are no footmarks showing that he walked away again.'

Nobody had thought of that at all. How very stupid! Barney frowned, very puzzled. 'Yes, we didn't think of that – we were so excited at finding strange footmarks that we never thought that there should be *two* sets; one coming and one going.'

'This is *horrid!*' said Diana. 'How can anyone come to our front door and knock, and then not go away? He's not standing there now! Then *how* did he go away?'

'For goodness' sake come and have your breakfast,' said Mrs Tickle, shivering in the cold. 'I'll have you all in bed with bad chills if you stay out here any longer. Leave Mr No-One and his antics to himself and come away in.'

They obeyed her, very silent. It certainly was very, very strange that there were no footmarks going away from the house – only one set, walking towards it! How did Mr No-One, as they all called the night visitor, go away if he didn't use his feet? It was a puzzle – a real mystery!

They sat down to breakfast, and helped themselves to hot porridge. Snubby remembered the fright he had had two nights before when he thought he had seen someone standing near the snow house while they were having their supper. He reminded the others.

'I bet that was Mr No-One too,' he said. 'And I bet that's his glove we found!'

'Oh, yes,' said Roger. 'I expect it was. Well, we now know he was a man with large hands and large feet, and he has probably got one odd navy glove. But what we *don't* know is why on earth he's messing about Rat-a-Tat House.'

'I wish he'd go somewhere else,' said Diana, pouring out large cups of milky coffee for everyone. 'And I hope to goodness he doesn't come knocking at our front door again.'

'Do you think we'd better telephone to my father and tell him about it?' said Barney. 'After all, this is my granny's house, and if anyone intends to burgle it, we ought to do something about it.'

'Yes, of course. We'll telephone and tell the whole tale!' said Roger. 'Good idea. Perhaps your father will come over and have a fight with Mr No-One, Barney.'

But when they went to telephone, there was no reply. The snow had brought down the wires, and until they were mended Rat-a-Tat House was completely cut off from everywhere!

Chapter Thirteen

A Few Interesting Things

'Well!' said Barney, hanging up the telephone receiver. 'That's that. We're cut off from everyone at the moment. Couldn't even get a doctor if we wanted one.'

'We could get to the village of Boffame somehow, if we had to,' said Roger.

'It would take us ages,' said Barney. 'All through that thick snow! I bet we'd get lost, too. All the countryside looks alike when it's covered with snow. We'd need skis to make any headway.'

'So we'll have to solve the Mystery of Rat-a-Tat House by ourselves!' said Snubby cheerfully. 'Oh, well, we're jolly good at mysteries, I think. We've had four already – the Rockingdown Mystery, the Rilloby Fair Mystery . . .'

'The Rubadub Mystery,' said Diana, 'and what was the other? Oh, yes, the Ring o' Bells Mystery.'

'We'll call this the Rat-a-Tat Mystery then, as Snubby said,' put in Barney. 'How weird – they all begin with R.'

'Is there any more bacon and eggs?' asked Snubby, hopefully.

'Certainly not,' said Diana indignantly. 'You've had twice as much as anyone else.'

'Oooh, I haven't. Have I, Loony?' said Snubby, looking hurt. Loony thumped his tail on the ground and licked Snubby's hand.

'Stop thumping,' ordered Diana. 'I don't want to hear any knocking or thumping or hammering for ages. Loony, stop it!'

'Does anyone feel like tobogganing today?' asked Roger. 'My legs feel quite all right now.'

Barney would have liked to skate all day long, but when the others voted for tobogganing he nodded too.

'Right,' said Roger. 'That's settled then. But don't let's choose such a steep hill for our tobogganing this time – it really is such a drag up.'

So they chose another hill, and dragged their toboggans up joyfully, after they had done all they could to help a rather silent Mrs Tickle. She wasn't at all happy about Mr No-One!

When they came to the top they had a fine view over the white countryside, and suddenly saw something they had not been able to see from the other hill they tobogganed down.

'What's that?' said Snubby, pointing to what looked like a small house, whose roof was white with snow. It stood very close to one bank of the lake, and, in fact, looked almost as if it were *on* the lake.

Everyone looked down at it. 'It's a boat-house, of course!' said Roger. 'Built partly on land and partly over water. There'll be boats in there, won't there, Barney?'

'Yes,' said Barney, remembering that his father had told him that boats were stored for use on the lake in the summer. 'I'd forgotten there was a boat-house. We might go and explore it when we're tired of tobogganing.'

The snow was beautifully crisp for tobogganing again and the children really enjoyed themselves – especially when Snubby went down the hill alone with Loony, and the toboggan struck something, leapt in the air and flung both Snubby and Loony into the snow. Poor Loony fell in so deep that he was lost to sight!

'Loony, Loony, where are you?' yelled Snubby in a

panic. 'Come and help, you asses, don't stand laughing your heads off there. Loony will suffocate in the snow.'

'Not Loony!' shouted Roger. 'He's having a nice little rest!'

Loony was, in fact, tunnelling under the snow, too out of breath even to bark. He popped up just by Snubby and made him jump. He leapt on him in delight and over went poor Snubby, deeper in the snow than ever, with Loony leaping about on top of him. The others laughed till they ached, but Snubby was most annoyed.

'Let's eat our morning biscuits in the boat-house – if we can get in,' said Barney when they began to feel tired and hungry. So they went over the snow to the boat-house, which with its white-painted walls and snow-clad roof, was really quite difficult to see from a distance.

It was shut and locked. 'Blow!' said Barney. 'We can't get in.'

They went to look in at a window, and saw three boats there, in the dimness of the shed. Snubby wandered right round the shed and then suddenly shouted.

'Hey, here's a broken window. We can get in after all.'

The others went round to him, but before he came to the broken window, Roger suddenly saw something else. Footmarks! Large ones, very much the same size as those they had seen in the drive.

'I say, we're on to something now,' said Barney, excited. 'Perhaps our Mr No-One lives here – trespassing in my father's boat-house. Anyone got a torch?'

No one had, which was a pity. Barney looked at the broken window and saw that he could easily get in without tearing his clothes. 'I'll just have a snoop round,' he said, and was up on the wooden sill easily and in at the jagged window.

The others waited eagerly. He soon came back with a

bit of news. 'Yes, I think our Mr No-One is staying here. One of the boats is lined with boat cushions, as if someone sleeps there. And I found an empty cigarette packet. Look!'

He gave the packet to Roger and then climbed deftly out of the window, his eyes shining. He looked at the large footprints again, just under the window. Yes, Mr No-One used the window to get in by, that was certain. Now, where did the footmarks go? They might lead to Mr No-One himself!

But the prints merely went to the front of the boat-house, which, instead of standing on piles in the water, as it usually did, was now standing in thick ice, for the lake was frozen. As soon as the footmarks reached the ice, they disappeared, of course, for no footprints showed on the ice.

'At least the footprints go *both* ways this time,' said Roger thankfully. 'Look, there are sets leading up to the window and sets leading away again – all jumbled up, but clear enough to see that the fellow came and went.'

'Who is he – a tramp?' wondered Diana. 'But why would a tramp come and knock at Rat-a-Tat House? And, anyway, how did he make footprints that only led there – and not away? That's been puzzling me all day!'

'Oh, let's not worry about that,' said Snubby, who had finished his biscuits and wanted to toboggan again. 'Come on – it's cold just standing here.'

They were all bright-eyed and red-cheeked when they went in for lunch, feeling quite ravenous.

'Has Mr No-One been knocking at the door again?' asked Snubby cheerfully, as Mrs Tickle brought in a dishful of chops surrounded by fried potatoes and tinned peas. 'Oh, I say – look at that! It makes me feel hungrier than ever.'

'That Mr No-One wouldn't dare to come in the day-time,' said Mrs Tickle. 'I've got my rolling-pin ready, and a kettle boiling on the stove. I'm ready for him if he comes banging at any door, front or back.'

They all laughed at the determined little woman. She laughed too. 'There you are – you get on with your lunch – and there's a big treacle pudding to follow so leave a bit of room for that.'

It was a lovely meal as usual, and the children felt lazy after it. But the day was again so beautiful that no one wanted a long rest. Soon they were on their way to toboggan again and spent the whole afternoon racing down and climbing up the snowy hills. They were very tired when they dragged themselves back to Rat-a-Tat House just as it was getting dusk.

'I can't find enough strength to throw a snowball at anyone,' said Snubby sorrowfully. 'As for Loony, he's so tired I'm having to drag him back on my toboggan, the lazy fellow.'

'Our snowman is still standing on guard over our snow house,' said Roger. 'Hallo, Mr Icy-Cold? Your hat's gone crooked. Pray let me put it straight for you.'

He tipped the old hat straight, and they all went on to the garden door to take of their wet boots and gloves. Mrs Tickle heard them and came to welcome them.

'You're late,' she said. 'I've had hot buttered toast ready for you for twenty minutes. Hurry up and wash, or the toast will be cold.'

'I can't even hurry for buttered toast,' said Snubby. 'I'm an old, old man, Mrs Tickle, bent and stooping, and my legs will hardly bear me. Oh, what tobogganing does to you!'

'Go on with you,' said Mrs Tickle. 'Bent old man you

may be, but you'll eat more than your share of the toast, I'll be bound!'

They all sat at the laden white-clothed table, enjoying their meal, with Diana pouring out huge cups of tea for everyone. They were happy but so tired that they could hardly tease one another. Loony flopped down under the table with an enormous sigh. He was very much afraid he would go to sleep before the titbits began to arrive for him below the table.

'Let's draw the curtains,' said Barney. 'I don't want to feel that Mr No-One is hiding in our snow house again and watching us while we eat.

Barney got up to draw them. Before he pulled them across the lighted window, he looked out into the darkness, pierced only by the rays of the bright oil-lamp. He swung round suddenly.

'I SAY! Our snowman's gone! He's not there!'

'Gone! But he can't be! Why, he was there when we came in, half an hour ago!' said Diana. 'Roger put his hat straight.'

'Well, he's not there now,' said Barney. 'Come and see. You can just make out the snow house – but no snowman! Gosh! What extraordinary things are happening? Where *has* Mr Icy-Cold gone?'

Chapter Fourteen

Another Mystery

The four children really were astounded at the disappearance of their snowman, especially as they had passed him such a short time ago on their way back to tea.

'Someone must have knocked him down,' said Barney at last. 'It's the only explanation. Snowmen don't walk away on their own – not even our nice Mr Icy-Cold.'

'Well, shall we got a torch and go out and see if he's been knocked down and made into just a heap of snow?' said Roger.

'Yes. And we may perhaps spy the person who spoilt him,' said Barney, getting his torch off the mantelpiece. 'We'll take Loony too; he'll soon smell out anyone hiding nearby, watching to see if we've noticed the disappearance of the snowman.'

'I don't see any *point* in knocking him down,' began Diana, really puzzled, and then she stopped. A cry had come from the kitchen, and then the children heard hurried footsteps running down the passage to the sitting-room. The door was flung open, and there was Mrs Tickle 'all of a shake' again.

'What's the matter?' cried Barney.

'The snowman! Your snowman! He came and peeped in at the kitchen window when I was having my tea,' panted Mrs Tickle. The children stared at her unbelievingly.

'But – Mrs Tickle – you must know that a snowman doesn't walk!' said Roger. 'It must have been a – '

'I tell you, it was your snowman, all white, and with that hat on,' said Mrs Tickle, sinking down into a chair. 'Such goings-on! We'll get back to Little Wendleman as soon as possible. You telephone your father, Barney.'

'The telephone is out of order,' said Barney, and Mrs Tickle groaned. Then she looked out of the window and gave a little scream.

'He's gone – your snowman's gone!' she said. 'I *thought* it was him, peering in at my window and frightening the life out of me. Hat and all.'

This was really very puzzling. None of the children believed for a moment that it actually was their snowman that Mrs Tickle had seen. But *who* was it? And why was he all in white? And how was it that their own snowman had disappeared so very suddenly?

'I believe that wasn't a snowman at all, out there,' said Mrs Tickle, nodding her head towards the window. 'He may have been once, but after that it was someone covered in snow, watching us.'

'Oh, no, Mrs Tickle!' said Barney. 'Honestly, we walked close by him this morning *and* this afternoon, and there is no doubt at all but that he was a snowman made of snow. Why, Roger even put his hat on straight for him. Didn't you, Roger?'

'Well, then – you explain to me how he walked away and came and looked in my kitchen window,' said Mrs Tickle fiercely. 'You tell me that!'

They couldn't. It was just as much a puzzle to them as to poor Mrs Tickle. Barney and Roger went out to the kitchen with her to see if the snowman was still doing some peeping. But he wasn't. Barney took his torch into the backyard and shone it everywhere, but there was nothing to be seen, except a jumble of footmarks all mixed up together – obviously Mrs Tickle's and some of theirs. It was impossible to tell if there were any others as well.

They came back, and Mrs Tickle firmly locked and bolted the door behind her. 'I won't have that snowman walking into my kitchen,' she said.

'It's a pity he doesn't,' said Snubby. 'He would go and warm himself at your big fire, Mrs Tickle; and in a few minutes all you'd have to do would be to mop up a big pool of water, and empty the snowman down the sink.'

Mrs Tickle had to laugh. 'You're a real caution, you are,' she said. 'Have you finished your tea yet?'

'Gosh, no!' said Snubby, quite shocked to think that he could have left his tea and forgotten about it. 'I was in the middle of my third piece of toast and butter.'

'You'd better go and finish it, then,' said Mrs Tickle, giving him a little push.

The children went back to the sitting-room to finish their tea. They all felt rather excited, but they found it difficult to believe that Mrs Tickle had seen anyone *really* like a snowman. It must have been a trick of the dusk.

'But that doesn't solve *our* problem – of why our snowman suddenly disappeared,' said Snubby.

'He might have melted,' suggested Diana. 'The weather might have got warmer. It feels like it.'

'You can't possibly tell what the weather's like sitting in this hot room,' said Roger. 'I'm sure it's as cold as ever. I hope it is, anyway. I want to go skating tomorrow.'

'Yes!' said Barney, beaming. 'Yes, let's all go skating.'

They had a very pleasant evening with no more disturbances. They thought that Mrs Tickle seemed a bit scared of being in the kitchen by herself, so they decided to ask her to come and have a game of Snap-Grab with them – that would cheer her up, and make her forget the snowman who had peeped in at her window.

They set the cork in the middle of the table and Roger dealt the cards. Whenever anyone saw that two cards were the same, he not only had to call 'Snap!' but had to grab the cork as well. This saved a great many arguments as to who it was who had called Snap first! Snubby grabbed at the cork so fiercely every time he called Snap that they made him go and fetch his gloves and put one on.

'You've scratched my hand twice,' complained Diana. 'You really are rough at this game, Snubby. I shan't play unless you wear a glove.'

So Snubby fetched his gloves and put one on his right hand. Now, when he grabbed the cork, he couldn't scratch anyone!

Miranda loved a game of snap, and kept trying to grab the cork herself when anyone yelled 'Snap!' Once she really did get hold of it and leapt away to the mantelpiece with it, holding it so tightly that Barney couldn't get it away from her.

'You really are naughty,' he said, but Miranda refused to give up the cork. She put it into her mouth and held it there, looking wickedly at Barney.

Snubby laughed. He got up and put a few old cards on the mantelpiece beside Miranda.

'Here you are,' he said. 'You can have a game of Snap all to yourself, cork and all, you little wretch! We've got another cork in the card-box.'

Miranda picked up the cards in delight, and began to chatter to herself. She took the cork out of her mouth as soon as Barney was safely settled again at the table, and set it down beside her. Then she began to deal out the cards.

'Look! Do look at Miranda!' said Diana, amused. 'She'll be yelling out 'Snap!' in a minute.'

But she didn't get as far as that, of course! She did, however, think that it would be more fun to play cards *with* someone, rather than by herself, and in a few minutes she leapt off the mantelpiece, cork in mouth, and cards in one paw. She scuttled along the floor to where Loony was lying in a deep sleep under the table, and woke him by biting his tail.

She dealt out the cards and put the cork on the floor. Diana, peeping under the table, went off into fits of laughter and Barney produced his uproarious laugh, that always set everyone else laughing too.

Loony wasn't at all pleased. He sniffed at the cork, looked scornfully at the cards and once more went to sleep. Miranda had to play on her own again.

Snubby soon had all the cards, as usual, though Mrs Tickle ran him very close. She was surprisingly good at grabbing the cork, much to Snubby's annoyance. It was, in fact, a very jolly evening, despite the upsets of two or three hours before.

'Bedtime,' said Mrs Tickle at last. 'And let's hope Mr No-One doesn't come hammering at the door again. If he does, I don't stir out of my bed. Let him knock all he likes.'

'And so say I,' said Roger, yawning. 'Yes, let's go to bed. Diana's nearly asleep already.'

They turned out the oil-lamp, collected Loony and Miranda (who still clutched her cards and cork), lighted their candles and set off upstairs. In half an hour's time the house was in darkness, and everyone was sound asleep, except Loony.

It is true that Loony was *asleep*, but tonight he had one ear open, which meant that one ear was awake, and so Loony was not really *sound* asleep. The upsets of the night before, and the excitement over the snowman had put him on his guard. He meant to keep one ear awake all night – just in case!

It was just about midnight when that one ear heard something unusual – not the crashing of the knocker on the front door this time – but a small sound, somewhere downstairs. Loony's ear took in the noise, and he awoke at once and sat up. Snubby was lost in a deep sleep, and took no notice. Loony ran to the door and listened.

Yes, something was going on downstairs. He ran to Snubby, and gave a little warning growl. Then he pawed at him. Finally he jumped up on to Snubby's middle – that always awoke him, as Loony very well knew.

It awoke him now and he sat up indignantly. 'Ass! What did you want to do that for? Haven't I told you . . . I say – what are you growling for?'

Loony's growl put Snubby on his guard at once. Aha! Perhaps someone was about to crash that knocker again, and Loony had heard footsteps. Right – Snubby would go down and watch for Mr No-One, and catch him hammering at that knocker. Grrrrrr! Snubby growled softly into Loony's silk ear – they would not go on the warpath immediately!

'Come on,' said Snubby. 'Something's up!'

Chapter Fifteen

Look Out, Snubby!

Snubby slipped on his dressing-gown, and looked across at Roger, shining his torch on him. He was fast asleep. Should he wake him? No, he would go down and pry around a little first, and then if there *was* anything exciting, he could come back and get Roger.

Loony was still growling in a low tone, his hackles up and his body stiff. There was no doubt that he could hear *something* going on.

Snubby began to feel excited. 'Adventures in the night!' he whispered to Loony. 'Come on, old fellow.'

They went out of the room quietly, and Snubby shut the door behind him. They crept along the wide landing, and came to the top of the stairs. Snubby shut off his torch and listened. He could hear sounds now – muffled sounds – he thought they came from the kitchen.

'Who's there?' he wondered. 'Mr No-One perhaps! Loony, we'd better go carefully. Gosh! It might be the snowman, of course. I never thought of that.'

Snubby would never have dreamed of thinking he might *really* meet a snowman, if it had been broad daylight – but somehow, in the dark, silent house, with queer sounds going on, it seemed quite possible that he might meet the snowman round the next corner. He tightened his dressing-gown belt, and went softly down the stairs, torch in hand.

Yes, the sounds quite definitely came from the kitchen. They were curious sounds, and Snubby couldn't quite make them out. There were bumps – and scraping noises – and grunts as if someone was carrying something heavy. What could be happening?

Snubby came to the bottom of the stairs and went down the hall towards the big kitchen door. Mrs Tickle always left it open at night, but now it was shut. Snubby crept towards it, Loony close at his heels, still growling very softly.

Snubby put his eye to the keyhole, but the kitchen was in darkness, except for what seemed to him to be a ray from a stationary torch. He heard a low voice, and then a bump from the far side of the kitchen. Snubby tried to think what was just there – was it the larder? No. Was it the cupboard where Mrs Tickle kept the crockery and pans? No. Of course – it was the *cellar*! He and Barney had noticed the door there, and had tried to open it, to see where it led to, but it had been locked.

'The cellar's locked, and I don't know where the key is,' Mrs Tickle had told them. 'I expect your granny has something stored down there, Barney. It was open when I was here last summer – your cousins were here boating and swimming. I expect your granny locked it when we all went home.'

But whoever was in the kitchen now had evidently got hold of the key to the cellar, because Snubby, straining his ears, could quite well hear someone going down the steps. What in the world was happening? Were thieves robbing the cellar of any goods stored there? What a time to choose – in the middle of a snowy spell, when there was no chance of a lorry or van to take them away.

Loony continued to growl, and Snubby got tired of looking through the keyhole. He suddenly decided that he would slip out of the garden door and go round to the kitchen window. He would have a much better view there.

'Come on,' he whispered to Loony, and they went back up the hall together. They passed the open sitting-room door and, in the light of the dying fire, Loony suddenly caught sight of the gleaming eyes of the bearskin rug. He backed heavily into Snubby and growled loudly.

'Look out!' whispered Snubby, almost falling over. 'What's the matter? Oh, it's the old bear. My word, doesn't he look life-like tonight!'

He was about to go on when a sudden idea struck him. Why shouldn't he drape the bearskin over him, and pull the head over his – if the men happened to see him looking in at the kitchen window, they would have the fright of their lives to see what appeared to be a live bear!

'Also,' thought Snubby, shivering, 'it would be nice and warm to wear. I expect it will be terribly cold outside.'

All thoughts of waking Roger went from his mind and he felt a tingling feeling run down his back as a tremendous excitement suddenly took hold of him. Yes, he would wear the bearskin. He would give those thieves a fright, and he would find out what they were doing. What a tale to tell the others! Snubby's chest swelled in pride, and he patted Loony on the head.

'I'm going to wear that bearskin,' he whispered. 'So don't get excited about it. The bear won't eat me!'

And then, to Loony's everlasting amazement, Snubby went to the bearskin, lifted it up, and draped it round his shoulders, with the big head on top of his! When he bent his own head the bear's head flopped down lower and it looked exactly as if it were alive.

It was very heavy – heavier than Snubby had imagined. But he was quite determined to wear it! Loony gaped at him, his tail well down. He couldn't understand this at all, and he was ready to leap on the bearskin if it showed any signs of biting Snubby or clawing him.

Snubby went slowly to the garden door, weighed down by the skin over his shoulders. He unlocked the door and he and Loony went out into the cold, frosty night. The snow was thick and deep as he went round the house to the kitchen entrance, Loony obediently at his heels.

The spaniel growled as they came near the kitchen door, and Snubby tapped him on the head. It was essential that the men should not hear anything. As they rounded the corner, they saw that the kitchen door was open – and, to Snubby's amazement, some hefty boxes, about the size of small trunks, were piled in the little kitchen yard.

He stared at them. They were only very dimly outlined in the starlight, for there was no moon, and Snubby could not make out anything at all except their size. What were the men doing with them – hiding them in the cellar?

'Or perhaps taking them *out!*' thought Snubby. 'Yes, of course – they are taking them out. That's why the cellar door was locked and the key was gone. These men must have come to the house while it stood empty, and hidden something down the cellar, knowing it would be safe in an empty house, with nobody to pry and peep.'

He stole past the boxes to the kitchen window, and peered inside, just as the snowman was supposed to have looked in at Mrs Tickle that evening. A torch lay on a table, its beam pointing towards the cellar door – which, of course, was open.

Loony did his best to peer through the window too, putting his paws on the sill. He almost choked himself trying not to bark – especially when a man appeared at the top of the cellar steps, going backwards as if he were helping another man to carry something heavy.

Snubby watched in excitement. Yes, it was another box – very heavy too. Good gracious, no wonder the men had locked the cellar door and taken the key! Mrs Tickle would have been amazed to find the cellar full of heavy boxes! Snubby supposed that the men hadn't had time to remove them before Mrs Tickle and the rest of them came down to Rat-a-Tat House – they must have thought that the house would certainly stand empty all the winter.

The first man came right out of the cellar followed by a second man; they carried a big box between them.

'Put it down for a moment, Jim,' said the second man, panting. He was fat, as Snubby could see in the light of the torch that lay on the nearby table, but he could not see the faces of the men at all.

Loony could bear this no longer. He suddenly gave a terrific growl, and the startled men turned to the window at once, one of them flashing a torch there. He almost dropped it when he saw a great bear's head, apparently looking in at them with gleaming, staring eyes – and, much lower down, just above the sill, another furry head, black this time, with another pair of gleaming eyes!

'Look! What's that? No, it *can't* be a bear!' said the man called Jim, in a startled voice. 'What is it, Stan?'

Snubby dropped down as soon as he saw the men had seen him, and so did Loony. 'Quick!' said Snubby. 'We must get back to the others, Loony, and wake them up.'

He slipped as he shambled along in the deep snow and went down on all fours, looking now for all the world like a real bear. Loony, glancing at him in amazement, half-wondered if the bear had eaten Snubby, for there was little to be seen of the boy now.

The two men rushed out of the kitchen door together, shining their torches. They saw the bear shambling along with Loony. One of them took out a revolver, but the other motioned him to put it away. 'We don't want to

101

rouse the whole household with the sound of a shot,' he said. 'Besides, somehow I don't think that bear is real.'

Poor Snubby didn't know what to do now. If he stood up to get along more quickly, the men would see that it was only someone wearing a bearskin, and not a real bear. On the other hand, he couldn't get along at all fast on all fours in the snow.

The bearskin solved his difficulties by slipping right off his shoulders, and the men at once saw that there was only a small boy on all fours in the snow. They were most relieved. Loony stood by Snubby growling in a most alarming way, ready to fly at the men at the word from the boy.

'Get up,' said the man called Jim, to Snubby. 'What's the meaning of this foolery?'

'Well,' said Snubby indignantly, standing up straight, 'I like *that*! What's the meaning of *you* delving about in our cellars in the middle of the night?'

'No cheek from you,' said the other man roughly. 'Get back into the kitchen at once – go on – and the dog too. And I warn you, if that dog begins to bark or try any funny business with his teeth, I'll kick him over the wall.'

'No, don't, said Snubby in alarm, looking at the man's great wellington boots. He hitched his dressing-gown round him and went back to the kitchen, glad to be in the warm, for it was freezing hard outside.

His heart was beating fast. What was going to happen now? Something very unpleasant, that was certain.

Chapter Sixteen

Down in the Cellar

Snubby went over to the fire that was still gleaming in the grate, and faced the men. His red hair stood on end, and he felt very scared. But he put on a bold face, and even tried to whistle.

The men stood together, talking in a low voice. Snubby's heart sank. They must be discussing what to do with him, and there were so many unpleasant possibilities! Could he make a dash for it? He eyed the door that led into the hall. he knew that it was locked, but the key was on his side. He *might* be able to dash over, unlock the door, open it and rush upstairs.

He suddenly made up his mind, and raced for the door, putting out his hand to turn the key. But the men were on to him like a flash. Loony, now thoroughly aroused, and eager to defend Snubby, bared his teeth and went for the men, snapping at their legs. But the thick rubber boots they wore went up to their knees and Loony only got mouthfuls of hard rubber.

Snubby yelled and slipped between the men, now making the open door that led into the yard – but Jim was there, to prevent him. Then Snubby saw the opened cellar door and ran to that. Down the stone steps he went, falling down the last four, with Loony on top of him. Snubby was up at once, and ran to the farthest corner, fumbling and stumbling in the dark, afraid that the men would be after him down there.

But no – they didn't come down the steps. There was

only the thud of the cellar door shutting, and then Snubby heard the turning of the key in the lock.

'Gosh! I've made myself a prisoner,' he groaned. 'I bet those fellows planned to lock me up here anyhow, while they go off with those boxes – they must be going to take them away somewhere. I wonder if they've got a van. No, how could they in this snow?'

He sat down on an old broken chair, and Loony pressed close to him. He didn't understand this at all. Why had Snubby come down here into this cold dark place? Why didn't he go back to his warm bed and let Loony cuddle against his legs? The spaniel gave a little whine, and Snubby patted his silky head.

'*Why* did you give that frightfully fierce growl, when we were looking in at the window, Loony?' He groaned. 'It was all because of that that we got caught. Honestly, you really *are* a loony dog!'

Snubby listened to see if there were any more noises upstairs. He rubbed his bruises and decided to go up to the locked cellar door and see if he could hear anything useful. So up he went, Loony pressing behind.

He could hear low voices, but could not make out a word. 'They're moving the box they put down in the kitchen,' he thought. 'Putting it outside with the others. I expect. What's in them, I wonder? And where are they going to put them? I might have found out all that if I'd been more sensible – or if Loony had.'

It was so cold and draughty at the top of the stone steps that Snubby went down to the cellar again.

'Looks as if we've got to spend the night here, Loony,' he said miserably. 'Blow! WHY didn't I wake Roger and let him come too? He'll go on sleeping all night long, and it won't be till Mrs Tickle comes down to the kitchen in

104

the morning that anyone will hear me yelling Brrrrrr! It's cold here!'

He flashed his torch round the cellar. It was very big and rambling. Shelves ran up to the ceiling here and there, and were laden with all kinds of stores, especially tinned food. Snubby stared at the labels – pineapple, peaches, pears, grapefruit – his mouth watered. What a pity he hadn't a tin-opener with him.

There was an old wringer there, and various broken chairs stood in corners. A space had evidently been cleared for the boxes, and Snubby could see where they had stood for they had left their outlines in the dust.

He shivered. What a horrid cold place this was. 'Loony, let's see if we can find something a bit warmer than the stone floor to lie on,' he said, and he and the spaniel went round the big cellar poking into everything.

They made a good find at last – an old mattress, rolled up and tied with rope. 'Good!' said Snubby. 'Got a knife to cut the rope, Loony?'

Loony wagged his tail, knowing this was a joke. Snubby had no knife, of course, in his dressing-gown, so he had to struggle with the knots. He got them undone at last and the mattress unrolled itself. Snubby lay down on it, gathered his dressing-gown round him and cuddled Loony, who was better than any hot-water bottle!

'Now we'll try and go to sleep, and hope that Mrs Tickle will hear me yelling in the morning,' he said. But it took him a long time to fall asleep. For one thing, he was very excited, and for another he was very cold. But he did sleep at last, Loony curled up against him as close as possible.

Nobody knew that Snubby was not in his bed. Upstairs the rest of the party slept soundly, the three children tired out with their day's sport. Mrs Tickle heard no sound either, and hardly stirred in her bed – till the alarm clock went off and awoke her.

She got up, dressed and went downstairs. The kitchen fire was still in, thank goodness, so she only had to rake the embers together and put on some coal. Then she took her brooms and dusters and set off to get the sitting-room clean and tidy, and to light the fire there too.

She was most astonished to find the bearskin rug gone. She stood and stared at the empty place where it usually lay and wondered what had happened to it.

'It's that dog Loony,' she decided. 'He must have come down in the night and fought it, and taken it off somewhere. Where has he put it? What a dog! I can't leave a duster or brush about anywhere but what he's off and away with them. I'll have to tie them all round my waist soon. Where *can* he have taken that bearskin rug?'

She didn't hear poor Snubby yelling in the cellar, because the sitting-room was a good way from the kitchen. She finished cleaning it and then went to mop and dust the hall.

Upstairs Roger was awake, and rather surprised to see Snubby's bed empty and Loony gone too. 'He must have dressed and gone out early,' he thought. 'No, he hasn't; his clothes are still there. Perhaps he's in Barney's room.

He went to see, but Snubby wasn't there either, of course. Barney was already half-dressed, looking forward to another day of skating. Roger looked round the room in surprise.

Isn't Snubby here?' he said. 'He's not in our room. His clothes are there, though.'

'I bet he's gone down to ask Mrs Tickle for a snack before breakfast,' said Barney, and Roger thought that was very likely.

Diana came out of her room fully dressed, as he went

back. 'Buck up, Roger!' she said. 'I'm going down to help Mrs Tickle.' And down she went. Barney followed almost at once. They met Mrs Tickle in the hall, just finishing the polishing.

'Hallo, Mrs Tickle!' said Barney. I hope the old snowman didn't visit you in the night!'

'Go on with you!' said Mrs Tickle. Are you going to lay the breakfast table for me, Diana, seeing that you're up nice and early?'

'Barney and I will do it together,' said Diana, going to the sideboard where the cloths were kept. 'Oh, where's the bearskin gone?'

'That dog Loony's taken it, I think,' said Mrs Tickle. 'Mad as a hatter, he is.'

She went off into the kitchen, and then, a minute later, she came hurrying back, looking puzzled and indignant.

'I went to shake my dusters in the yard,' she said, 'and bless us all, if the bearskin isn't lying out there in the snow! But how COULD Loony have taken it through a locked door?'

'Isn't Snubby downstairs?' asked Barney in surprise. 'He's not in his room – we thought he'd probably gone down to the kitchen to ask you for a snack. You're sure he's not in the larder, Mrs Tickle?'

Mrs Tickle began to look astonished. 'No. I've not seen Snubby – *or* Loony – this morning and yet there's the bearskin out in the snow. Perhaps Snubby's playing some joke?'

'He's an ass,' said Barney impatiently. 'What can he be up to? He *must* be somewhere in the kitchen, Mrs Tickle – hiding for some reason of his own.'

Diana, Barney and Mrs Tickle went back to the kitchen, and Roger, coming downstairs, joined them. As soon as they were inside the room, they stopped in surprise. From somewhere came a voice – Snubby's voice – yelling loudly. And with it came a hammering on the other side of the cellar door.

'Help! Help! Open the cellar door. Help! MRS TICKLE, ARE YOU THERE? HELP!'

'Good gracious! It's Snubby – down in the cellar, of all places,' said Barney, and ran to the door.

'But it's locked,' said Mrs Tickle. 'And there's no key to it, you remember. How could Snubby get in? And look – there's no key *now*.'

Barney was at the cellar door, tugging at the handle. 'Snubby! Why are you in there? Where's the key? There's none this side.'

'Oh! They've taken it with them, the beasts!' said Snubby, with a groan. 'I might have guessed. Can you break the door down, Barney?'

Everyone was astounded to know that Snubby was locked in the cellar! And who were 'the beasts' who had apparently taken the key – a key that hadn't been there before, as Mrs Tickle very well knew.

'Try the key of the kitchen door, or of the door into the hall,' said Diana, suddenly remembering that the keys at home were often interchangeable. 'Quick, Roger, get them. Snubby must be freezing cold in there.'

Roger got the two keys, and oh, what a bit of luck – the kitchen door fitted the cellar lock! He turned it and out came poor Snubby, with Loony barking madly at his heels.

Chapter Seventeen

Barney Thinks Things Out

'Snubby! How did you get in there?'

'What happened? Gosh, you look cold!'

'Come over to the fire, Snubby; your hands are like ice.'

Everyone spoke at once, and Diana dragged the shivering Snubby to the fire, which was now blazing well. Mrs Tickle was simply amazed that he should have been in the cellar all night. Whatever next!

Snubby got as close to the fire as he could and held his hands out to the flames thankfully. 'My word, it was cold down in the cellar,' he said. 'If I hadn't had Loony for a hot-water bottle I'd have been frozen stiff.'

'But, Snubby, how did you get locked in there? What were you *doing*, wandering about at night!' cried Mrs Tickle.

'I had an adventure,' said Snubby, beginning to feel pleasantly warm, and very much the centre of attention. 'I heard a noise in the middle of the night and came down to see what it was. . . .'

'Snubby, how brave of you,' said Diana, admiringly. 'I couldn't possibly have done that.'

Snubby went on with his tale of the night's doings; how he had looked through the locked kitchen door, and had had the idea of going to look in at the kitchen window clad in the bearskin, and had gone out of the garden door and round to the window.

'There were boxes out there, piled up,' said Snubby, 'and the kitchen door was open wide.'

'But I locked it!' said Mrs Tickle, amazed. 'And what's more, I bolted it too!'

'Well, it was open,' said Snubby. 'Is it locked now?'

Barney went to look. 'Yes, locked *and* bolted! They must have got in somewhere else, and opened the kitchen door from inside. And then, when they went, they must have locked and bolted it again on the inside, and gone out the way they came in.'

'Probably a window somewhere. We'll look in a minute,' said Roger. 'Go on, Snubby.'

Snubby told the rest of the tale. How he had been caught and how he had bolted down the cellar steps to escape the men, who had promptly locked him in.

'The box I saw them carrying up the cellar steps must have been the last one,' he said. 'There aren't any more boxes like it down there. I had a look. My word, it was cold in the night; I was lucky to find an old mattress to sleep on.'

It really was an extraordinary tale. Nobody knew quite what to make of it. So many peculiar things had happened since they had been at Rat-a-Tat House, but this last one, of boxes hidden in the cellar, and taken away in the middle of the night was the most puzzling of all.

'I suppose all the peculiar things fit together somehow,' said Barney, when at last they were in the sitting-room having breakfast, with Snubby now dressed and comfortably warm again. 'But the question is – how?'

'Yes, how does Mr No-One, banging at our door in the middle of the night fit in with the Somebody who watched us by the snow house one night?' said Roger.

'And how does the walking snowman fit in too?' wondered Diana. 'Why should he wander about and look into the kitchen window, frightening Mrs Tickle out of her wits?'

'I rather think I know!' said Barney suddenly. 'Yes, I'm beginning to see how all the happenings can fit together like pieces in a jigsaw.'

'What do you mean?' said Roger, surprised.

'Don't talk to me for a bit while I think it out,' said Barney, buttering a piece of toast. 'It's just beginning to dawn on me.'

Snubby was eating his fifth piece of toast, and was now feeling extremely pleased with himself and his adventure. He was even inclined to boast, but this the others would not allow.

'It wasn't *really* very clever to hear a noise in the night and go down by yourself instead of waking me and asking me to come with you,' said Roger. 'If I'd been with you we might even have caught the men, locked them into the cellar in the same way that they locked *you* in! You never know.'

'I think I've got it,' announced Barney suddenly. 'Yes, I think I begin to see things now.'

'What? Tell us,' said Diana eagerly.

'Well, listen. Coming down here was quite a sudden idea of my father's and grandmother's,' said Barney. 'To all intents and purposes the house was closed till next spring – shut up and empty. Well, along comes someone who wants a very, very good place to hide something in – perhaps stolen goods – perhaps smuggled goods. I don't know – '

'And what could be better than an empty house which won't be visited for months,' cried Roger. 'Yes, go on, Barney.'

'Right. They decide to bring their goods here, and probably plan to hide them in our cellar till it's safe to

111

take them to wherever they want to,' said Barney. 'So they break in somewhere, or get a key that will unlock one of the doors, and one night they arrive here with car, or van, or lorry – '

'And carry those boxes I saw down into the cellar,' said Snubby. 'Gosh, yes! That's it. Meaning to collect them in their own good time! And they locked the cellar door and took away the key just in case anyone should come here to do a bit of cleaning and perhaps even pop down into the cellar, and discover what was hidden there.'

'Exactly,' said Barney. 'It certainly was a splendid hiding-place. No one would see the van or lorry arriving in this lonely spot, far from any other house – no one would see the boxes being unloaded and taken into the house – and no one would see them being taken away again when the right time came.'

'And then suddenly we come and spoil all their plans, said Diana. 'What a shock it must have been for them to hear that we had arrived to stay for a while. How do you suppose they heard?'

'Oh, probably someone in Boffame village told them,' said Barney. 'Or they may have come along to have a look to see if their hidden goods were all right, and discovered us here.'

'And one of them spied on us in the snow house,' cried Snubby. 'And dropped his glove there.'

'But I don't see how Mr No-One, banging at the knocker, fits in,' said Diana, puzzled. 'Or the walking snowman that went and peeped in at Mrs Tickle's window last night. Somehow I don't *think* she made that up.'

'She didn't,' said Barney. 'I'll tell you how I think Mr No-One, the knocker, and the snowman all fit into the picture. I think they were meant to *frighten us away* – so that we would go off, and leave the coast clear for them.

112

They would be able to load up their lorry again, or whatever it was they used – and hide the goods somewhere else.'

'Gosh!' said Snubby, lost in admiration at Barney's explanations. 'You're right. Mr No-One was simply one of those men – Jim or Stan – hammering away at the knocker to make us think it was the old legend coming true. I nearly did think it too – we were all scared to death.'

'It's a wonder we didn't leave at once,' said Diana. 'Mrs Tickle would have loved to go, I know.'

'Yes, but to the man's great annoyance, we still stuck here – and they had to watch us tobogganing all day yesterday, instead of rejoicing to see us pack up and go.'

'We couldn't go, anyway,' said Roger. 'Unless a car came to fetch us, and we couldn't get Barney's father over because the telephone is out of order.'

'They wouldn't know that,' said Barney. 'So they tried to scare us once more, by dressing up in a white sheet, or something like that and stealing the snowman's hat, and then peering through the window at poor Mrs Tickle.'

'No wonder she was scared,' said Diana. 'We all thought she made it up, or was quite mistaken, but she wasn't. Poor Mrs Tickle! How awful to see the snowman peering through the window, hat and all.'

'And when we still didn't get in a panic last night, I suppose they gave up trying to scare us and decided to get the boxes out in the middle of the night, hoping we wouldn't hear, and hide them in a safer place,' said Barney. 'But old Snubby heard them, and rather messed up their plans.'

'But not enough to *ruin* them,' said Roger. 'They've got the stuff away all right, that's clear. I wonder what it was.'

'I think we ought to try and find out,' said Barney. 'This may be something pretty serious, you know. If only we could telephone my father! I wonder how long it will be before the telephone wires are mended.'

'Ages, I expect,' said Diana. 'What do you plan to do now, Barney?'

'I plan to follow the tracks the men made carrying those boxes away,' said Barney. 'They'll show easily over the snow.'

'Well, we'll have to buck up then,' said Roger. 'Look the sky's full of snow, and it's beginning to fall already. Any tracks will soon be covered.'

'What I want to know is how Mr No-One made tracks to the front door, and got away without leaving another set,' said Snubby. 'Who'll tell me that?'

Nobody bothered to answer him. They were all rushing to get their hats and coats to go and find the tracks the men made when they took away those big heavy boxes.

Chapter Eighteen

On the Trail

Diana stayed behind to tell Mrs Tickle a little of what Barney had said, and to carry out some of the dirty dishes. Mrs Tickle, looking astonished, tried to follow all that Diana was saying, but she soon gave it up.

'All I know is, there's very funny goings-on here,' she said. 'And I don't like it. If the telephone was all right, I'd phone Mr Martin and tell him it's dangerous to stay here and get him to fetch us. Knockings in the night, and wandering snowmen, and Snubby locked in the cellar! It just isn't right.'

'Never mind, Mrs Tickle,' said Diana, comfortingly. 'I don't think we'll have any more "funny goings-on" now – if Barney's right in what he says. So you needn't be scared, or carry your rolling-pin about with you.'

'Indeed I shall – it goes with me wherever I go,' declared Mrs Tickle, brandishing it. 'Upstairs and downstairs.'

'And in my lady's chamber,' Diana, with a laugh. 'All right, you do what you want to do, Mrs Tickle. *I* think you've been marvellous.' And with that she went out to join the others. They were examining the snow house, and the place where the snowman had once stood.

'Look, Di,' said Barney, as she came up. 'The snowman has simply been knocked down and then trodden on. The only things left are his two feet.'

'And someone's broken down the back wall of the snow

house,' said Roger. 'Walked into it, probably, or leaned on it when he was watching us through the window.'

'AND we've found out how Mr No-One walked through the snow to the front door, and apparently didn't go back again,' said Snubby. '*I* worked that out, actually.'

'Oh, the clever boy!' said Diana, amused at Snubby's boasting. 'How did Mr No-One do it?'

'Well, watch. I'll go to that tree through the snow, and come back, and yet you'll see only one set of prints,' said Snubby, 'and *all* going one way!'

'Go on, then, show me,' said Diana disbelievingly. Snubby grinned. He walked slowly to the tree, making well-defined footmarks in the snow – and then, when he reached the tree, he stopped. He looked carefully over his shoulder to see the last footmark he had made, and put his foot in it; then the other foot into the neat print, and the next.

'He's walking backwards, and putting his feet into the same footmarks he's already made,' said Diana, astonished. 'What an idea!'

'Yes. So there is only *one* set of footprints all going to the tree, though Snubby has gone there *and* back,' said Roger, as Snubby arrived beside Diana again, grinning all over his freckled face.

'And that's how our Mr No-One managed to puzzle us, when he walked up to our front door in the middle of the night, and hammered on it, and apparently didn't go back again,' said Barney. 'He just walked backwards in the prints he had already made.'

'It was clever of you to find that out, Snubby,' said Diana. 'I never thought of that. I say, it's snowing quite hard. Have you looked yet to see if you can follow the tracks the men made when they carried off the boxes?'

'No. We'll go and do that now,' said Barney. 'If we

don't, the tracks will be covered. Let's take our toboggans with us, then we can do a bit of sliding down the hills again. Skating's no use at the present moment.'

But when they got to the outdoor shed where the toboggans were kept, they had a great shock. The toboggans were not there!

'Blow!' said Barney. 'Who's taken those?'

'Stan and Jim, I bet,' said Snubby, feeling quite brilliant. 'AND I know what for.'

The others stared at him. 'You don't mean – you don't mean they've taken them to drag away those boxes,' said Roger. 'Oh, goodness! I hope you're not right.'

But Snubby *was* right. When they made their way to the back door, outside which he had seen the big boxes set ready to take away, they found the toboggan tracks deeply indented in the snow there.

'Look – here's one set – and another,' said Barney. 'The runners of the toboggans have cut right down into the snow, almost to the ground.'

'Yes. That's because those boxes were so heavy,' said Snubby. 'I bet those men saw our toboggans out in the shed there when they were snooping round, and one of them suddenly had the bright idea of using them to carry away the boxes. They'd be far too heavy to carry between them for any distance.'

'Snubby's quite a detective,' said Roger, half in earnest and half joking. 'Get away, Loony; you're spoiling the tracks we're following. Go and play with Miranda.'

But Miranda didn't want to play with Loony. She was sitting on Barney's shoulder, trying to catch the snow-flakes as they floated down round her. She couldn't make out why they disappeared as soon as she caught them.

'Let's see if we can follow the tracks now,' said Barney. 'They may go to that boat-house – you never know.

117

They'll be easy to follow, because the men can't have taken all the boxes at once on the toboggans – not more than two at a time, I should think – so they'd have to come to and fro a good many times, and makes quite a track over the snow.'

'Well, the tracks are beginning to go already,' said Diana. 'The snow is falling so thickly. Look, they go right round the house. Come on, let's follow them.'

They began to follow the deeply-rutted tracks made by their toboggans. Snubby was feeling quite worried in case they would not find the toboggans; he had been so much looking forward to some more fun on them. Blow those men! What silly tricks would they be up to next?

The tracks led around the house and down the drive and then out of the gate. They led across the road and over the bank beside the pond. Then they led round the pond to where the boat-house was.

'There you are! We *thought* the men might have made the boat-house the next hiding-place for the boxes,' said Barney, pleased.

'I'm surprised they didn't realise we could easily follow their tracks,' said Roger.

'Well, they probably knew a thick fall of snow was coming, and they hoped the tracks would be hidden,' said Barney. 'Look – there's the boat-house. Let's go carefully in case the men are there.'

So they went very carefully indeed, not talking or laughing, and not allowing Loony to bark even a small bark. The boat-house loomed up, all white, with a new layer of snow on the roof.

The toboggan tracks, still deeply indented in the snow, led right round the boat-house to the front of it, where the lake itself began. There the tracks stopped.

'It looks as if the men brought the boxes here, and

unloaded them into the boat-house,' said Barney, in a low voice. 'I wonder where our toboggans are?'

'Look! Is that them over there?' cried Snubby suddenly. 'Loony, go and look.'

Loony leapt over the snow to where the newly-fallen snow was half covering something brightly coloured. He scraped at it and barked loudly as the children walked towards the snow-covered heap.

'Yes, it *is* our toboggans,' said Diana. 'They emptied them, and then threw them into the snow, hoping they would soon be hidden. I hope they haven't damaged them.'

The children pulled them out. No, they were quite all right, although the paint had worn off where the heavy boxes had scraped them.

'Well, that's *something*, at any rate!' said Diana thankfully. 'I was afraid we might not find them again, and they're such beauties.'

'What are we going to do next? Look in the boat-house?' said Snubby eagerly. 'The men can't be there, or surely they would have yelled at us.'

'Well, we can at least go and peep through that broken window,' said Barney. 'I wonder how the men got the boxes into the boat-house. I suppose they have a key to the big doors that open above water-level to let the boats out in the summer.'

They went round the boat-house to the broken window. Barney looked boldly inside, but it was so dark in there that snowy morning that he could not make out even the outline of the boats. He felt for his torch, but he had left it behind.

'Blow!' he said. 'Oh, you've got yours, Snubby – good.' He flashed it quickly through the window, and all round the shed. There was no one there at all; at least, no one

119

that he could see. 'Empty!' he said. 'Not a soul here. The men must have gone off, now that they have disposed of the boxes. I expect they think they've hidden them so well that no one will discover them. They don't know that we've spotted this old boat-house for a hiding-place.'

'Can you see the big boxes anywhere, Barney?' said Snubby, trying to peer in through the window too. 'Let *me* look!'

'There's nothing to see in the way of boxes,' said Barney. 'But there wouldn't be. I expect they are under one of the boats, or covered with tarpaulins – sure to be, in fact. I bet they're here somewhere.'

'Well, let's get in and look,' said Roger. 'We ought to be able to find them – it's not a very big place. Gosh, what a thrill to come across them! Do let's explore the boat-house, Barney. After all, it belongs to your family, so we won't be trespassing. Do let's.'

Chapter Nineteen

Rather Disappointing

Barney did not need much persuading. As for Miranda, she didn't even wait for him to say yes. She leapt in through the broken window, and bounded here and there, looking at this and that with the greatest interest.

Barney began to break away the few remaining bits of broken glass in the window. 'Very sharp edges!' he explained. 'I don't want any of you to get bad cuts. Diana, you be very careful. Roger will help you up and I'll help you down inside the boat-house.'

'I don't see *how* we can cut ourselves,' said Snubby, impatient at having to wait. 'We're all wearing thick gloves and boots. Buck up, Barney!'

Barney leapt inside the boat-house, and then Roger helped Diana up, and Barney helped her down. Roger followed and then Loony was handed up, and, last of all, Snubby came.

The boat-house was very dark indeed, for the daylight hardly penetrated through the dirty windows. And, in any case, it was a dark day with the sky full of snow; quite a different day from any they had had.

The children had two torches, and with them they began to look all over the boat-house. It was a typical place for keeping boats, full of all kinds of gear, ropes, tarpaulins and half-empty tins of paint. It smelt musty, and the boats were fast-locked in the ice. They had once floated in water there in the boat-house, but now their keels were no longer afloat, they were ice-bound. Barney quickly realised that there was no possible chance of finding any boxes under the boats. He set to work to look under the tarpaulins and sails that lay about here and there.

'I don't believe the boxes *are* here,' said Diana, at last, tired of floundering about the dirty boat-shed without finding a single box.

'I'm beginning to think the same,' said Barney, puzzled. 'After all, Snubby said they were big ones, and there were a lot of them, and they just *can't* be here. We've hunted everywhere.'

It was very disappointing indeed. 'We followed the toboggan tracks here, where they ended, and yet we can't see any sign of the boxes,' said Diana. 'Could the men have hidden them anywhere under the snow, do you think?'

'Well, they *could*, I suppose,' said Barney. 'But even one box would need a big pile of snow to hide it, and a lot of boxes would certainly make quite a mountain under the snow. Still, we can look.'

So the next thing they did was to flounder about in the thick snow round the boat-house. They felt sure that the men would not have carried such heavy boxes very far. Loony leapt about like a mad thing, not knowing what they were looking for, but hoping it might be something eatable. Miranda watched him from Barney's shoulder, wishing they could go home to the nice warm fire. She didn't like the snow that kept falling, falling, falling.

There were *no* boxes hidden anywhere round or about the boat-house. Snubby was most disappointed. What a waste of a morning! He was amazed when Barney said it was time to go back to lunch.

'Do you mean to say we've spent the whole morning looking for those beastly boxes?' he said, in disgust. 'No tobogganing – no skating – not even a spot of snowballing. What a waste. Well, anyway, I'm at least going to have a slide on the pond.'

'It's got a covering of snow now. You won't be able to slide properly,' said Diana.

But Snubby was on the pond, making a little slide of his own. Whooooosh! He slid along quite well and then fell over and slid the rest of the way on his trouser-seat.

As he was turning over to get up, he felt something under his hand and grasped it. What was it? He looked to see and gave a little exclamation.

'A cigarette packet – like the one Barney found in the boat-house. One of the men must have thrown it away last night, when he arrived at the boat-house with the toboggans.'

He went back to the others and showed them the packet. 'Same as before,' he said. 'The man must have chucked it away over the lake.'

Barney took it to compare with the packet he had found in the boat-house. 'Just the same,' he said. 'Hallo, it's not empty. It's half-full! Look!'

He was right. 'Wasteful fellow, throwing away cigarettes,' said Snubby. 'I shall really have to speak to Stan or Jim about it when I next see them!'

'Ass,' said Roger, 'I say, isn't it snowing fast! By the time we've had our dinner all tracks will have been covered with another fall of snow. It's a good thing we followed the toboggan tracks when we did.'

'Not that it did us much good,' said Diana. 'We didn't find a sign of the boxes. I wonder where they can be. Well, I suppose they simply *must* be somewhere in the boat-house.'

They were quite ravenous when they got back to Rat-a-Tat House. Mrs Tickle was looking out anxiously for them. 'You're late,' she said. 'I began to think you'd got lost in the snow.'

'Has Mr Icy-Cold been wandering about again, or Mr No-One?' asked Snubby. 'What – nobody been peeping in at your window? Life is getting dull for you, Mrs Tickle.'

'Go on with you,' said Mrs Tickle, giving Snubby a push. 'You've got far too much to say. My word, how wet you are! You'll have to change your things before you sit down to your lunch.'

'Oh, blow!' said Snubby. 'There's such a nice smell coming from the kitchen. What is it, Mrs Tickle?'

'You go and get those wet things off,' said Mrs Tickle. 'And dry Loony too. What a mess he's in. Stop pouncing at my feet, Loony. Stop it, I say! And just you take one more of my dusters away and I'll put you in the dustbin.'

Soon all the children were sitting down to hot vegetable soup. Miranda was given an apple, and nibbled it daintily, sitting on Barney's shoulder. But when she came to the black pips in the middle she was not so dainty. She picked them out with her tiny finger and dropped them into Barney's soup.

'I don't know *why* we keep you and Loony,' said Barney, fishing out the pips. 'I really don't. Pests, both of you.'

The monkey took hold of the lobe of Barney's ear, put her mouth close and chattered in a whispery voice. Barney listened gravely.

'All right. As you apologised so very nicely, I won't say anything more, Miranda.'

Diana chuckled. It always amused her when Miranda whispered into Barney's ear, and Barney pretended to know exactly what the little monkey had said.

After rather a big meal, the children sat round the fire talking about the peculiar happenings of the last few days.

124

There was no point in going out, for the snow was still falling, and they even had to light the oil-lamp because the day was so dark.

Mrs Tickle came in to see what they planned to do. 'Don't you go out again,' she said. 'You might easily get lost in this. I can hardly find the way from my back door to the dustbin.'

They all laughed. 'Mrs Tickle,' said Snubby, 'there's something worrying me. How are you going on for food? No tradesmen can come here, and we certainly can't get to Boffame village now.'

'That *would* worry Snubby, of course,' said Diana. 'Food is his biggest interest.'

Mrs Tickle laughed. 'You don't need to worry,' she said. 'I brought in a car-load of things from Boffame village when I came. Old man Hurdie at the post office, he said we were in for more snow, and told me to take all the food I could. Our larder is as cold as a refrigerator, and things keep fresh for a week. The bread's too stale to use now, though, so I'll bake some myself.'

'Good idea,' said Snubby, approvingly. 'Shall I come and help you?'

'No, thank you,' said Mrs Tickle. 'I don't want you messing about with my bread. All *you* want to do is to go and poke your nose into my larder. Just like my Tom, you are.'

'What's going to happen if this snow goes on and on, and we get even more snowed up?' wondered Roger.

'I don't quite know,' said Barney. 'I wish we could telephone. I can't see that we can do anything except stay here till my father thinks it's time we came home, and somehow finds a means of transport.'

'A large sleigh and a few husky dogs is what we really

125

want,' said Diana. 'You know, the dogs the Eskimos have.'

'Yes, a sleigh with bells on,' said Snubby. 'Jingle-jingle-jing – '

R-r-r-r-ring! Rr-r-r-r-ring!

A sudden, shrill ringing noise made them all jump. Then Barney gave a shout and leapt to his feet.

'The telephone bell! The wires must have been mended. *Now* we can get on to somebody and tell them about the extraordinary happenings here. Hallo, hallo?'

Everyone sat up eagerly. Yes, it was Barney's father, anxiously asking how they were all getting on.

'Fine, Dad, fine!' said Barney. 'But, I say, Dad, listen. Some very peculiar things have been going on here. . . . Yes, *peculiar* things, I said . . . What? . . . Yes, I'll tell you if you hang on. Actually, I don't quite know what we ought to do about them. Well, here goes. . . .'

And Barney launched into the story of the last few days and all their strange happenings. What a tale it was!

Chapter Twenty

The Telephone at Last!

Mrs Tickle came running eagerly when she heard the welcome sound of the telephone bell once more. She and the others stood round Barney while he told the curious tale of the happenings at Rat-a-Tat House.

Barney's father was astonished.

'But what *is* all this?' he said, his voice ringing clearly through the telephone, so that even the others could hear it. 'Disturbances in the night – breaking into the house and taking things from the cellar. Why was it locked when you came – it never is! And whatever had these fellows got hidden down there? Barney, is there anything more to tell me?'

'Yes, but I've told you all the *Important* things,' said Barney. 'Can you possibly come down here, Dad? We are pretty well snowed up, and I'm not sure if a car can get through now. Thank goodness the telephone wires are mended.'

'Yes, thank goodness,' said his father. 'Your grandmother was so worried about you all that I really think she was planning to put on my old skis and ski over hill and dale to you.'

'Good old Granny!' said Barney, proud of the old lady. 'I wouldn't be surprised to see her arriving here on skis – or even on a sledge drawn by reindeer. But Dad, *is* it possible for a car to get through now, do you think?'

'No, we couldn't risk it,' said his father. 'Not today, at any rate, with more snow falling. We'd probably get stuck in a snowdrift, and be marooned there for days. Why, some of the villages that are completely snowbound are having to be helped by helicopters. They drop food down, as you know. By the way, you've got plenty, haven't you?'

'Oh, yes,' said Barney. 'Dad, are you going to tell the police? I don't know what is in those boxes they hid in the cellar here, but it's quite certain they couldn't have got them away far, because no van or lorry could stir from here; so they must be hidden somewhere near, though goodness knows where.'

'Yes, I thought that too,' said his father. 'I shall telephone the police at once, and let you know what they say.'

Everyone was very thankful that the telephone wires were mended again. It was a real relief to be in touch with the outer world now that such strange things were happening. Barney put down the telephone and smiled round at the others.

'My father's on the job now,' he said. 'We needn't worry at all.'

'Well, I'm glad to hear *that*,' said Mrs Tickle, as they all turned to go back to the warm sitting-room. As they went, they heard the little 'ting' sound from the telephone that meant that someone had lifted the receiver. Barney swung round at once. It was Miranda, pretending to chatter into the telephone just as Barney had done!

'You little mimic,' said Barney, snatching it from her paws and putting it back into place again. 'Why we put up with you and Loony I really don't know.'

Miranda scampered into the sitting-room and sat on the top of the bear's head, looking very comical. Then she pretended to whisper something into the bear's ear.

'That monkey – she's a real comic!' said Mrs Tickle.

'Well, Barney, I'm relieved to think your father knows everything. What's he going to do?'

'Tell the police,' said Barney promptly. 'But what they can do at the moment I don't know – nobody can get through the thick snowdrifts, Dad says.'

'Anyway, the men are not likely to worry us any more,' said Diana. 'They've got their goods, whatever they are, so we needn't expect any more rat-a-tatting, or snowmen wandering about.'

'That's true,' said Roger. 'Anyway, I expect the men have gone off somewhere now they've hidden their boxes. It must have been very cold and uncomfortable sleeping in the boat-house.'

'Well, they can't have gone far in this thick snow,' said Barney, looking out of the window. 'They're probably hiding in some outhouse or other, but I wonder what they do for food?'

'Don't forget that the cellar had plenty of tins on its shelves,' said Snubby. 'They could help themselves to those when they took the boxes.'

'So they could,' said Roger. 'I never thought of that. And you know, we've never discovered yet how they got into the kitchen. We know they didn't come through the kitchen door, because Mrs Tickle locked *and* bolted it, so even if they had a key, they couldn't have opened it.'

'I'm going to have a look,' announced Snubby. 'A little detective work! Come on, let's see who can find out how the men got in.'

Mrs Tickle remembered that she had bread to make, and hurried back to her kitchen. The others began to go round the different rooms and try the windows to see if they were all closed and fastened.

'They're all well and truly shut, and fastened tight,'

said Barney. 'All the downstairs windows, anyhow. I simply can't imag . . .'

He stopped as Mrs Tickle came running into the room looking excited.

'I've found out how they came in,' she said. 'Through my larder window! It's never had a very good catch, and they've forced it, so that they could climb in. Then they shut it after they went, and I never noticed that the catch was broken.'

They all went to examine the broken catch. 'Yes, you're right,' said Snubby. 'They got in this way. My word, what a big larder this is, Mrs Tickle. And, I say, look at that pie. When is that for?'

'You keep your fingers off my shelves,' said Mrs Tickle, pushing Snubby out. 'And who said you could take that jam tart? You're a caution, you are!'

Barney was glancing up at the top shelves. 'I suppose nothing has been taken from here by the men, has it?' he asked. 'They'd be glad of food now.'

Mrs Tickle fetched a chair and stood on it to look at the shelves above her head. 'I don't know exactly what was here,' she said. 'There were tins and bottles and packets which I didn't touch. And, yes, they've taken a few things. I can see marks in the dust where tins or something stood. Yes, I think they took a few tins. Well, I never did!'

'Taking food off the shelves and boxes from the cellar. They'll be sleeping in our beds next,' said Snubby 'You'd better look out, Mrs Tickle.'

'I'm certainly going to look *under* my bed to-night – with a rolling-pin in my hand,' said Mrs Tickle fiercely.

'We'll let Loony do that,' said Snubby. 'He'll simply *love* to go hunting under everyone's bed. Won't you, Loony?'

'Wuff!' said Loony, joyously, and tore up the stairs as if he meant to begin that very minute.

They all went back into the sitting-room, and gazed out of the window. What a change in the weather! No clear sky, no pale, clear sun, no view over the gleaming lake; only endless snowflakes falling from a leaden sky.

'I don't envy those men, Stan and Jim, wherever they are,' said Snubby. 'They must wish to goodness we'd never come down here. I bet they planned to shelter in Rat-a-Tat House if it got too cold in the boat-house.'

'They probably hoped to remove those boxes by lorry sometime this week,' said Barney. 'Their plans have certainly been upset. I do wonder where they hid those heavy boxes. They *can't* be very far away. They could never carry them any distance.'

'It's odd,' said Roger. 'They put them on our toboggans and dragged them down to the boat-house, then took them off the toboggans and hid them. But where?'

'I'm tired of thinking about it,' said Diana. 'Let's play a game. Let's have a jigsaw battle. We've brought plenty, haven't we?'

'Yes,' said Snubby. 'I'll get four. They're in the cupboard.'

Soon they were all sitting at the big round table, each with a box of jigsaw pieces. 'Go!' said Roger, and they all emptied out their pieces quickly, and began to sort them at top speed.

'I always pick out the blue sky bits first,' said Diana. 'Snubby, you've dropped a piece on the floor already.'

Miranda was a little nuisance when jigsaws were being done. She was fascinated by the tiny coloured pieces, and longed to help.

'*Don't*, Miranda.' said Snubby, exasperated. 'That

131

piece doesn't go there. Now you've knocked out another piece. Barney, put her on your shoulder.'

But she wouldn't stop there, and Diana thought that the only sensible thing to do was to give the little monkey a jigsaw of her own to play with, so she fetched another from the cupboard.

Miranda was delighted and proud. She settled down on the table, her jigsaw pieces spread in front of her, and fiddled about with them, chattering in her little monkey voice. Mrs Tickle could hardly believe her eyes when she came in with the tea-tray later on, and saw her.

'Well, I never!' she said. 'That monkey beats everything. Are you ready for tea – or shall I leave the tray here till you've finished?'

'I've won!' said Snubby, fitting in his last piece. 'I'm first! What do I get? The biggest slice of chocolate cake, and more scones than anyone? I've won!'

And just then the telephone bell rang again urgently – r-r-r-r-ing – r-r-r-ring – r-r-r-ring-ring! Ah, what was the news from Barney's father?

Chapter Twenty-One

Diana has an Idea

Barney ran to the telephone at once. Had his father told the police? What had they planned?

'Hallo!' he said. 'Hallo! . . . Yes, it's me, Barney, Dad. . . . Yes, I'll listen carefully.'

He stood with his ear glued to the telephone, nodding his head and saying 'yes – oh, yes' now and again in an excited manner, his eyes sparkling. The others crowded round trying to hear what was being said, but Barney had clamped the receiver so close to his ear in order not to miss a single word, that they could make out very little.

Snubby could hardly stand still, he wanted so badly to know what Barney's father was saying, and at last he heard Barney say goodbye.

'Right, Dad. I'll do all you say, you can depend on me. I'll tell Mrs Tickle too. I say, how *very* exciting! See you tomorrow. Goodbye!'

He put the receiver back and turned to the others, his eyes still shining.

'What did he say, what did he say?' almost shouted Snubby.

'I'll tell you. Come into the sitting-room,' said Barney. 'Mrs Tickle! Oh, there you are! You come too. I've got exciting news.'

They all went into the sitting-room, Loony as excited as the rest, though he didn't know what about. Miranda jigged up and down on Barney's shoulder, a piece of jigsaw puzzle still in one tiny paw.

They all sat down, and Barney began:

'My father got in touch with the police and told them everything. The police were *very* interested indeed. My father says he thinks they know what is in the boxes, but they didn't tell him. They're coming down here tomorrow morning to investigate.'

'Tomorrow – in this snow!' said Roger, looking out of the window where the snow was still falling gently. 'No car would get through.'

'They're coming by *helicopter*!' said Barney. 'And we've got to prepare a landing-place for them.'

'Whew!' said Snubby. 'This *is* exciting! How do we do that?'

'Well, there's a big lawn at the back of the house,' said Barney. 'Very big, and quite flat, of course. And we're to clear as large a space as we can in the middle of it, so that the helicopter won't land in deep snow.'

'Let's go and begin now,' said Snubby, leaping up, quite forgetting that it was almost dark.

'Ass,' said Roger. 'Shut up, and let Barney go on.'

'We're to mark the landing place somehow,' said Barney. 'With dark cloths, or something.'

'We can take down all the navy-blue curtains upstairs,' said Mrs Tickle at once, as excited as the rest. 'We can clear a big square and lay the curtains all round it. If they're likely to blow away we can weight them down with something heavy – tins of food, or something like that.'

'But how many people are coming?' said Diana. 'I thought helicopters couldn't take many.'

'Three people are coming,' said Barney. 'My father, an inspector of police, and a sergeant, I think, Dad said. It's the only way they can come, and the inspector says its absolutely *essential* that they should get those boxes.'

'What can be in them?' wondered Snubby, jigging up and down in his chair just like Miranda. 'I say, isn't this a thrill? I hope those men won't hear the helicopter coming.'

'Dad says it doesn't matter if they do,' said Barney. 'He says they'll merely think it's been sent to drop food or to see if we're all right. Anyway, he says it's more important at the moment to find the boxes than the men.'

'Whew!' said Snubby. 'Let's have another hunt for them then. We *know* they can't be far away; they're too heavy to carry any distance.'

'Well, we did look all round and about, and in the snow and in the boat-house,' said Diana. 'Honestly, I don't think the men could have carried them any distance at all, once they took them off the toboggan.'

'No. That's quite true,' said Barney thoughtfully. 'I've puzzled about that too. We know quite well where the toboggan tracks ended – by the lake-side.'

'I suppose,' said Diana suddenly, 'I suppose . . . No, it couldn't be that.'

'Couldn't be what? What have you thought of?' said Barney at once.

'Well, we found that the toboggan tracks ended by the lake-side, and we found the toboggans themselves nearby in the snow,' said Diana. 'But it's quite possible, I suppose, for the men to have slid the toboggans *across* the lake, to the bank on the other side, and have hidden the boxes there. And then slid the toboggans all the way back to where we found them in the snow?'

The others stared at her, taking in this new idea. Barney slapped his knee and made Miranda jump in surprise.

'Yes! Yes, it's not only possible, it's very, very likely. If you remember, the lake was free of snow that night. We'd been skating on it all day, and the toboggans would

135

slide over it easily enough. And then the snow fell and hid any tracks made over the lake! Even a thin layer would hide any cuts made by the runners of the toboggans as they slid over the ice, weighted down by the heavy boxes.'

'And I've thought of something else,' almost shouted Snubby, making Loony jump this time. 'That cigarette packet I found some way out on the lake – with cigarettes still in it. It wasn't thrown there by the men, it was *dropped* by one of them as he pulled a toboggan along.'

'Yes. That's right,' said Roger, clapping Snubby on the back. 'That puzzled me too. Now you've solved *that* little mystery, Snubby. Of course, it was *dropped*, not thrown. I say, I wish it wasn't dark. We could go across the lake and hunt for hiding-places somewhere on the opposite bank.'

'Let's take our torches and go,' said Snubby, jumping up and making Loony bark.

'No, certainly not,' said Mrs Tickle at once. She had been listening to all this in astonishment, not uttering a word. But now she had *her* little say. 'Going out into the thick snow at this time of night, when it's pitch dark and freezing cold – you'd all be lost, and frozen to death by the morning.'

'Stuff!' cried Snubby, too excited to listen to reason. 'I'm going. Come on, Barney.'

'No, Snubby, Mrs Tickle's right,' said Barney. 'It would be a mad thing to do. We can easily wait till morning. We'll have to be up early. It will take us ages to clear the thick snow off the lawn, and make a square big enough for the helicopter to land in safety.'

'We'll have to find spades,' said Diana.

'There are some in the gardener's shed,' said Mrs Tickle. 'We'll get them out tomorrow. Now, look, don't

136

you *want* any tea? The buttered toast and the scones will all be cold.'

'Gosh! I'd forgotten all about tea. However could I do that?' said Snubby, sounding most surprised. 'Di, lay the cloth quick. I'll help to set out the things. Buttered toast all going cold. What a thing to happen!'

Mrs Tickle laughed and went back to the kitchen to get the tea made in the big brown teapot. That Snubby! Just like her Tom, he was, always hungry, always one for a joke. She heard the patter of feet and looked round quickly. It was Loony, and even as she turned she saw him make off with her hearth brush. By the time she had put down the kettle and teapot she was holding he had disappeared upstairs. Goodness knew where he would put that brush!

Tea was a most excited meal, with everyone discussing helicopters, police, possible hiding-places for the boxes on the other side of the lake, and where Stan and Jim, the two men, could be.

'They might be with the boxes,' said Snubby, putting potted meat on to his fourth pieces of toast. 'They might have built themselves a snow-house like ours, and have made a fine hide-out, with plenty of our tins for food, and snow for water.'

'In that case we'd better go carefully,' said Diana, alarmed. '*I* don't want to find those two men. Let the police do that. But I'd love to find the boxes.'

'We'll take the toboggans with us when we go across the lake tomorrow,' said Roger. 'Then if we *do* find the boxes we can bring two back, one on each toboggan. Wouldn't the police be pleased to see them!'

They were not at all tired that night, for they had had too little exercise, and Mrs Tickle found it very difficult to get them to bed. She badly wanted to go herself, for she had baked and cooked a good deal that day, and was tired. She peeped in at the sitting-room door at half-past nine.

'Aren't you ready?' she said. 'I've lighted all your candles for you out here. Please come quickly.'

'Right,' said Barney, hearing the tired note in Mrs Tickle's voice. 'You go on up, Mrs Tickle. We're just coming. We'll knock at your door to tell you we're safely upstairs.'

They talked for ten minutes more and then went into the hall to get their candles, but not one was alight! The hall was in complete darkness.

'Don't turn out the oil lamp!' shouted Barney to Diana. 'Someone's blown out our candles. NOW what's up? Surely our Mr No-One isn't up to his tricks again. It's pitch-dark here in the hall. I'll just feel about for the candles and see what's happening.'

'Oh, *dear!*' said Diana. 'Surely we're not going to have any upsets tonight! Buck up, Barney. Wait, I've got a torch. I'll shine it round the hall and see if anyone's about.'

She shone it nervously round the dark hall. And yes – someone *was* hiding there. The beam fell on a small furry head, peeping out from behind the back of a chair, with two bright eyes gleaming mischievously.

'It's *Miranda!*' cried Snubby. 'Oh, you little wretch! *You* blew out all the candles, didn't you? Loony, get her!'

But before Loony could get near her the little monkey was bounding up the stairs in glee, chattering away in delight. Aha! *She* had played a trick that Loony would never even think of.

138

Chapter Twenty-Two

Here Comes the Helicopter

Next morning dawned clear and bright. The snow had ceased falling, and once again the sun shone from a clear, pale-blue sky. All the children were pleased, because this would make things much easier for the helicopter.

They were up nice and early, and gobbled their breakfast. Diana went to help Mrs Tickle with the washing-up, and the boys brought in the wood for the fires. Then they went to look for spades in the big gardener's shed not far from the kitchen. It was locked, but Mrs Tickle gave them the key. They unlocked it and looked round for spades.

'Good!' said Barney, as his eyes fell on quite a selection. 'Big ones and little ones. Here, have this nice little one, Snubby.'

'Don't be a fat-head,' said Snubby, annoyed. 'I'm as strong as you are – stronger, if anything.'

Diana and Mrs Tickle came out to join them as they were arguing about the spades. Mrs Tickle rolled up her sleeves and chose a hefty spade. Barney looked at her admiringly. Whatever she did, she did *very* thoroughly.

They went to the lawn, their spades over their shoulders. The snow was quite thick and deep here – about two feet, Barney thought. 'Let's mark out a good-sized square,' he said. 'And begin to clear it at once.'

They marked out the square, and then began to shovel away the snow vigorously. It was very hard work. Snubby began it much too vigorously and was forced to take a rest before the others did. 'You should have taken the small spade as I told you,' said Barney, his blue eyes twinkling.

They soon had quite a good piece of the middle of the square cleared. 'It's big enough for a helicopter to land here now,' said Roger, considering it carefully. 'Though it would be a pretty near thing. Mrs Tickle, what about you and Diana going to get those dark curtains now, and we can lay them round the clear patch as soon as we hear the noise of the helicopter. We don't know when it will come, but we'll go on digging hard till it does.'

Mrs Tickle and Diana disappeared indoors. They came out in half an hour with armfuls of the dark curtains, taken down from the upstairs rooms.

They laid them down in a heap and joined the boys in their digging. No helicopter arrived, and soon the diggers felt as if they simply MUST have another rest. Barney was digging in his shirt-sleeves now, and seriously considering working bare-backed, he was so hot.

Mrs Tickle went indoors and brought out some buns and ice-cold lemonade. Nobody wanted a hot drink just then! They ate and drank eagerly, for the exercise had made them very hungry and thirsty. Then they set to work again.

'It's a quarter to twelve,' said Mrs Tickle, at last. 'I think I'd better go in and make some soup, and peel potatoes, and so on. With three extra lunches, we'll need plenty of food. Diana, you come too; you've done enough digging.'

'Yes, go and help Mrs Tickle,' said Barney, who saw that Diana was getting tired. 'We've not much more to do. There's a fine big clear place for the helicopter to land now.'

Diana went in to help Mrs Tickle, and the boys resumed

their shovelling. Certainly they had made a big enough landing-place now. Barney felt quite proud of it.

Then, through the clear, frosty air, there came a distant throbbing. The boys looked up. It must be the helicopter.

'Quick! Spread out the dark curtains!' shouted Barney, suddenly excited. 'And don't you dare to run off with any, Loony – or you either, Miranda!'

Mrs Tickle and Diana came running out as soon as they heard the helicopter, and helped to put the dark curtains all round the big, cleared square of lawn. They could now see the machine quite clearly – not a very big one – its vanes spinning above it.

It came nearer and nearer, and the noise grew louder. 'It's coming down! It's seen our marked-out square!' shouted Snubby, in intense excitement. 'Here, helicopter, here; this way, this way!'

Carefully and gracefully the helicopter descended to the clearing. It came to earth with hardly a jerk, and the sergeant, who was piloting it, jumped out first. He grinned round at the excited children.

'Fine!' he said. 'We saw our landing ground miles away. Splendid!'

Then came Barney's father, Mr Martin, and last of all the trim, burly inspector, with a grim mouth, but kind eyes twinkling under bushy brows.

'Well!' he said. 'Good morning to you all. You've had a little excitement, I hear.'

Mr Martin smiled round, glad to see everyone looking well and cheerful. 'I'd never have to let you come if I'd known you were going to be snow-bound like this,' he said. 'Come along – let's go into the house and talk.'

Off they went, and Mrs Tickle became very busy indeed in the kitchen, while the others filed into the sitting-room to exchange their news.

The inspector and the sergeant listened to everything with great interest, the sergeant taking notes all the time. The children had to tell the story over again right from the very beginning. The inspector asked many questions, and was pleased with the clear, ready replies.

'Intelligent children, there,' he said, turning to Mr Martin, who had sat silent, astonished once again at the strange story. He turned back to the children.

'Mr Martin says you tried to find the boxes, after the men had taken them away, but couldn't,' he said. 'Have you any idea at all where they *could* have been taken?'

'Yes, sir,' said Snubby eagerly, and he told him of their latest idea – that the men had slid the toboggans across the lake, taking the boxes to the other side. 'But the snow hid their tracks across,' he said, 'so we actually thought that they had taken the toboggans no farther than the boat-house; we never thought of them going across the frozen lake. And I found a half-full packet of cigarettes out on the lake, too; they must have dropped it there on their way across.'

Now the inspector and the sergeant were sitting up straight. 'Ah!' said the Inspector, 'now this is something. It's obvious that the men couldn't *carry* the boxes far, so . . .'

'Sir, what's in the boxes, do you think?' asked Snubby, longing to know.

'We'll have to wait and see,' said the inspector tantalisingly. 'If it's what we hope it is, we shall be very, very pleased.'

Mrs Tickle appeared in the doorway. 'I hope I don't interrupt, gentlemen,' she said politely. 'But I've got a meal all ready to bring in, if you'd like it now. Or I'll keep it hot for you.'

'No, no – we'll have it now, Mrs Tickle,' said Mr Martin

142

at once. 'Very good of you to think of it. Have you much more questioning to do, Inspector?'

'None,' said the inspector, and the sergeant snapped the elastic band round his black note-book, and put his pencil away. 'But we'll do a little searching this afternoon, if you children will show me the lake and the boat-house and all the rest. We may be able to find those boxes.'

'Oh, good!' said Snubby, rubbing his hands. 'I say, things are getting pretty exciting, aren't they?'

'Very,' said the inspector, smiling at the red-haired, freckled boy with the spaniel at his heels.

'I'll go and help Mrs Tickle,' said Diana, and Roger went too. Miranda leapt off Barney's shoulder and scampered out of the door as well, much to the astonishment of the two policemen.

'She's gone to help herself to something she fancies,' said Barney, grinning. 'She's probably lifting the lids off the dishes to see what's inside.'

Mrs Tickle had provided a very good lunch indeed – 'quite smashing,' as Snubby said – and stayed in the room to help to serve such a large company. The two policemen stopped being rather ponderous and sharp-eyed, and joked and laughed as cheerfully as Mr Martin did. Altogether it was a most enjoyable meal, especially for Loony, who was provided with an astonishing amount of scraps under the table.

Miranda was thrilled, because besides a big steamed jam sponge pudding, there was a dish of pineapple and tinned cream, and Barney had to keep his eyes on her. She loved pineapple and would help herself out of the dish whenever she thought there was nobody looking.

'And now,' said the inspector, having thoroughly enjoyed the lunch and the company too, 'now I think we'd better get down to business. We will all go out and

143

you will show me the boat-house, and anything else I need to see. Then we will trek across the frozen lake to the other side, and see if we can find where those boxes are hidden.'

All was excitement immediately. The four children rushed to get their coats and scarves, while the three men lighted cigarettes and waited for them.

Soon they were all ready, with Loony rushing about madder than usual, holding a small duster in his mouth, and defying everyone's efforts to get it from him. Miranda waited her chance and dropped down on his back as he rushed past. In anger and surprise Loony turned on her and barked, and the duster dropped from his mouth.

In a trice Miranda had it in her paw, and was up on Barney's shoulder again, stuffing it down his neck for safety.

'What a pair!' said the inspector, chuckling. 'As bad as a couple of children.' Everyone laughed – and then out of the house they went, stopping to show the inspector the enormous lion's head knocker on the front door.

'H'm. Those fellows badly wanted you out of the house, didn't they?' said the inspector, eyeing the knocker. 'Well, come along; we've got a lot of work to do this afternoon.'

Chapter Twenty-Three

Snubby Stubs his Toe

The children took the three men down to the boat-house first of all, and showed them the broken window there, and the place where the toboggan tracks had ended.

'And that's where we found the toboggans, over there, almost hidden by the snow,' said Snubby, pointing.

The policemen went into the boat-house and searched for a while, saying very little. They came back, and shook their heads.

'Impossible to hide anything much there,' said the inspector. 'But there's no doubt the men hid there, by the number of cigarette ends and spent matches. Now, let's go across the lake. Scrape the snow away a bit here and there, in case we can find any tracks on the ice underneath.'

They scraped here and there, but could find no tracks of the toboggan runners. They reached the other side of the lake and began a systematic search. The inspector allotted searching spots to each of them. The drifts of snow were high in places, and it was just possible that the boxes might have been hidden there.

It was tiring work, stamping in the drifts and searching in the snow for anything hard, such as a box. They soon exhausted the spots the inspector had allotted and went farther afield, but here the snow lay perfectly smooth and unbroken, and it was fairly obvious that no big boxes were hidden there, or the snow would have lain unevenly.

'Well, we don't seem very successful, do we?' said Mr

Martin, disappointed. 'We've pretty well examined the whole of this bank of the lake. The rest of it has bushes growing down to the edge, and it's unlikely the men would go there.'

'I think we'd better give up for this afternoon,' said the inspector. 'I don't imagine that the men will try to retrieve their boxes while it's so difficult to get transport – such as a lorry – to take them away by road. Wherever they are, those boxes will have to remain hidden till the roads are clear of snow. THEN the men will lose no time in collecting them from their hiding-place and getting them away one night.'

'Right,' said Mr Martin. 'We'll go back to Rat-a-Tat House for tea then. It is getting dusk now. We can hardly see what we're doing.'

They turned to go back across the lake. The weather had turned warmer, and in places the snow was now melting fast. They came to the lake and stepped on it to go back to the boat-house.

Mr Martin and the two policemen went first, talking together. Snubby and Loony came last, shuffling through the snow that lay on the frozen surface.

Snubby suddenly stubbed his foot against something hard, and gave a yell of pain.

'What's up?' said Barney.

'I've stubbed my toe,' said Snubby, standing on one foot and holding the other. 'Oooh, I felt it right through my rubber boot!'

'Don't make such a fuss,' said Barney. 'Just a bit of frozen snow, that's all.'

'It was *not*,' said Snubby, indignantly, and immediately began to hunt for whatever it was he had stubbed his toe on. He soon found it, and uncovered it.

'Here, look, Barney!' he shouted. 'It's a great piece of

146

solid ice. LOOK! *Not* a bit of frozen snow. No wonder it hurt my toe.'

Barney turned back impatiently, and looked at the piece of ice Snubby had uncovered. It was rather curious – large, circular, and thick, and lay flat on the frozen surface of the pond. Barney stared at it in surprise.

'Why is it round like that?' he said. 'What a *peculiar* piece of ice.' He looked at it more closely and then gave a yell that startled Snubby considerably.

'Hey, Dad! Inspector! Come back here a minute – quick!'

Snubby stared at Barney as if he had gone mad, and Loony rushed round in circles, barking loudly as he always did if there was any excitement about. Mr Martin and the two policemen turned in surprise and made their way back as quickly as they could. 'What is it?' said the inspector. 'Have you found something?'

'Yes, this piece of ice,' said Barney. 'Look – perfectly round, and quite large. It's been sawn out of the icy surface of the pond.'

'Ah! *Now* we're getting warm,' said the inspector, and knelt to examine the circle of ice. 'Perfectly round – done with a saw, of course, as you say. But why? Aha! This is very interesting. What a pity it's getting so dark! Let me see, now. Could you boys run back to the house and get torches and some spades to shovel away the snow just here on the ice? We must see where this circle was sawn from.'

Tremendously excited, the four children raced back to the house, grabbed torches, found spades, and raced out again, hardly replying to Mrs Tickle's astonished questions.

Torches shone on to the snow near where Snubby had

found the round piece of ice. Shovels were used vigorously to shovel away the snow round about.

'We'd better be careful not to fall into the hole made when this piece of ice was cut out,' said Roger.

'No fear of that,' said Mr Martin. 'The water below would have frozen again almost immediately.'

In under five minutes there came a yell from Barney. 'I've found the place. this must be it. Look!'

They went to him, and shone their torches at his feet. There, uncovered by the snow was a circle of ice clearly defined on the surface of the pond, showing where a round piece had been removed, and where the water had frozen again.

'It looks rather like one of those round drain-covers you see in the road,' said Diana. 'Goodness! Do you think – do you possibly think – that the men shoved the boxes down under the ice, knowing it would freeze again and hide them safely?'

'Looks like it,' said the inspector grimly, peering down at the new circle of ice, so neatly filling in the place where the first one had been removed. 'What an ingenious idea! Stan and Jim are evidently men with brains.'

'What shall we do, sir?' asked the Sergeant, with great interest. 'It's getting very dark.'

'I think we can safely leave things till tomorrow,' said the inspector. 'The men are not likely to try to remove the boxes from the lake until the weather is good enough to arrange for a lorry to collect them. We'll be along here tomorrow and have a little excitement sawing out another piece of ice ourselves, and probing down into the water below.'

Everyone felt very excited, but rather disappointed that they would have to wait till the next day. 'I shan't sleep tonight for thinking of it,' said Snubby. 'Sir, we could do

148

it all right now, surely. I'll get a saw, and there are plenty of candles.'

'Ass! They'd blow out,' said Roger. The inspector didn't even bother to reply to Snubby. He led the way back to Rat-a-Tat House, feeling very pleased. Nobody took any notice of the way Snubby limped, and he felt cross. If he hadn't stubbed his toe so painfully against that big round piece of ice, nobody would EVER have found that most ingenious hiding-place. He thought they might at least sympathise with him over his toe.

Mrs Tickle had to hear the news of course, and was surprised and excited.

'To think of that now,' she said. 'Making a hole in the ice and dropping the boxes down. What a thing to do! Well, I must say those men are full of ideas. What with hammering at the knocker in the middle of the night to scare us away, and pretending to be the snowman walking round and about! I'll be glad when you've got them safely under lock and key, Mr Inspector, sir.'

'So shall I,' said the inspector grimly. 'Very glad indeed. Of course, we don't know for certain that we *shall* find the boxes down there, nor what they contain. But I'm hoping – yes, I'm certainly hoping.'

'Fancy having to wait a whole night before we find out,' complained Snubby bitterly. 'Loony, what about you and me slipping off at midnight and finding out for ourselves? Are you game?'

Loony was game for anything, of course, and said so, but the inspector did not approve of such fantastic suggestions.

'Nobody is to go near the pond again until the sergeant and I go tomorrow morning,' he announced. 'We will all have a nice quiet evening, and look forward to some good luck tomorrow.'

Certainly the evening passed pleasantly enough, for the inspector proved to have a fund of astonishingly interesting stories. Snubby listened open-mouthed to the ways of the police in tackling crime.

'My word!' he said, in awe, as the inspector described the capture of a particularly clever spy. 'I'm *never* going to do anything wrong, *never*. Nobody has any chance at all against people like you, Inspector. I think I'll join the police force when I grow up. Loony would be awfully good at tracking thieves, I bet he would.'

'He's just tracked down another of Mrs Tickle's brushes,' said Diana. 'Look – it's her hearth-brush again. Loony, have you no interests in life besides brushes and dusters?'

Loony deposited the brush at Snubby's feet as if he were bringing him a really fine bone. Snubby frowned at him.

'Idiot! Here am I praising you up to the inspector and you do a silly thing like this. Take it back at once, and apologise to Mrs Tickle. Quick, before Miranda gets it!'

Mr Martin laughed. Snubby always amused him. 'Time you went to bed,' he said. 'Remember, we may have some difficult work to do tomorrow.'

Chapter Twenty-Four

The End of the Mystery

Snubby was up first the next morning, with Loony racing round his feet. Mrs Tickle came downstairs a few minutes after Snubby, and found him trying to rake out the kitchen fire and light it for her.

'I couldn't sleep a minute longer,' he explained. 'I can't think why the inspector isn't up. Surely it is his duty to get on with this job as soon as possible?'

'You're a caution, you are,' said Mrs Tickle. 'Leave that fire alone, now. You've made ten times more mess than I do. Go and wake the others, because breakfast is to be earlier than usual.'

'Thank goodness for that,' said Snubby, and went back upstairs with Loony at his heels.

Breakfast that morning seemed a waste of time to the four children – even to Snubby, who liked a very big one, and could always be counted on to finish up the last piece of toast. But today he was as impatient as the others.

At last, armed with two saws and some thick rope, the little party set off to the lake. Miranda was on Barney's shoulder and Loony was finding that now the snow had melted on the lake, the surface was slippery again, and his legs most unaccountably slid away in all directions, making him feel most ridiculous.

They came to where they had discovered the newly-frozen circle of ice on the lake; close beside it was the loose piece on which Snubby had stubbed his toe. The inspector nodded to the sergeant, who knelt down and tried to insert the end of the bigger saw into the ice.

It wasn't easy, but at last the saw was really working, and the sergeant was puffing and panting as he sawed round the frozen circle. At last it was done – the circle was complete.

The sergeant inserted a wedge and heaved up the round piece of ice he had sawed round. Up it came, and he deposited it beside the first one. Everyone peered down into the icy water.

'I can see *something*,' said the sergeant, his head almost in the hole. 'I can just about reach it, sir, I think.'

He put his arm down into the water and groped about. His hand felt a rope and he pulled at it. Up it came and he dragged it out of the hole.

'It's fastened to something down below, sir,' he said, tugging at it. 'We'll have to heave hard, I'm afraid.'

'Tie that rope to ours,' said the inspector. 'Double ours to make it strong. Come away from the hole, boy – you'll fall in.'

Snubby removed himself in disappointment. The sergeant knotted the two ropes together, and then he and the inspector did a little heaving.

'Something's coming up,' panted the sergeant, pleased. 'Whoa-steady, here she comes! Anyone else like to help pull? It's very heavy.'

The edge of a box now showed through the big hole – then the top of it. And with another heave the big box came right over the edge of the hole and slid along the ice. The sergeant promptly fell over backwards, much to Loony's joy.

Everyone gazed at the box. 'Yes,' said Snubby joyfully. 'That's one of the boxes the men took out of the cellar. Hurrah!'

152

'Shall I open it now, sir?' asked the sergeant, getting up carefully. The inspector nodded, whereupon the sergeant produced a most interesting collection of tools in a leather case. How Snubby wished he had a set like that!

With a great deal of care and manipulation the sergeant at last got the lid open, and the children stared down inside. The box had been quite water-tight, apparently, for there was no moisture inside. Something gleamed up brightly as the children bent over to look.

'Guns!' said Snubby, in awe. 'I say, look at those guns!'

The inspector and the sergeant looked at one another and nodded. Yes, this was what they had been hoping for and expecting. Mr Martin nodded too.

'Good work!' he said. 'Let's hope we've got all the guns down there that those fellows stole from the army camp. I suppose they were going to be shipped out of the country secretly, and used against us somewhere.'

'I *say*! Mrs Tickle won't at all like the idea of having had dozens of guns stored in her cellar,' said Snubby. 'She's really scared of them. Are we going to get up the whole lot? Look – there's a rope hanging down from this one, into the water. Is it tied to the next box? Are they all tied to one another?'

'Shut up, chatterbox,' said Barney, eager to catch every word said by the three men. This was a serious business – traitor's business!

A thought struck him. Traitor's business – that rang a bell in his mind. Yes – what was that old legend? – the knocker, the lion's head knocker was never sounded unless there was a traitor in Rat-a-Tat House! And there *was* a traitor when that knocker sounded – it was sounded by the traitor himself. Barney made up his mind to tell the others this idea as soon as he got them alone. Very, very curious!

153

'Fetch your toboggan, boy,' said the inspector to Snubby. 'We'll drag this box back to the house for further examination. As for the other boxes, we'll leave them till I can get men down here to look at them. Their contents are probably exactly the same as this.'

Snubby sped off and brought back his toboggan. They lifted the heavy box on to it and Snubby and Roger dragged it over the slippery ice. What a find!

'What about the other boxes, sir? Suppose the thieves come and get them!' said Snubby.

'They won't come until the snow has gone and they can get a lorry down the roads,' said the inspector. 'And a few men to help them.'

'But aren't you going to set a watch, sir?' said Snubby. 'I mean, you don't know when they might come.'

'The first *lorry* that gets through to this district will be watched,' said the inspector good-humouredly. 'And just in case you think we don't know our business, I can tell you that as soon as the lorry is loaded with the guns, and the men drive off, it will be stopped, searched and driven off to the nearest police station. Does this meet with your approval?'

'Oh, sir!' said Snubby, actually blushing. 'I know you know your business – I just thought – well, those men may come along and get those boxes out, and – '

'But don't you think it is a good idea to let *them* drag them out, and load them into the lorry, so that we haven't anything to do but drive it to the police station?' said the inspector. 'Or would you like to take on the job of getting them out yourself?'

'Oh, *no*, sir,' said Snubby. 'I – well – er – er . . .' And he dried up completely, annoyed at being laughed at by the burly inspector.

The inspector and the sergeant, with the box of guns,

took off in their helicopter after lunch. The children were sorry to see them go – everything had been so very exciting! They waved till the helicopter was a speck in the sky and then went indoors.

'Dad, are you going to stay on with us?' said Barney, delighted to have his father with them.

'Yes, I thought I would,' said Mr Martin, smiling. 'If I shan't spoil the party.'

'Oh, *no*,' said Diana, who liked Barney's father very much. 'We'd love to have you. I'm sorry the snow is going, though – there won't be much more tobogganing or snowballing – but there'll still be skating.'

'My father skates marvellously,' said Barney, with the note of pride that was always in his voice when he spoke of his father. 'Dad, isn't Cousin Dick coming after all? Didn't his cold get better?'

'Yes, but there wasn't room in the helicopter for him too,' said Mr Martin. 'So it will be just me and the rest of you.'

'Good!' said Barney, pleased. 'Jolly good! I wonder if we'll still be here when those men come to get their guns from the lake. I do hope so.'

'Yes, I expect we shall,' said his father. 'That will be another bit of excitement to round off a most exciting holiday. My word, fancy your coming down here for a bit of winter sport just when the men had hidden their stolen guns in our cellars. What a shock it must have been for them to see lights in the house all of a sudden.'

'Snubby *really* solved most of the mystery,' said Diana generously. 'If it hadn't been for him things wouldn't have turned out so well.'

'Your're right!' said Snubby, beaming. '*I* heard the noise in the night and went down and found the boxes . . .'

'I bet it was *Loony* who growled or something,' said Roger. 'And don't forget that you managed to get yourself well and truly locked up.'

'And it was Snubby who knocked his toe against that round piece of ice and made us realise where it came from and set us on the track of the guns,' went on Diana. 'Yes, and it was Snubby who found that cigarette packet half full of cigarettes.'

'In fact, we might almost say that Snubby solved the mystery of Rat-a-Tat House!' said Mr Martin, smiling at Snubby's delighted face. 'He deserves a reward. Anything you'd particularly like Snubby?'

'Yes,' said Snubby at once. 'There's something I badly want to do – can I do it?'

'What is it?' asked Mr Martin cautiously.

'I want to go and bang that lion's head knocker on the door,' said Snubby. 'CRASH it down, like Mr No-One did that night. You've no idea what it sounds like, Mr Martin.'

'Ass,' said Barney. 'Let him do it, Dad. He won't be happy till he does bang that knocker. Little things please little minds, you know.'

'That knocker is an ENORMOUS thing,' said Snubby indignantly. 'Come on, Looney – let's go and have a bash.'

'Tell Mrs Tickle what you're going to do, for goodness' sake,' called Diana, 'or she'll go up in smoke. And Barney, hang on to Miranda. Look, she's up on the mantelpiece with her snap-cards again, bless her!'

Snubby went to the front door and opened it, Loony at his heels. 'Loony,' said Snubby solemnly, 'I and I alone, solved the Rat-a-Tat Mystery – and we're telling the world we did it. Stand ready!'

He lifted the huge knocker with both hands and then hammered with all his might on the door.

RAT-A-TAT-TAT!   RAT-A-TAT-TAT!   RAT-A-TAT-TAT!

All right, Snubby, we heard you. Now do go and sit down and be quiet!

The Ragamuffin Mystery

First published in a single volume in hardback in 1951 by
William Collins Sons & Co Ltd.
First published in paperback in 1970 in Armada

Chapter One

Off In The Caravan

'This is going to be just about the most exciting holiday we've ever had!' said Roger, carrying a suitcase and bag down to the front door. 'Diana, bring that pile of books, will you, before we forget them?'

Diana picked them up and ran down the stairs after Roger. At the front door stood a caravan. Diana stood and gloated over it for the twentieth time.

'Fancy Dad buying a *caravan*!' she said. 'And oh, what a pity he can't come with us, after all!'

'Yes – after all our plans!' said Roger. 'Still, it's a jolly good thing Mummy didn't back out, when she heard Dad had to go off to America – I was awfully afraid she would! My heart went into my boots, I can tell you.'

'Same here,' said Diana, stacking the books neatly on a shelf in the caravan. 'Have we got our bird-book – we'll see plenty of birds on our travels, and that's my holiday task – writing an essay on "Birds I have seen".'

'Well, don't forget to take the field-glasses then,' said Roger. 'They're hanging in the hall. I say – what did you think about Mummy asking Miss Pepper to come with us, now that Daddy can't manage?'

Miss Pepper was an old friend of their mother's. The children were fond of her – but Roger felt rather doubtful about having her on a caravan holiday with them. 'You see – she's all right in a *house*,' he said to Diana. 'But in a small caravan, with hardly any room – won't she get fussed? We shall be so much on top of one another.'

'Oh well – Mummy must have someone to take turns

at driving the car that pulls the caravan,' said Diana. 'And she'll be company for Mummy, too. She's quite good fun – if only she won't keep making us be tidy, and wash our hands and knees a dozen times a day, and . . .'

'What are you two gossiping about?' said their mother, hurrying out to the caravan with some more things, 'If we're going to start off at eleven, we'd better hurry! We've got to pick Miss Pepper up at two o'clock, you know – and that means going over thirty miles an hour if we don't start punctually. Too fast for a car with a caravan!'

'I wish Daddy was coming,' groaned Diana, helping her mother to pack in more luggage. 'Miss Pepper's all right – but Daddy's such fun on a holiday.'

'Yes – it's a pity,' said her mother. 'But at least we haven't got to put up with Snubby this time!'

'Gosh yes – Snubby with us in a small caravan – and Loony too – would be just about the limit!' said Roger. 'Who's he staying with these hols?'

Snubby was their cousin, a ginger-haired, freckled, snub-nosed twelve-year-old boy. He had no father or mother, and so spent his holiday with one or other of his aunts and uncles. Snubby by himself was bad enough, but with his quite mad dog, Loony, a beautiful black spaniel, he was enough to drive even the most patient aunt and uncle out of their minds.

'He's staying with Auntie Pat, I think,' said Diana. 'Isn't he, Mummy? I bet he's driving her crazy. Last time he stayed with her, Loony got a passion for goloshes, and he took every single one from the hall cupboard and hid them in the rhododendron bushes . . .'

'And the gardener couldn't believe his eyes when he saw them, and he called Snubby, and Snubby asked him why he had sown golosh seed under the rhododendrons!' said Roger, with a sudden snort of laughter.

'Good old Snubby! He *is* a pest, but honestly you can't help laughing at him half the time,' said Diana. 'I bet he wishes he was coming on this caravan holiday with us.'

'Well, thank goodness he's not,' said their Mother. 'Pack those rugs in the corner there, Diana. I really think that's about all. Now I'll go in and see that we've got absolutely everything – and if we have we'd better start.'

She hurried indoors. Diana looked round the neat little caravan, wondering how long it would be before it was anything but neat! She and her Mother and Miss Pepper were to sleep in it at night, and Roger was to sleep in the back of the car. What fun to travel round the countryside, going where they liked – not knowing what county they would sleep in at night – waking up when they liked. Yes – this was going to be something *like* a holiday!'

'There's just one thing I do *wish*,' said Diana to Roger, as they went indoors to say goodbye to their cook and daily woman. 'I wish and wish that old Barney was coming with us.'

'Gosh – so do I!' said Roger. 'And Miranda his monkey too. Dear little Miranda. We haven't seen her for ages.'

'Well, Barney's been travelling about with his father,' said Diana. 'I wonder if he often thinks how he travelled about before – you know, when he was a child and didn't know who his father was, and went about with the people of circuses and fairs. He did plenty of travelling then!'

'And now he's found his father – and a real family of his own – and he's no longer a poor circus boy, all alone in the world,' said Roger. 'And Miranda isn't a lonely little monkey, going everywhere with him, often hungry and cold – but a spoilt little pet, loved by every single one of Barney's family! And thank goodness, Barney hasn't changed a bit.'

'No – he's still the same kind, strong Barney,' said Diana. 'I do hope we see him these hols. Mummy!

Mummy, where are you? We really ought to start, you know.'

'Just coming!' called their mother, hurrying downstairs. 'I remembered I must find the sunburn lotion, in case we all get too burnt for words, in this hot weather. Go and say goodbye, dears – and then we'll start.'

Diana and Roger said goodbye to their cheery old cook, and she pressed a bag into their hands. 'Just a few of my special sugar biscuits to keep you going till dinner-time,' she said. 'Have a good time! And see and look after your mother; she's tired after all the packing up.'

At last they were in the car, and it moved slowly towards the front gate, pulling the caravan behind it. Fortunately the gates were wide and the posts were not even scraped. Away they went down the lane, the caravan running smoothly behind them, rocking just a little now and again when they went over a rut. Soon they were out on the main road – the holiday had begun!

They stopped for a picnic lunch on the way, and then drove on towards Miss Pepper's. 'We shall be late,' said Roger, 'but it doesn't matter, Mummy – Miss Pepper would be *most* surprised if we were punctual!'

'I dare say – but she's sure to be quite ready ten minutes beforehand,' said his mother. 'And I shall feel just as I used to when she looked after me in my teens – very very guilty!'

Miss Pepper was waiting for them on her doorstep, her suitcases beside her. She looked as tall and thin as ever, but her eyes twinkled as usual behind their glasses, and she smiled warmly.

'Well, here you all are, bless you!' she said. 'And wonder of wonders not more than fifteen minutes late! Had your dinner?'

'Yes, Miss Pepper,' said everyone, and Roger leapt out to take her luggage. He stowed it away in the caravan.

'What a fine caravan!' said Miss Pepper approvingly. 'Well, well – I never thought I'd ever sleep in a caravan – and here I am, quite looking forward to it!'

'I'll drive on for some way,' said the children's mother. 'Then you can take a short turn at driving if you will. We thought we'd make for that lovely little lake at Yesterley. The children can bathe then. Isn't it a mercy it's such glorious weather?'

'It certainly is,' said Miss Pepper, settling herself in the front seat. 'Dear me – it seems strange not to have Snubby with us. He's always come with the children when I've been with them before.'

'He's staying with Auntie Pat – and I expect he's driving her mad,' said Diana. 'All the same, I wish his dog Loony was with us – darling Loony – I do love him.'

'H'm,' said Miss Pepper, doubtfullly. 'I'm fond of him too – but I don't think I should be fond of him long if he went for a caravan holiday with us. He's not a very *restful* dog.'

It was very pleasant driving along that sunny day, with three weeks stretching before them, lazy, lovely weeks, full of picnics, bathes, ice-creams – and perhaps sleeping out in the open air instead of in the caravan? Roger made up his mind to suggest it that very first night – not for his mother or Miss Pepper, just for himself and Diana.

The car purred on and on – where would they stop for the night? Nobody knew and nobody cared. The caravan rolled on behind them, and every now and again Roger looked back to make sure it was still safely there.

'We're going to have fun!' he said to Diana. 'For three whole weeks – nothing but fun!'

167

Chapter Two

Very Unexpected!

For five days Roger and Diana had a truly wonderful time. For two nights they stayed by the lovely blue lake at Yesterley, and picnicked and bathed. Miss Pepper surprised them all by producing a bathing suit, and bathing too – and what was more she was a very fine swimmer indeed!

'Goodness!' said Diana, lying panting on the white sand that edged the lake. 'Goodness! I had a swimming race with Miss Pepper – and she beat me. And look, she's still swimming, and I've had to come out and rest.'

'She's jolly good,' said Roger. 'So's Mummy, actually. I wish I could float as long as she can – she just goes on and on – and yet it's not salt water! She must waggle her hands about, or something.'

'This is the kind of holiday I like,' said Diana. 'Wasn't it fun last night, sleeping out on the heather? Did you hear that owl hooting just by us? It nearly made me jump out of my skin.'

'Didn't hear a thing,' said Roger. 'I just shut my eyes – and never knew anything till you shook me awake this morning. How long are Mummy and Miss Pepper staying in the water? I'm hungry.'

They were all hungry those first five days, even Miss Pepper, who became quite ashamed of the enormous appetite she suddenly discovered.

'I do wish you wouldn't look so surprised, you two, when I take a third helping,' she said. 'You make me feel greedy – and really, it's only just that I'm very hungry.'

'Aha! *Snubby* would like to hear you say that!' said Roger. 'You always used to tell him he wasn't *really* hungry when he wanted a third helping – but just Plain Greedy!'

'Dear Snubby!' said Miss Pepper. 'I do wonder how he is getting on these holidays. Let me see now – your Auntie Pat hasn't any children, has she – so Snubby won't have anyone to play with. I'm afraid he may make himself a bit of a nuisance.'

'More than a *bit*,' said Diana. 'He can behave like a lunatic when he's bored. He thinks of the most awful things to do. Don't you remember how he thought he'd sweep our chimney one day, when it smoked a little, and then . . .'

'Don't *talk* of it,' said her mother, with a groan. 'I can't bear even to remember that day. I know your father nearly went mad, and chased Snubby round and round the garden with the chimney brush.'

'And fell over Loony,' said Diana.

'Yes. Funny the way Loony *always* gets under the feet of anyone who's angry with Snubby,' said Roger. 'Remarkably clever dog, Loony.

Each night the four of them sat in the caravan and listened to the news on their portable radio. They hadn't seen a single newspaper since they had set off on their holiday, but as Miss Pepper said, it didn't do to cut themselves off *completely* from everything.

'Someone might have landed on the moon – or started a war – or had an earthquake,' said Miss Pepper. 'We had better listen in just once a day.'

On the fifth night, they were as usual sitting in the caravan, listening to the evening news on the little radio. The children listened with only half an ear, until the announcer came to the weather. that was *really* important! Was the weather *still* going to be warm and sunny?

169

The news came to an end. It had been very dull – a new strike – a long speech by somebody important – a new kind of aeroplane tested – and then there came a message that made them all sit up at once.

Miss Pepper was just about to turn off the radio, when the voice spoke urgently.

'Here is a message, please, for Mrs Lynton, who with her children, is on a caravan tour. Will she please telephone Hillsley 68251 at once, as her sister is dangerously ill? I will repeat that. Here is a message for . . .'

No one spoke for a few seconds, or even moved, as the message was repeated. Then Diana whispered. 'Mummy – it's us they are trying to reach! You're Mrs Lynton – and oh Mummy, does it mean . . .'

'It means that something's happened to your mother's sister – your Aunt Pat,' said Miss Pepper, getting up at once. 'Don't worry too much, my dear – we'll drive straight off to a telephone box, and find out what's wrong.'

'Oh dear – what *can* have happened?' said Mrs Lynton, looking very pale. 'I'll have to go back – I'll have to go to Pat. Oh, I feel quite dazed.'

The children felt dazed too. What a dreadful thing to happen in the middle of a lovely holiday! Poor Auntie Pat – what *could* have happened – 'Dangerously ill' – that sounded very frightening.

'You two children stay here in the caravan,' said Miss Pepper briskly, taking charge as usual. 'I'll drive your mother to the nearest village and we'll telephone. We'll get back here as soon as possible. Cheer up, Diana – don't look so upset, dear. It may not be as bad as it sounds.'

In two minutes Miss Pepper was driving the car down the lane, the children's mother sitting silently beside her. Roger and Diana went outside the caravan, and sat down in the heather. It was a very light night, and, although they could not see to read, they could just see each other's faces. Diana was crying.

Roger gave her a quick hug. 'It mayn't be so bad,' he said. 'I expect Mummy will have to go back, though. We'll have to as well, I suppose.'

'But how can we?' wept Diana. 'Cook's away now, and the house is shut up. There'd be nobody there.'

'I'd forgotten that. And what about old Snubby?' said Roger. 'He can't stay at Auntie Pat's if she's ill – or gone to hospital. What's to happen to *him*?'

'And to us too,' said Diana. 'Mummy will certainly stay to look after Aunt Pat. She's so fond of her. Oh what an *awful* thing to happen in the middle of such a lovely holiday!'

It seemed a very long time before their mother came back with Miss Pepper. The children heard the car coming in the darkness and stood up at once. They ran to it as soon as their mother got out.

'But it wasn't their mother! It was Miss Pepper – and it wasn't their car either, it was a taxi!

'Oh – what's happened? Where's Mummy?' cried Diana.

'Gone off in the car to see to your auntie,' said Miss Pepper, paying the taxi-driver. 'She's had a fall and hurt her head, and the doctors thought she might die. But they've just given your mother a better report of her, and have asked her to get back as soon as she can, as your aunt keeps calling for her.'

'Oh! Poor Mummy!' said Diana, thinking of her mother driving fast through the night, all alone, worrying about her sister. 'Oh, Miss Pepper – do you think Auntie Pat will be all right?'

'From the doctor's latest report, I should think she *will*,' said Miss Pepper, comfortingly. 'So don't fret too much. It's silly to cross bridges before you come to them. Mummy sent you her love, and she says she'll give us the latest news in the morning, if I go into the village to telephone. It's not very far.'

'Will Mummy come back here, and go on with our holiday?' asked Roger.

'No. No, I think I can say that quite definitely,' said Miss Pepper. 'I'm pretty sure she will want to stay with your Aunt Pat till she's really on the mend. We had no time to decide exactly what to do – but I'm afraid you'll have to put up with *me* for a bit, my dears! I promised your mother I'd be with you till she can have you home again.'

'But – what are our plans now, then?' asked Roger feeling rather dazed. 'We've this caravan – but no car – and our house is shut up. Will we leave the caravan here and go and stay with *you*, Miss Pepper?'

'I really do *not* know, Roger dear,' said Miss Pepper. 'Shall we leave everything till tomorrow? Things like this do happen, you know – and then we often find out how strong – or weak – we are! Your mother now, was full of courage as soon as she got over the shock; she was ready to face up to anything!'

'What about poor Snubby?' said Diana. 'He's staying with Auntie Pat. Oh, Miss Pepper – Auntie Pat didn't fall over Loony, did she?'

'No – she slipped off a ladder,' said Miss Pepper. 'Now – I'm going to open a bottle of orangeade, and find those chocolate biscuits and macaroons we had over from lunch – and we're going to have a nice little supper.'

The two children felt glad to have Miss Pepper with them. She was cheerful and brisk, and even made one or two little jokes. Roger felt more cheerful too, after his supper, but Diana was still scared and upset.

'Roger, would you like to sleep in your mother's bunk

tonight in the caravan with Diana and me?' Miss Pepper asked. 'I expect Diana would like you in here with us tonight.'

'Yes. Yes. I'd like to sleep here instead of in the open,' said Roger, and Diana nodded, pleased. Now if she was awake in the night and felt scared and sad, she could talk to Roger. Brothers were good to have when things went wrong!

Soon the caravan was in darkness, while three people tried to get to sleep. What news would the morning bring? Good – or bad? And what was going to happen to their holiday?

Chapter Three

Good Old Barney

Next morning Miss Pepper was up bright and early, and woke the two children. 'Wake up!' she said. 'We'll have breakfast and then I'll pop down to the village and telephone your mother. Did you sleep well?'

'Yes, I did,' said Diana, rather surprised, for she had felt sure that she wouldn't sleep at all. Roger had slept well too, and both of them felt more ready to face up to whatever news they would hear.

Miss Pepper made the tea, and Diana cut the bread. Soon they were eating cold ham, and drinking the hot tea. 'Though really, why we don't have orangeade this hot morning, instead of this scalding tea, I can't think!' said Diana.

Immediately after breakfast Miss Pepper set off briskly to the village. She was back in half an hour and the children, who were anxiously looking out for her, ran to meet her, most relieved to see a smile on her face.

'Better news,' said Miss Pepper at once. 'Your mother arrived safely, and your aunt was so glad to see her – and she has taken a turn for the better already.

'Good, good, good!' said Diana, thankfully.

'Apparently she fell from the top of a ladder when she was tying up some ramblers on the wall,' said Miss Pepper. 'And she hit her head on the stone path. Nothing to do with Loony at all! She's in hospital, and your mother is with her. And I'm afraid your mother will have to stay away for quite a while, because there is no one to look after your uncle – so your mother says she'll spend part

174

of her time seeing to your uncle and the other part with your aunt.'

'Oh. Then what's to happen to *us*?' said Diana at once.

'Well, I suppose I'll have to try and hire a car and take the caravan back to my own home,' said Miss Pepper. 'You'll have to come with me, I'm afraid, as your own house is shut up. I'm sorry, dears – very very sorry. This is a horrid end to what was going to be one of your very best holidays. But I honestly don't see what else we can do.'

'I don't either,' said Roger gloomily. 'And I think it's jolly good of you to take all this trouble for us, Miss Pepper. I'm sure you don't want us in your little house! Oh dear – isn't this all horrid!'

'Diana can come with me to find out about a car,' said Miss Pepper as they cleared up the caravan and made up the bunks. 'And Roger can stay here with the caravan. That be all right, Roger?'

'Of course,' said Roger, still gloomy, and watched Miss Pepper go off to the village again, Diana by her side. What a mess up of a glorious holiday! Miss Pepper was good and kind – but the thought of living for two or three weeks in her tidy little house filled Roger with dread.

'We'll be too bored for words!' he thought and then reproached himself for being unkind. Whatever would they have done without Miss Pepper just now! 'We *might* have gone to stay with old Barney, if he hadn't been touring about the country with his father,' his thoughts ran on. 'Oh well – we'll just have to make the best of things, I suppose.'

Miss Pepper and Diana came back in an hour's time, looking depressed.

'We can't get a car anywhere in the village,' said Miss Pepper. 'So we telephoned the nearest town, and somebody is going to try there for us. I do hope we shan't

175

have to take some old crock that will break down halfway home! I'm not really very good at driving cars I don't know.'

Their caravan was set on a heathery hill, just off the road, not far from a farmhouse. The farmer had given them permission to stay on the hill – and, about three o'clock that afternoon, the three saw him coming up to their caravan.

'Oh dear – I hope he's not going to turn us off!' said Miss Pepper in a fright.

The farmer came slowly up to where they were all sitting outside the caravan, his dog at his heels.

'Good afternoon, Ma'am.' he said, in his pleasant country voice. 'There be a message come for you, sent to my farmhouse by the post office. Telegram it be.'

He held out the orange telegram and Miss Pepper took it, suddenly frightened. She tore it open and read it. Then she looked round at the two waiting children, puzzled.

'Listen,' she said, 'it says "Wait till you see us tonight, Barney".'

'Wait till you see us tonight!' echoed Diana, and her face suddenly lighted up. 'Oh, Miss Pepper! Barney and his father must have heard about Auntie Pat's accident, and how Mummy had to go to her, leaving us here! And they're coming here tonight! Oh, how WONDERFUL!'

'They must have heard the message on the radio last night, when we did!' said Roger. 'And they rang the Hillsley telephone number and found out what was happening. Miss PEPPER! Everything will be all right now! Barney's father will arrange about a car and everything. Oh, thank goodness!'

Diana gave a long sigh of relief, and her heart suddenly lightened. Barney was coming – and his nice father. Now things would soon be settled for them. Perhaps they could go and stay with Barney?

'Thank you,' said Miss Pepper to the farmer, and he nodded, and left, his dog still at his heels.

'*Wait till you see us tonight!*' said Diana, quoting the telegram again. 'That must mean that they are driving straight to us, wherever they are – and must be rather far away, or they would arrive before tonight. Good old Barney! Now we can just sit back and not worry.'

'You two had better go down to the river and have a bathe,' said Miss Pepper. 'It's so hot today. I won't come with you, because someone had better stay with the caravan. Go along now, and have a good swim. It will do you good.'

So off went Roger and Diana, feeling considerably happier because of Barney's telegram. How good it was to have friends – how very very good!

'We shall see dear little Miranda too,' said Diana happily. 'The best thing about animals is that they don't seem to change, as human beings do! Miranda must have looked the same ever since she was a year old!'

They had a long bathe, and then lay in the warm heather to dry. They were hungry when they got back to the caravan. 'Any news of Barney yet? Or another telegram?' asked Roger. Miss Pepper shook her head.

'No – but Barney said *"tonight"* in his telegram, you know. We shall have to wait in patience. I'm sure they must be down in Cornwall, or up in the north of Scotland or in the Welsh mountains – somewhere quite far away from here, anyway.'

'I'm not going to bed till they come,' said Roger firmly.

'I can't really expect you to!' said Miss Pepper. 'But I hope it's before twelve o'clock!'

The evening drew on, and the sun began to sink low down in the west. At every far off sound of a car going by on a distant road, the three of them stiffened and listened – but car after car purred by in the distance and not one stopped, or came in their direction.

Then at last, just as it was getting really dark, the sound of a car jolting over the rough road next to the old farmhouse came to their ears. 'That *must* be Barney!' said Diana in excitement. They listened anxiously.

The car stopped – and then, a few minutes later they heard it starting up again in the silence of the evening. It was coming over the rough track that led to them!

'It's Barney! It must be!' cried Roger, leaping up. 'The villagers must have sent them to the farm, and the farmer has told them where we are. Barney! BARNEY! BARNEY!'

An answering shout came to their ears. 'Hey! We're coming! The track's rough, though!'

Soon a big car came to a stop beside the caravan, and a tall figure leapt out; Roger and Diana ran to meet it – and to greet dear old Barney, with little Miranda the monkey on his shoulder, chattering excitedly.

'Hallo, hallo!' cried Barney, and hugged both Diana and Roger. 'Sorry to be so long coming – we were right away in Scotland! Heard the news on the radio last night, of course, and telephoned to your mother at Hillsley. How are you?'

'Oh, BARNEY, it's so lovely to have you,' said Diana. 'We simply didn't know WHAT to do when Mummy had to go off and leave us. Is that your father getting out of the car now?'

'Yes. We can leave everything to him,' said Barney, very happy to be with his friends again. 'Every single thing! He's got a marvellous plan. Hallo, Miss Pepper! Isn't this a surprise?'

'It certainly is,' said Miss Pepper. 'Ah, here's your father! Good evening – it *is* good of you to come to us like this!'

'We'll soon fix up some plans,' said Barney's father

178

shaking hands. 'Sorry about this trouble. Let's go into that fine caravan of yours and talk.'

And in they all went, Miranda the monkey too, chattering loudly, leaping from one shoulder to another and making Roger and Diana laugh in glee. Good old Barney – dear little Miranda – it really was wonderful to see them again!

Chapter Four

A Wonderful Idea

It seemed quite a crowd in the little caravan. Miss Pepper lighted the safety-lamp, and they all looked at one another, blinking. Barney's brilliant blue eyes shone as he looked round at everyone. He was as brown as a berry, as usual, and his grin just as wide as ever!

His father spoke to Miss Pepper. 'We rang up again tonight to see how Mrs Lynton's sister was, and she is just a little better – and will certainly recover well now – but it will take time.'

'Thank goodness it's better news,' said Miss Pepper. 'It was such a terrible shock last night. I am so glad to see you, Mr Martin – I really was worried about what to do for the best.'

'Well, don't worry any more,' said Mr Martin. 'What I propose is that I should hitch my car on to your caravan and . . .'

'And take us home?' said Roger. But our house is shut up, Mr Martin!'

'Yes, I know that,' said Barney's father. 'And I know too that it must be a great disappointment to you, to have your three weeks' holiday broken up – so I think that if you all joined Barney – or let him join you, which ever way you like to put it – that would solve your difficulties.'

'You mean – we could have your car to drive the caravan about?' asked Miss Pepper. 'Oh dear – if you mean *me* to drive it, Mr Martin, I'm afraid I couldn't. It's so *big*, and . . .'

'No, no – I didn't mean that,' said Mr Martin. 'I'll

explain. Barney and I are on a week's holiday – and it is almost up, because I have to get back. What I propose is that I hitch up to your caravan, and we go off tomorrow and find some really nice place for you all to stay in – somewhere near a little inn, perhaps, so that you and Diana can sleep indoors there, and the two boys can sleep in the caravan, and . . .'

'Oh! What a WONDERFUL idea!' said Diana, her eyes shining. 'Some place by the sea, perhaps?'

'We'll see,' said Mr Martin, smiling at her excited face. 'If we can find a good spot tomorrow, I'll leave you all there, with the caravan, and drive back home. Miss Pepper will keep an eye on you, I know! When the time comes for you to leave, I'll drive up and fetch the caravan. What do you think of that?'

'Oh – too good to be true!' said Roger. 'I honestly thought we'd have to go home and look after ourselves in an empty house! It's awfully good of you, sir – and of course, solves all our problems – except one!'

'And what problem's that?' asked Mr Martin.

'Well – about Snubby,' said Roger.

'What's going to happen to him?'

'Can't he come with us?' said Diana, eagerly. 'There's room in the caravan for three – or he could sleep in whatever inn or hotel Miss Pepper and I go to.'

'Dear me – I'd forgotten about Snubby!' said Mr Martin. 'Of course he can come too. He was staying with the aunt who's ill, wasn't he, poor fellow. We'll telephone your mother and tell her to send him up to us, when we've decided where you're going to stay.'

Diana heaved a great sigh. 'I was so worried about everything,' she said. 'And now all the troubles are smoothed out. Thank you very much, Mr Martin. And to think we'll have Barney and Miranda with us too!

Miranda, do you hear that? You're coming on holiday with us now!'

Miranda heard her name, and chattered in delight. She leapt to Diana's shoulder and pulled her hair gently, pretending to whisper into her ear.

'You dear, funny little thing,' said Diana, fondling her. 'Fancy having you with us too – what a treat!'

'Can I offer you some cocoa – or some orangeade?' asked Miss Pepper. 'I'm afraid there's nothing very exciting to give you for supper.'

'Oh, I nearly forgot!' said Barney, getting up. 'We've got a whole lot of stuff in the car. We didn't stop to have meals at hotels today, we just bought bread and ham and fruit and tomatoes, and ate them as we drove along. We so badly wanted to get here as soon as possible. I'll go and bring some of it in.'

'How lovely!' said Diana. 'I don't know why, but I suddenly feel frightfully hungry.'

'It's because your worries are gone, dear!' said Miss Pepper. 'I feel a bit hungry myself too! It is truly good of you, Mr Martin, to come to our aid like this.'

'Ah well – you've been kind to Barney many a time,' said Mr Martin. 'Hey, what's that monkey doing?'

'Oh – she's got my sponge!' said Diana, with a delighted giggle. 'Miranda, give it to me! Oh look, she's washing her face with it, just as she's seen me do at times. Miranda, that's *my* sponge!'

'Now she's put it into her mouth!' said Miss Pepper. 'Oh, the naughty little thing! Surely she's not thinking of eating it, Diana!'

Barney deftly removed the sponge, and scolded the little monkey, who at once covered her face with her arms, and sat in a corner giving little moans.

'Don't pretend like that!' said Barney, going out of the

caravan. 'You're not a bit sorry. I'll be back in half a jiffy, everyone. See Miranda doesn't get your soap, Di!'

Barney was soon back with paper bags and tins. Then they all settled down to a first-rate supper of ham, tomatoes, cheese, ripe plums and orangeade.

'What are you going to do tonight – about sleeping, I mean,' said Miss Pepper to Mr Martin. 'It's such a lovely night, I expect the children will sleep out of doors again, on the heather, with a rug around them. But you won't want to do that, Mr Martin.'

'No. I'd rather go to the little inn in the village,' said Barney's father. 'Barney can stay here with you, of course. I'd like to telephone Mrs Lynton tonight and tell her we'll have Snubby as soon as we can. Tomorrow we'll decide where we'll go – and then I'll let Mrs Lynton know where to send Snubby. Well – I'll say goodnight, I think. I can see Diana yawning her head off!'

'Good night, sir,' said Roger, 'and thanks most awfully. See you tomorrow!' Everyone went to the car to see Mr Martin off, and soon he was jolting slowly over the little track that led back to the farmhouse.

'And now it's bed for all of us,' said Miss Pepper briskly. 'My word, I feel different now – everything straightened out so well! I just wish your mother hadn't had her holiday spoilt, though she won't mind so long as your aunt is on the mend!'

The two boys went out to find a thick patch of heather. 'We'll wash in the stream tomorrow morning,' yawned Roger, settling down on a rug. 'Here – there's enough rug for you and Miranda, Barney.'

Miranda cuddled up into Barney's neck, chattering in his ear. He was sleepy and didn't answer, and she tweaked his hair.

'Now look here, Miranda,' said Barney, undoing her

tiny fingers from his hair, 'I will *not* have you pulling my hair when I want to go to sleep. Settle down!'

And Miranda settled down meekly, her small brown face hidden in his neck. Barney patted her and smiled. What a funny little thing she was!

Miss Pepper and Diana slept in the caravan with the door wide open for air. Miss Pepper sighed with relief as she closed her eyes. Things were turning out better then she had hoped!

In the morning quite early, Mr Martin was back again in the car, complete with new-laid eggs, new-made bread, butter and fresh milk from the farm. 'And very nice too!' said Miss Pepper approvingly. 'Miranda – leave that egg alone!'

'I've been looking at a map,' said Mr Martin, after breakfast, and spread a large one out on the heathery ground, where they had all sat having breakfast in the warm sun. 'The thing we have to decide is where to go! Any ideas, anyone?'

'Somewhere by the sea,' said Roger at once. 'If this hot weather goes on, we'll want to bathe.'

'Not in a big town,' said Miss Pepper. 'Somewhere small and countrified.'

'Somewhere where I can watch birds,' said Diana. 'I've got a holiday essay to write on "Birds I have seen".'

'Oh, don't start talking about that essay again!' said Roger. 'I bet you don't watch for a single bird the whole time!'

Diana glared at him, and Miss Pepper hurriedly interrupted. 'There are birds everywhere, Diana – we really don't need to look for any *special* bird-haunt. Barney, what kind of place would *you* like?'

'Well – I hate modern holiday spots, where there are crowds of people,' said Barney. 'I'd rather go to some quiet old place – where we can laze about in old clothes, do exactly what we like, and not have to bother with anyone else at all.'

'I think we are all pretty well agreed then,' said Miss Pepper. 'But where shall we find a place like that in the middle of summer? Most places by the sea are so crowded now.'

'We'll go somewhere on this hilly Welsh coast, I think,' said Mr Martin, tracing a route with his finger. 'It's lovely country round there. I vote we start off straightaway, and cruise along by the sea – and we'll stop as soon as we find the place we want. Come along – let's pack up and go at once!'

Chapter Five

A Halt For Ice-Creams

Before long they were all on their way. Mr Martin's car was a big one, and there was plenty of room for them all. The caravan swayed along behind, and Mr Martin had to keep remembering that his car was pulling it, and try not to swing round corners too fast!

They drove until lunchtime, and then had a picnic by the roadside, in a little wood. They looked at the map again. 'Soon be by the sea,' said Mr Martin, following the map with his fingers. 'Then we'll look out for a likely spot for you. We'll drive straight through all the big seaside towns, and dawdle along the coast looking for what we want.'

'This is fun!' said Diana. 'Oh, Miranda – you'll be sick! Barney, that's the fourth plum she's taken.'

Barney took away the plum, and Miranda flew into a rage. She leapt onto his head, pulling one of his ears till he shouted. Then she was sorry and tried to creep down his neck, under his shirt.

'Really, you can't help laughing at the naughty little thing!' said Miss Pepper. 'What shall we do when Snubby arrives with that mad spaniel Loony, I don't know! There'll be no peace for anybody!'

'Well, I must say I'm as pleased we haven't that pair in the car with us yet,' said Mr Martin, rolling up the map. 'A mad dog, an idiotic boy, and a naughty monkey would certainly be too much for any driver!'

They drove off again. They came to a big seaside town packed with trippers, noisy and full of litter. 'Straight through here,' said Mr Martin firmly. 'And the next one too. After that we come to a lonely part of the coast, and we'll keep our eyes open.'

Through that town they went, and then right through the next, without stopping. Ah – now they were leaving behind the crowded part of the coast, and coming to deserted bays, lonely sweeps of sand, tiny villages, fishing hamlets. Hills rose up from the coast, and the car had to take a roundabout route, going slowly because of the caravan behind it.

'This looks more like what we want,' said Diana, looking out of the car window at the sea on one side and hills on the other. 'Mr Martin – do you think we could stop for an ice-cream sometime? I'm simply too hot for words, even with all the windows open!'

'Good idea!' said Mr Martin, and he stopped at the next village – a tiny place that ran down to the sea. But there was no shop that sold ice-cream! 'You go on to Penrhyndendraith,' said the woman they asked. 'That's got a fine ice-cream shop there. And if the young ones want a bathe, you tell them to go to Merlin's Cove – there's the finest bathing there in the kingdom.'

'That sounds fine,' said Roger, and they once more drove on. Round the coast they went, with the sea splashing on one side, and the mountains on the other – for now the hills had grown higher, and some of them towered up into the sky.

'Grand country!' said Mr Martin. 'Now – where is this Penny-denny-draith place. Ah – that looks like it – see, built on the slope of the hill.'

They came to Penrhyndendraith. It was a truly picturesque place, a fishing village, with a dozen or so old cottages built along the seafront and others straggling up the slope of the hill behind.

Above the cottages on the hill rose a strange old place

with curious turrets and towers. It was set right against a cliff-like hill, so that the back of it had no windows at all. Some of it was falling to pieces, and it looked in places as if only the ivy held it together!

A signboard was set over the great old doorway, but it was too far away for the children to read what was on it. Diana was more interested in finding the ice-cream shop than in looking at the half-ruined building on the hill. She jogged Mr Martin's arm gently. 'Look – would that be where the ice-cream shop is?' she asked, and pointed to the crooked row of cottages.

Mr Martin stopped the car near them. 'Well, as I can see only one that looks like a shop, that must be it!' he said. 'Yes – see what it says over the door. "Myfanwy Jones, General Dealer".'

'And look – it says "Ice-Cream"!' said Roger. 'In the corner of the window, see? Come on – let's get out of the car.'

So out they jumped and went to the little shop. What a curious place it was! Inside it was very dark, and there was little space to stand, because of the hundreds of things that the shop sold! The goods were piled on the floor, they hung from the walls, they swung from the ceiling!

'It must sell simply everything in the world!' said Diana in astonishment. 'Eatables, drinkables, china, pots and pans, fishing-nets, Miss Pepper, it's like a shop out of an old fairy-tale!'

'And here's the witch!' whispered Roger, and got a frown from Miss Pepper, as an old woman waddled behind the small counter. Her face was a mass of wrinkles, and her snowy white hair was tucked away under a little cap of black net. But old though she looked, her eyes were startlingly bright and piercing.

She spoke to them in Welsh, which they didn't understand. Diana pointed to a card that said "Ice-Cream" and the old lady nodded, and smiled suddenly.

'Two? Three? Four?' she said in English.

'Oooh – twenty!' said Roger at once, and everyone laughed, the old woman too.

'How big are your ice-creams?' asked Diana. The old woman took a scoop and scooped some from an ice-box – a good large helping, which she slapped between wafers.

'Ah – I think two each will be enough for the children,' said Miss Pepper, 'and one each for the grown-ups. What about Miranda, Barney?'

'Oh, one for her,' said Barney. 'She'll probably put most of it on the top of her head, because she's so hot!'

'There is a big seat outside,' said the old lady, nodding her head, as the children took the ice-creams, and they took the hint and went to sit on the hard old wooden bench.

'Not much taste – but VERY creamy and deliciously cold,' said Barney. 'Miranda, please go and sit on the ground. I DO NOT like you to dribble ice-cream all down my neck. Nor do I like it held against my ear. SIT ON THE GROUND!'

The little monkey leapt down to the ground, chattering, holding her ice-cream tightly in her paw. The old lady who was very interested in Miranda, came out to watch her.

'Very good little monkey,' she said, in her lilting Welsh voice. 'You come far?'

'Quite a long way,' said Barney.

'You go far?' said the old lady.

'We don't know. We are looking for somewhere quiet to stay,' said Barney. 'Somewhere near here, perhaps. It is such a lovely country. We don't want a big place, with big hotels – but perhaps a quiet old inn, and . . .'

'Ah, then you go up there, see?' said the old lady, and pointed up to the strange, half-ruined place they had seen on the hills. 'Quiet, very quiet – and the food is, it is so good, so good. And here, it is beautiful, with the sea so blue, and the sand so white, and . . .'

'But – is that old place occupied then?' said Mr Martin, astonished. 'I thought it was just an empty ruin.'

'No, no – my son, he keeps it,' said the old lady proudly. 'It is an inn, sir, you understand? And what food! Big men come here, sir, important men – they say how good the food, how good!'

Nobody could believe that important people would stay at the half-ruined place. The old woman saw that they did not believe her, and she grasped Mr Martin's arm.

'I speak the truth,' she said. 'To my son's inn come Sir Richard Ballinor, and Professor Hallinan, and . . .'

Mr Martin knew those names; 'One is a famous botonist, and the other is a well-known ornithologist – a man who studies birds,' he told the astonished children. He turned to the old lady.

'There are many flowers here, then?' he said. 'And rare birds?'

'Yes, many, many – up in the hills – and round the coves and on the cliffs,' said the old lady, nodding her head. 'Big men come to study them, I tell you, sir. My son, he knows them all. His cooking pleases them, sir, it is good, very good. You go to stay there too, sir? He has not many people now, it is a good time. Very good cooking, sir.'

'Well – we might as well go up and see the old place,' said Mr Martin, taking out some money to pay for the ice-creams. 'Thanks very much, Mrs Jones. We enjoyed your ice-creams. Is there a road up to the old inn?'

'It is very rough, sir. You must go slowly,' said the old woman, smiling delightedly at the thought that they were really going to see her son's place. 'Cooking very good sir, very very good.'

They all went off to their car. 'She's got good cooking on the brain,' said Roger. 'I wonder what the old place is like? It *might* be fun to stay there – there's all we want here, really – fine bathing . . .'

'Wonderful walks, I should think,' said Barney, who loved walking. 'And a jolly fine view.'

'Fishing,' said Roger, watching a small fishing-boat on the bay, its sails filling out with the wind.

'No trippers,' said Miss Pepper.

'And birds for me!' said Diana happily.

'You and your birds!' said Roger scornfully, and Diana immediately gave him a punch.

'Well – up to the inn we go!' said Mr Martin, as they started off slowly up the steep track, leaving the caravan behind for the time being. 'And what shall we find there, I wonder?'

Chapter Six

Penrhyndendraith Inn

The car crawled up the steep hill, on the zig-zagging track. The higher they went, the more magnificent the views became.

Diana gasped when she looked down the hill and saw the wonderful bay, and the great stretch of heaving sea beyond.

'Oh, *look*!' she said. 'How lucky the people are who live in that old inn, Miss Pepper, and look out on that view every day. And see – the view across the hills is glorious too – are those mountains beyond?'

'Yes. And beautiful ones too!' said Miss Pepper. 'Did you ever see such a blaze of heather – why, the hills look on fire with it! My goodness me – I can't help hoping that it will be possible for us to stay in the inn. I've never seen such views in my life!'

At last they reached the old inn. It really looked rather like a half-ruined castle! The great sign above the open door gave its name.

PENRHYNDENDRAITH INN

'Goodness knows how it's pronounced,' said Diana. 'I say – isn't it dark inside! What do we do? Ring the bell?'

'Yes, if there is one – but there isn't,' said Roger, looking all round. 'No knocker either. What do we do? Yell?'

'IS ANYONE HERE?' shouted Barney obligingly, and they all jumped at his enormous yell. A small boy with an untidy shock of hair came running round a corner, followed by a great grey goose. He shouted out something to them in Welsh, and then disappeared into the open doorway, followed by the waddling goose.

'Well – I *imagine* that he and the goose have gone to find the owner of the inn,' said Miss Pepper. 'Ah – here comes someone!'

A lively little woman came hurrying up the hallway to the door, followed by the small boy, the goose still tagging along behind.

'Good afternoon,' said Mr Martin politely. 'Er – Mrs Jones down in the village told us of this inn, and . . .'

The plump little woman smiled all over her face, and rattled out an answer at top speed.

'Oh yes, sir, yes, sir, that would be my mother-in-law, sir, she knows this place well, and a good inn it is, no doubt about that, sir, we get important people here, sir, you should just peep into our visiting books, oh, the fine manes that are there, and my husband, Llewellyn, he is the best cook in the world, sir, he went to London to learn his cooking, sir, in one of the big hotels, very good cooking, oh very . . .'

'Er – what I wanted to ask,' put in Mr Martin, afraid the the lively woman would never stop, 'what I wanted to know was . . .'

'Oh yes, sir, you ask me anything,' said the woman, smiling and nodding. 'Come in, sir, won't you, and see what a wonderful place this is, and oh, the cooking, sir, well can you smell what's baking now, sir? That's my husband, sir, he's always cooking, he's . . .'

This sounded exactly as if her husband was being baked, and Diana gave a sudden giggle. They followed the woman into the great dark entrance, the boy and the goose behind them. Talking all the time, she showed them an enormous, rather delapidated dining-room, and then took them up some stone stairs, uncarpeted, to the bedrooms.

'The beds are comfortable, sir, the view is fine, just you look, sir, did you ever see anything like it?'

Certainly the view was wonderful, and everyone gasped to see it. 'And we don't charge a great deal, sir,' rattled on the little woman. 'You come to us, sir, if you want to stay in these parts, I tell you the cooking is fine, sir, very good cooking!'

Miranda the monkey, stopped the flow of talk quite suddenly, by flinging herself on the grey goose's back. The goose was simply amazed, and began to cackle so loudly that it made everyone jump. The small boy ran to take the monkey off its back, and Miranda promptly jumped on to his shoulder. He screamed in fright and Miranda leapt back to Barney.

'Sorry about that,' said Barney to the surprised woman. 'It was just that Miranda wanted to see what sort of creature the goose was. I don't believe she's seen one before. Er – is the goose *safe*?'

The great bird was advancing on him, its enormous wings flapping, cackling at the top of its voice.

'Take Waddle away,' said the woman crossly to the small boy. 'He must not come indoors. Always I am telling you that.' She turned to the others, but before she could begin one of her long speeches again, Mr Martin spoke firmly to her.

'This is my son, and these other children are his friends. This lady, Miss Pepper, is with them, but I go back home today. Another boy, and a dog, will come soon. Can you let them have meals here – and a bed for Miss Pepper and Diana? The others would sleep in a caravan we have.'

'Oh, sir, it would be an honour, it would be a pleasure to have them!' cried the talkative little woman. 'My name is Mrs Jones, sir, Mrs Llywellyn Jones, and certainly we will look after them all, they shall have the best food, sir, they shall go fishing with our men, they shall have picnics – and very good cooking, sir, and . . .'

'Well, thank you,' said Mr Martin, and turned to Miss Pepper. 'Would you like to stay here, Miss Pepper? I can see already that the children approve!'

'Yes, Mr Martin. I think this is just what we're looking for,' said Miss Pepper. 'The views and the walks will be enough for me – and as for the children, if they can fish and bathe and explore, that's all *they'll* want! Yes – I'd like to stay here.'

'Good, good, good!' cried Diana, and gave Miss Pepper such a sudden hug that she gasped. 'And Snubby will love it too, I know he will. When will he come, Mr Martin?'

'I'll telephone your mother as soon as I can, and arrange for him to come tomorrow, it possible,' said Mr Martin. 'He can come by train to the nearest big town, and then get a taxi to bring him here. And let's hope Loony gets on all right with that goose – what's his name – Waddle!'

'Well – what with Loony the spaniel, Miranda the monkey and Waddle the goose, we may have rather a hectic time,' said Miss Pepper, with a laugh. 'But I've coped with Snubby and Loony before, so I've no doubt I can manage!'

'You go now? You go back home?' said Mrs Jones anxiously to Mr Martin. 'You will not stay to have supper here, and taste the very good cooking?'

'No. I think not,' said Mr Martin. 'I'll go down and pick up the caravan and bring it up here, now that I know the others will be staying. Perhaps I could just have a cup of tea before I leave?'

'You shall, sir, yes, you shall have tea and good, buttery scones!' said Mrs Jones, and fled down the stairs as if she could smell the scones burning in the oven!

'Whew – what a non-stop talker!' said Roger. 'We're going to have some very one-sided conversations, I can see!'

'I don't mind. I like her,' said Diana. 'She goes on and on like a babbling steam, but she's quite interesting. Oh, I *am* glad we're going to stay here. Sniff the air, Miss Pepper – isn't it clean and – and – mountainy? I wonder what Snubby will say – I'm sure he'll love it.'

'Roger – you and Barney come down and help me with the caravan,' said Mr Martin. 'It may be a bit awkward getting it round those zig-zaggy corners – you'd better walk behind and yell to me if I'm not giving it enough room to swing round.'

'Right, sir,' said the two boys, and went down to the car with Mr Martin. They hopped in and went off to fetch the caravan, Miranda jigging excitedly on Barney's shoulder. Miss Pepper and Diana took the opportunity of peeping into the other bedrooms. 'They really look a bit like cells, with their stone walls and stone floors,' said Diana. 'Let's choose one with the best views, Miss Pepper.'

So they chose one with two windows, one window looking out over the sea, and the other into the mountains that rose one behind the other for miles. There were two small beds there, and the stone walls were partly draped with thick old curtains. A great chest stood against one wall, and Miss Pepper looked at it with interest.

'That must be pretty old,' she said. 'Our few belongings will be quite lost in there. And look at the ancient fireplace, Diana – you could almost put one of the beds in there!'

Diana went to the fireplace, and put her head up the chimney. 'I can see the sky!' she called. 'It's a most *enormous* chimney!'

A voice spoke to them from the door. It was Mrs Jones,

nodding and smiling. 'I will show you a better room,' she said. 'This is not so comfortable as the others.'

'But we *love* the view here,' said Miss Pepper, smiling. 'And it really looks very comfortable!'

'No. It is not the best room. Come, I will show it to you.'

And she took Miss Pepper's arm, and led her to another room, a little larger and better furnished. The view, however, was not nearly so beautiful.

'No. I'd rather have the other room,' said Miss Pepper firmly. 'Because of the view, you know.'

Mrs Jones looked suddenly sulky. 'I do not like you to have that room,' she said. 'It is not the best room. I will give you this one.'

But Miss Pepper was used to having her own way, and shook her head with a polite smile. 'No. I have chosen the other room. Now we will go down and see if Mr Martin has the luggage!'

And down they went to the great entrance, where Mr Martin and the boys were already waiting with the car and the caravan, having put the bags and suitcases down on the battered stone steps.

'What about my cup of tea?' said Mr Martin to Mrs Jones, smiling. 'And then we'll just fix up terms, and I'll go!'

'Your tea – your beautiful scones!' cried Mrs Jones and rushed off down the dark passageway, presumably to the kitchen. 'Wait just one minute, sir, just one minute. The cooking here is . . .'

'Very good!' finished everyone at once, and Mr Martin chuckled. 'What a woman! I should think she probably talks all night long in her sleep, wouldn't you?'

Chapter Seven

'Cooking Good! Very Good Cooking!'

When Mr Martin had gone, all the three children waving to him madly, and Miranda waving too, Roger put his hand over his tummy.

'Whew! What a tea Mrs Jones gave us! I never tasted such marvellous scones in my life! I had six!'

'Cooking good – very good cooking!' quoted Diana. 'Even Miranda had two scones. What's the time – just gone half past five, not too bad. What shall we do?'

'A little unpacking, please,' said Miss Pepper promptly. 'And a little arranging. I see that your father has put the caravan round the side of the inn, Barney, on that level piece. Is it safe there? There's such a slope down this hill.'

'I'd better put heavy stones under the wheels,' said Barney. 'In case that small boy thinks up anything funny! He looks a bit of a monkey to me. Come and help me, Roger.'

While the boys went to drag big stones to the wheels, Miss Pepper and Diana went upstairs to their room. They expected to find their luggage in the room with two windows that they had chosen, but it wasn't!

'Well! Don't tell me that Mrs Jones has put it in the Best Room that she kept trying to force on us!' said Miss Pepper crossly. 'Go and look, Diana.'

Diana went off to the Best Room, and came back at once. 'Yes, it's there! What a nerve, really. She *knew* we said this one!'

'Well, we'll just go and get the suitcases and bring them

here,' said Miss Pepper, deciding that Mrs Jones must be kept firmly in her place, and do what her guests asked. So in half a minute the suitcases were in the room they had chosen, and were being unpacked. There were great drawers in the chest, and the clothes were hurriedly arranged inside.

In the middle of it there came a knock at their door. 'Come in!' called Miss Pepper, in the briskest voice.

In came a tall man with thick, untidy hair, wearing glasses and a surly look. 'Good evening,' he said, 'I am Mr Jones, the innkeeper. You have the wrong room. Please come this way to our Best Room.'

'I've already chosen this one,' said Miss Pepper. 'It's quite empty and I prefer the view. You have no guest staying in it, I know.'

'Madam, you will not like this room,' said Mr Jones, looking even surlier.

'Please don't be so mysterious,' said Miss Pepper, deciding that however well Mr Jones cooked, she was not going to like him. 'Why shouldn't I like this room?'

'There are sometimes noises in the night,' said Mr Jones solemnly.

'Oooh, how thrilling! What *kind* of noises?' asked Diana. 'Howls – yells – moans – or what?'

'You laugh,' said Mr Jones angrily. 'But you will not laugh in the dark of night, when the noises come.'

'Well, we'll see what they are like,' said Miss Pepper, slamming a drawer of the chest shut. 'Then we'll know whether to laugh or not. If you're trying to tell me the room's haunted or something, you're wasting you time. I don't believe in things like that.'

Without another word Mr Jones walked out of the room. Miss Pepper looked at Diana. 'Well – if I wasn't such an obstinate woman, I'd move out into the other room!' she said. 'This is obviously a guest room, and I see no real reason why we shouldn't have it if we want it. Even the beds are made up and are all ready to sleep in!'

Soon all their clothes were stowed away and they went down to see how the boys were getting on. Miss Pepper peeped into the caravan and was astonished and pleased to see everything put away so tidily.

As she stood there talking to the boys, the great grey goose came round the corner, cackling loudly. Behind it came the small, untidy boy, whistling.

He went right up to the caravan and had a good look inside. The goose looked in too, and made as if to climb in.

'Oh no, you don't!' said Roger, and gave it a small push. 'Geese not allowed in here!'

The goose hissed and flapped its wings. The boy put his arms round its neck, and it quietened down. He stared solemnly up at Roger with great dark eyes.

'What's your name?' said Diana, amused.

'Dafydd,' said the boy.

'Oh – David,' said Diana. 'Come and look inside the caravan. Haven't you ever seen one before?'

Dafydd didn't understand what she was saying, but took her hand and went inside the van. He fingered everything with his dirty little hands, and finally took up a small comb from a hair-brush and slipped it into his pocket.

'No, no, Dafydd!' said Barney. 'That's *my* comb, old son! Put it back!'

But Dafydd shook his head, and picked up a tube of tooth-paste. He examined it with interest. Then he suddenly felt something touching his pocket and looked down. It was Miranda, slipping a paw in, and taking out the comb! She was not going to allow anyone to steal Barney's belongings!

She leapt on to Barney's shoulder, chattering angrily,

and began to comb his thick hair. Dafydd stared at her, frowning, rather scared. He said something in Welsh, something rather rude, and shook his little fist at Miranda, who immediately danced about on Barney's shoulder, saying plenty of rude things back to him in monkey-chatter.

'Cackle-cackle,' said the goose outside, and flapped its wings impatiently. Miranda felt sure that it, too, was saying something rude, and she leapt straight off Barney's shoulder down to the floor, and then, with another flying leap she was on the goose's back, clinging to its neck, chattering loudly.

The goose was so astonished that it fled at once, hissing like a dozen snakes, with Miranda riding it. Barney roared with laughter, and Dafydd at once battered him with his small fists, angry that anyone should make fun of his goose.

'Now, now,' said Barney, holding Dafydd's small fists in one of his hands. 'That's enough! The monkey won't hurt your Waddle. You go after him, and I'll call back the monkey. And listen – you're NOT to come inside our caravan if we're not here. Do you understand?'

Dafydd shouted something that nobody could understand, kicked Barney on the ankles, wrenched his hands away, and was out of the caravan like a streak of lightning, yelling for Waddle.

'Well – what do you think of *that*?' said Barney to the others. 'I vote we keep our caravan locked when we're out anywhere. What a little rascal!'

'His mother ought to keep him in order,' said Miss Pepper. 'A few good slaps would do him a world of good. Taking that comb right under our noses! We'd better keep our room locked too, Diana, when we're out. Ah, here comes Miranda, looking pleased with herself!'

Miranda did feel pleased with herself. She had put that flappy goose in its place! She had ridden on its back all the way to the cowshed a little way up the hill, the goose cackling at the top of its voice.

'You'd better behave yourself, Miranda,' said Diana, 'or Dafydd will be after you! Him and his precious goose! What a pair!'

'Well, the goose will have to mind its p's and q's when Snubby comes with Loony,' said Barney. 'I can't see either of them putting up with Dafydd and Waddle for long, if they *don't* behave themselves.'

'You two boys will be quite comfortable in the caravan at nights,' said Miss Pepper. 'The bunks are very good. Diana and I have got the room we wanted – the one with the heavenly view – though Mr Jones tried to scare us out of it with tales of noises in the night!'

'Oh, have you seen him?' said Barney. 'He's not what you might call very merry and bright, is he? Roger and I thought he must have some secret sorrow, he looked so glum! But he's no right to try and scare you with tales of noises at night, Miss Pepper.

'Oh, he and his wife are proud of their Best Room, as they call it,' said Miss Pepper. 'He just hoped that a silly fib about noises would make us change rooms, that's all. I don't expect he has even *noticed* what wonderful views our room has!'

'Well, I don't mind noises, or pet geese or light-fingered small boys, so long as we get Good Cooking, Very Good Cooking! said Diana. 'We shall see what supper's like.'

Well, supper was Wonderful! Miss Pepper stared in amazement at the beautifully cooked meal. It began with chicken soup, went on to a fine joint of beef with mounds of roast potatoes, garden peas and the first runner beans, and finished with an ice-cream pudding set round with dainty biscuits of all kinds!

'I *say*! This is the best meal I've had since Daddy took us out to a big hotel in London!' said Roger. '*Look* at this ice-cream pudding – there's enough for a dozen people. Are we supposed to eat it all, Miss Pepper?'

'Well, supposed to or not, I've no doubt you will!' said Miss Pepper, and they did! Miranda had the last little biscuit off the dish, and sat nibbling it on Barney's shoulder as Mrs Jones came in, beaming, to clear away.

'You like your supper?' she enquired, and laughed to hear the loud chorus that answered her.

'Cooking good, VERY good cooking!'

Chapter Eight

'Hallo, Snubby!'

They were all sleepy after their wonderful supper, and were yawning widely when Mrs, Jones trotted in with the silver tray on which coffee cups were set.

'Dear me!' said Miss Pepper, surprised to see the gleaming silver and the steaming coffee. 'Who would have thought that a little country inn like this would do everything so well! No wonder "Big People," sometimes come here, as Mrs Jones boasted! Coffee, anyone?'

'Anything to keep me awake!' said Barney, with a most tremendous yawn. 'Miranda, that sugar is NOT for you. Smack her paw, Diana, please. She's as bad as that monkey of a Dafydd.'

Far away, somewhere in the depths of the great dark hall, a bell shrilled. 'The telephone!' said Miss Pepper. 'I hope that's to say you aunt is getting on well, Diana.'

Mrs Jones appeared. 'Someone for you, Miss Pepper, please,' she said, and out went Miss Pepper, hoping for good news. She was soon back.

'That was your uncle,' she said to Roger and Diana. 'Barney's father got held up, and found he couldn't get back to your aunt's home tonight – so he telephoned your uncle, and told him to send Snubby off to us by train early tomorrow. Snubby is absolutely too thrilled for words, he said, and Loony promptly went mad!'

Everyone laughed. Roger rubbed his hands together. 'Good old Snubby! Funny we should be so pleased to have such a pest with us, but things always seem to happen when Snubby and Loony are around. What time will he arrive?'

'Probably by the half-past twelve train, at Dilcarmock, five miles from here,' said Miss Pepper. 'It's not a bad train. I'll telephone to order a taxi to meet him and bring him here. Your aunt is going on well, so your uncle sounded quite happy.'

'He'll feel even happier tomorrow when he's got rid of Snubby,' said Roger. 'Last time he stayed there Snubby kept pretending to be a Christy minstrel with a banjo and made banjo noises all day long. Uncle and Aunt nearly went crazy!'

Miss Pepper groaned, remembering the holiday at Rubadub when Snubby had fancied himself at playing all kinds of instruments, not only banjoes. 'I only hope he doesn't take it into his head to be a Christy minstrel here,' she said. 'Anyone want any more coffee?'

Nobody did. One by one they yawned again, and Miss Pepper laughed. 'Let's all go to bed,' she said. 'It's getting on for nine o'clock and we've had a very long day. Off to the caravan, boys – and sleep well! See you at breakfast time. It's at half-past eight, so if anyone wants an early morning bathe, there'll be plenty of time.'

'Right. I'm half asleep already,' said Roger, getting up. He gave Miss Pepper a sudden hug that surprised her. 'I think you're a brick to stay on with us like this after our caravan holiday broke up!' he said. 'I hope to goodness you don't hear any unpleasant noises in the night!'

'Well, we'll lean out of one of our windows and yell if we do!' said Miss Pepper, pleased at the sudden hug.

'This will be your last peaceful night, boys,' said Diana, with a grin. 'Tomorrow you'll have Snubby in the caravan with you, and mad-dog Loony!'

The boys left, and Miss Pepper and Diana went upstairs, meeting Mrs Jones on the way. 'A truly wonderful supper, Mrs Jones,' said Miss Pepper. 'Your husband is surely a trained chef?'

'Oh, yes indeed,' said Mrs Jones proudly. 'It was in London Town that he was trained, Miss Pepper, at a big, important hotel. We were so happy there. I was chambermaid, and he was second chef. I wanted to stay – but no, Mr Jones he wanted to come back here, where he was born. His cooking is good, very good!'

Miss Pepper nodded, said goodnight and went on up the stairs, half wondering whether she would find their things removed from their room-with-a-view to the Best Room. But no – their cases were still in the room they had chosen. Good! Miss Pepper was also pleased to see that there was a key in the door.

'Now we can lock our room when we leave it,' she said to Diana, 'and can be sure that that monkey of a Dafydd won't come in with his cackling goose and pocket whatever takes his fancy!'

She and Diana were soon in bed and fast asleep. Were there any Noises in the Night? There might well have been, even if only the wind in the chimney, but neither of them would have heard a thunderstorm that night! The beds were comfortable, the room was airy, and they slept so soundly that they only awoke when Mrs Jones came knocking at their door with cans of hot water.

Breakfast was as good as supper had been. Cold ham, boiled eggs, hot toast, homemade marmalade, creamy butter, and scalding hot coffee . . . Miss Pepper looked at the table with much approval.

'Snubby will like this place,' said Roger, taking his second boiled egg. 'Have you phoned about a taxi for him yet, Miss Pepper?'

'No, there's time enough after breakfast,' said Miss Pepper. 'Did you and Barney bathe? I should imagine you did by your appetites!'

'Well, we didn't!' said Roger, with a grin. 'We slept like logs – and I don't think we'd have wakened when we did if that young Dafydd hadn't come peering in at the caravan window and wakened up Miranda. She leapt out of the window and chased Waddle the goose all over the place, and what with Dafydd's yells and the goose's cackles, we woke up with an awful jump! Why doesn't someone smack Dafydd hard?'

'Someone's going to, if he doesn't look out,' said Barney grimly, rubbing his hands together.

Miss Pepper went to phone for a taxi for Snubby. 'I've ordered one to call here at 11.30,' she said. 'I thought you three would like to go in it to meet Snubby. It's the only one in the village, apparently, so it's probably a poor old crock.'

'Right,' said Barney, pleased at the idea of meeting Snubby at the station. 'We'll have time to go down for a bathe, then. Are you all coming? Merlin's Cove is supposed to be the best bathing place, apparently.'

Mrs Jones agreed that it was indeed the best place, when she came in to clear away the breakfast. Dafydd and Waddle also came in with her, and Waddle immediately pecked at a piece of toast left on one of the plates. Mrs Jones didn't say a word of reproof – but Miranda did! She snatched the toast out of the goose's beak, and then pulled her tail feathers hard, chattering angrily all the time.

Dafydd aimed a blow at the monkey, and Barney was immediately beside him, holding his hands tightly.

'No! Do you want to be bitten? Miranda has very sharp teeth. I will show you them. Come here, Miranda.'

Dafydd stared at the monkey's sharp teeth, and turned away, gabbling in Welsh.

'He says your monkey must not hurt his goose,' said Mrs Jones, clearing away. 'Dafydd, go away. You are not to come in here now that we have visitors. Take Waddle with you.'

Dafydd went out sulkily, Waddle following behind. 'Waddle was just a little gosling when Dafydd had him,' said Mrs Jones. 'He broke his leg, and Dafydd mended it – he put a stick, like so – and tied it well. And Waddle's leg mended, and now he will not leave Dafydd, and what a trouble the two are, I give you my word, and what is the use of my scolding him, he hears only what he wants to hear, he does only what he . . .'

It looked as if Mrs Jones was launched on one of her never-ending speeches, and Miss Pepper interrupted her firmly.

'We would rather that Dafydd and Waddle did not come into the dining-room or into our bedroom,' she said.

'But how can I stop them?' argued Mrs Jones, deftly folding up the tablecloth. 'They go where they please, they . . .'

'Not when *we're* here! said Miss Pepper. 'Er – have you ever tried a good smack, Mrs Jones.'

'A smack! A smack is no good with that one!' said Mrs Jones. 'Even if you could get near him with a smack! Like an eel he is, like a slippery eel, and as for Waddle, he is as bad, the way he walks where he wants to walk, and cackles when he wants to cackle, and . . .'

But there was no one to listen to her! The room was empty, the boys had slipped out to bathe, Diana had gone too, and Miss Pepper had hurried quietly out of the room! Mrs Jones went on talking for a long time before she saw she was alone – and even then she didn't stop, but talked away to herself as she carried out the tray to the kitchen.

The boys couldn't find their bathing things, and there was a great to-do at once. 'Miss Pepper! MISS PEPPER! Ask Di if she's got our things with her, will you?' shouted

Barney, as he saw Miss Pepper at her bedroom window. 'Ours aren't in the caravan, that's certain.'

Diana hunted hurriedly in the drawers where she had put her clothes, and a last found the boys' bathing things. She threw them out of the window, and one pair caught on a rambler growing up the wall.

'Ass!' shouted Roger. 'Now I'll have to get a ladder. Why can't girls throw properly!'

'Oh dear – if you don't hurry up, the taxi will be here,' said Miss Pepper, looking at her watch. She called down to the boys. 'I don't think you'd better bathe, after all – you'll miss Snubby's train if you do!'

And then, what a surprise! A piercing, very well-known voice came to their startled ears – surely, surely, it couldn't be SNUBBY'S?

'HALLO, EVERYBODY! HERE I AM!'

And someone came up the slope to the inn – someone very dirty indeed, with straw sticking out of him at every corner and a black dog careering at his heels.

'Snubby! We were just going to meet you!' yelled Roger. 'How did you get here? Your train isn't even due in yet! How AWFUL you look! What in the world have you been doing?'

Chapter Nine

Hot Bath For Snubby!

Snubby marched up to the astonished Roger and Barney, grinning all over his freckled, snub-nosed face. His ginger hair was very wind-blown indeed!

Diana and Miss Pepper ran downstairs most amazed. How like Snubby to arrive so unexpectedly!

'Have I given you a surprise?' he said. 'I thought I should!'

'Snubby – how did you get here so soon? And why are you so *filthy*?' said Miss Pepper. 'Hallo, Loony – good gracious, *you're* all covered in straw too!'

'Well, Uncle got me a ticket for an awful slow train,' said Snubby, rubbing his dirty face with an even dirtier handkerchief. 'And I heard there was a very early one, so I decided to catch that. You see, Uncle was getting pretty fed up with me, really. I arrived at Dilcarmock ages ago, and I got a lift in a cart that was loaded with straw and stuff for Penrhyndendraith, or whatever this place is called. Gosh, it crawled, though, and the straw was frightfully prickly.'

'Snubby, you look too awful for words,' said Diana. 'Honestly, I've never *seen* such a tramp!'

'Well, I did think you'd all be more pleased to see me,' said Snubby, sounding hurt. 'I tell you, I couldn't stay with Uncle any longer. He just glowered at me till I amost changed into a worm. Darling Miranda, are *you* pleased to see me?'

The little monkey leapt on to his shoulder and put her

tiny paws down his neck, chattering softly. Yes – she was very pleased to see Snubby – and Loony too!

Loony was tearing all round the place, sniffing into every corner. He had given everyone a really good lick, and was now interested in all the new smells. And then, quite suddenly, he saw a most fearsome creature coming towards him, hissing like a dozen snakes!

It was Waddle, of course. Waddle, who detested dogs and cats – and monkeys! Waddle considered that the inn belonged to him and to no one else, and woe betide any strange creature who dared to sniff around his domain!

Loony took one look at Waddle and backed away hurriedly. What in the world was this creature? Bird? Animal? Snake? Its head and neck and voice seemed to be those of a snake – but it had wings! Loony let out a terrified yelp and ran to Snubby.

'Don't be an ass, Loony – it's only a *goose*!' said Snubby – and then promptly ran for shelter himself as Waddle, cackling, hissing and flapping, descended upon him and Loony too!

But little Miranda was not going to have her friends scattered like this, and entered into the battle with delight! She flung herself on Waddle's back and clasped her neck as she had done once before, chattering at the top of her voice.

Then it was Waddle's turn to run, and off went the goose into the house, waddling more quickly than ever a goose waddled before, cackling as if the house was on fire! Miranda clung to her tightly, and the goose could not shake her off.

Loony recovered his courage and raced after them, barking madly. Mr Jones, coming to see what the noise was about, met the goose and Miranda with Loony immediately behind them, and was promptly bowled over.

He sat down very suddenly indeed, knocked over by the heavy goose, and then trodden on by the surprised Loony.

Miss Pepper put her hands over her face, and groaned. WHY did things like this always happen when Snubby was around? He had only to appear, and the whole world seemed at once to go crazy. And now there was Mr Jones, tall and thin and dour, getting up from the stone hall floor, rubbing himself angrily.

'Oh, Mr Jones – I hope you're not hurt,' said Miss Pepper, hurrying to him. 'The goose frightened the dog, and then the monkey frightened the goose, and the dog ran after them both, and, and . . .'

'And the cow jumped over the moon,' said Snubby with a hoot of laughter. Mr Jones took one look at him and raised his voice.

'Get out of here, you dirty little tramp! Go where you belong, into the gutter! Don't dare to come up to this inn, where decent folk stay!'

There was a surprised silence, while everyone stared first at Mr Jones, and then at Snubby. Snubby glanced down at his dirty clothes apologetically, and then looked beseechingly at Miss Pepper.

'Er – this is a cousin of Diana and Roger Lynton,' said Miss Pepper. 'The one whom Mr Martin arranged to come and stay, you remember. He's had a long – and er – a very dirty journey. He needs a – a wash.'

Mr Jones glared at them all, and limped back down the hall without a word. Miss Pepper took hold of Snubby.

'You're going to have a hot bath,' she said. 'And I'm going to scrub you from head to foot – you – you dirty little tramp! *Really*, Snubby, I *cannot* imagine how anyone can get as filthy as you look.'

'Where's that goose gone?' said Snubby, pretending not to hear. 'I can't stop old Loony from going for him if he appears again.'

'Don't worry about Loony – he'll retire into the darkest corner he can find, if he sees Waddle,' said Miss Pepper, keeping a firm hold on Snubby and propelled him towards the hall door. 'Thank goodness the creature has disappeared and Miranda's recovered herself. I do wish you'd caught the proper train, Snubby, and not caused all this sensation! We don't want to be turned out of this place. The cooking is so . . .'

'Very very good!' finished Barney, with a grin. He put his arm round Snubby's shoulder. 'Cheer up! Where's your luggage? Get out a bathing suit and come and bathe with us – you'll soon be clean then.'

'No,' said Miss Pepper at once. 'I don't see why he should make the sea absolutely black! Is that all the luggage you've got, Snubby – that small case there? My goodness – you can't have much in it.'

'Well, I thought Roger could lend me what I've forgotten,' said Snubby amiably, going indoors with Miss Pepper. 'Gosh, I feel a bit tired now. Come on, Loony. Is there anything to *eat*, Miss Pepper? I do feel awfully empty. I say, what a place this is! I thought it was a ruin, till the van-man told me it was the inn I'd asked him to drop me at. I say, I do hope I'm going to sleep in the caravan with the others, I . . .'

'Snubby! *Stop* talking for a minute,' said Miss Pepper quite fiercely. 'I want to ask for some hot water for you. Stay here while I go to the kitchen. Don't dare to move from there, because if Mr Jones sees you again he might quite well pick you up and throw you into the sea – and I wouldn't blame him either!'

'I say – you *are* peppery this morning, Miss Pepper darling!' said Snubby, surprised. 'And I'd so looked forward to seeing you again, too. I never . . .'

But Miss Pepper was gone, walking quickly down the dark hallway to the equally dark kitchen, which was huge and rather forbidding. Mrs Jones was there, doing some washing-up in an enormous sink.

'Oh, Mrs Jones – do you think I might have a very large can of hot water?' asked Miss Pepper. 'The children's cousin has arrived and he's really *very* dirty.'

'I will get it at once for you, certainly I will,' said Mrs Jones, reaching for an enormous jug. 'I will bring it up to the bathroom, Miss. In two minutes it will be there.'

Miss Pepper, thankful that Mrs Jones did not chatter on and on as she usually did, went to collect Snubby, determined that he should not escape her.

'You dirty little ragamuffin!' she said as she saw him patiently waiting for her on exactly the same spot where she had left him, Loony sitting beside him. 'You look as if you've just been sweeping a chimney! I never did know anyone who could . . .'

'Get dirty wherever he goes and whatever he does,' finished Snubby with a grin. 'I wonder how many times you've said that to each of us, Miss Pepper! Where's the hot water?'

It wasn't long before Snubby was clean and shining all over, even to the backs of his ears. It wasn't any good protesting that he could wash himself, Miss Pepper was determined to get him really clean. Loony sat beside the bath, watching in alarm, half afraid that it might be his turn next!

'Now dry yourself, and I'll go and find something for you to eat,' said Miss Pepper. '*Look* at the bath-water – what a disgrace! It will take you quite a bit of time to clean the bath!'

Snubby sighed. He thought it was very hard that no matter what he did, he got into trouble. He rubbed himself dry and talked to the listening Loony.

'She called me a *ragamuffin*! What do you think of that, Loony? Except that it sounds a bit like something to eat,

214

it's a horrid name to give to anyone. *Ragamuffin!* Now what am I supposed to put on? Those clean clothes, I suppose – my own vest, Roger's old shorts – and this looks like Barney's shirt, it's so big! Loony, you don't know how lucky you are to be born a dog, and be able to wear the same old fur coat all your life. Like to try this vest on, old thing?'

Loony retreated to the door at once, and scratched at it, whining, suddenly afraid that it might enter Snubby's head to pop *him* into the bath.

'I'm not ready yet, old chap,' said Snubby, looking down into the bath, where the dirty water had already left a black line all round the sides. 'I say, Loony – come and look at this! I've got to clean this bath, and it will take me *ages!*'

Loony put his paws up on the side of the bath and looked down at the water, wagging his tail. He didn't mind looking, so long as he wasn't going to be bathed in it. He couldn't imagine why *anyone* ever had baths. Snubby suddenly sniffed, and bent down over Loony. 'You know, you smell pretty awful,' he said. 'I've a good mind to pop you in too, and . . .'

But very fortunately for the scared Loony, Miss Pepper's voice suddenly sounded outside the door.

'Snubby! What in the world are you doing? Aren't you dressed *yet*? I hope you've cleaned the bath. There is a piece of meat-pie, and some bread and cheese downstairs, if you hurry!'

Snubby hurried at once. He let out the bath water, and hurriedly tried to remove the black line round the bath with the flannel Miss Pepper had given him, finished dressing, and grinned at Loony as he opened the bathroom door. 'Loony – I have a feeling we'll enjoy being here. We're going to have quite an exciting time!'

Well, Snubby, you're right. But perhaps it will be rather *too* exciting!

Chapter Ten

Snubby Gets Into Trouble

Snubby thoroughly enjoyed his first day at Penrhynden-draith, and so did the others. They went bathing that lovely morning, and found Merlin's Cove. It was a truly lovely place.

The sands were almost white there, and as smooth as silk to walk on. When the tide was up it swept right into all the caves that made up Merlin's Cove. These ran either a little way or a long way into the high rocky cliff, and two were labelled 'DANGEROUS.'

'Ha – let's see why they are dangerous,' said Snubby, peering into one, and was at once firmly taken by the arm by Barney.

'Any fatheadedness on your part, and you go straight back to another of your uncles and aunts,' he said. 'Do you want rocks falling on your head – or to lose your way forever in a maze of cliff tunnels? Aren't you ever going to grow up, Snubby?'

Loony ran a little way into the dark, low cave, and then turned his head as if to say, 'Come on, Snubby!' but Snubby yelled to him at once.

'Come back, ass! Aren't you *ever* going to grow up?'

They explored some of the other caves, and found most of them shallow, going back only a little way. They bathed twice, and lay in the sun. Miranda hated the water and wouldn't go near it, though Barney at last persuaded her to paddle, and held her paw like a child.

Loony splashed past her, and, once out of his depth

and swimming, turned his head as if to say 'Monkeys are poor creatures! *They* can only paddle!'

'It looks as if we're going to have a pretty good time here,' said Roger, lying on the sand, leaning on his elbow. 'Look – are those fishing-boats coming in? Aren't they lovely?'

They were! They all had brown sails of different shades, and come smoothly in on the wind, the tide taking them to the little jetty not far off. The children scrambled up to go and see the catch. Miranda waited till Loony had come out of the water, and was vigorously shaking himself, and then leapt straight on to his back, clinging there with all her might, jigging up and down as if wanting a ride.

This was an old trick of Miranda's, and one that Loony didn't approve of at all! He set off at top speed hoping the little monkey would be bumped off, but she clung on for dear life, winding her tail round his tummy.

'Loony, roll over on the sand, you idiot!' shouted Snubby, 'Have you forgotten how to get her off!'

Loony promptly rolled over, and Miranda had to leap off, scampering to Barney quickly before Loony could catch her. The children laughed, and ran over to the jetty. They watched the great catch of fish being emptied. There were some large crabs among the catch, and Miranda was most interested in them as they began to walk off sideways.

She tapped one, and almost had her paw caught by one of its big claws! After that she and Loony kept well away from the crawling crabs.

They were all very hungry by dinner time, and went back through the little straggling village and up the slope of the hill to the old inn. They passed the ice-cream shop, and Snubby at once wanted to go in and buy ice-creams when he heard how the others had sampled them the day before.

'No, you'll spoil your dinner,' said Barney. 'Do come on. I feel quite hollow inside with hunger.'

Miss Pepper had had a peaceful morning, except for twenty minutes when Mrs Jones saw her wandering round the old garden of the inn, and came out to talk non-stop. Miss Pepper made up her mind that she would rather go down to the beach with the children than risk being found by Mrs Jones again!

It really was a very pleasant first day, marred only by an accident to Snubby's clothes – or rather to the shirt and the shorts which belonged to Barney and Roger.

Barney suddenly saw that his nice shirt, which had been almost new, was torn right down the back. He felt very cross.

'What on earth have you done to ruin my shirt like that?' he demanded. 'It's my newest one – I hadn't even worn it myself! I didn't mind lending it to you till you had your own clothes sent on – but I do think you might have been more careful with it! And gosh – look at Roger's shorts! Have you sat down in a patch of oil or something? You *are* in a filthy mess!'

Snubby tried to screw himself round to see the shorts. 'I wondered what that horrible smell was that seemed to follow me around,' he said. 'Well, I never! When *could* I have sat in oil? I'm awfully sorry, Roger – and sorry about your shirt too, Barney.'

'Well, I don't know what you're going to do tomorrow for clothes,' said Roger. 'Borrow a skirt of Diana's, I suppose! I'm certainly not going to lend you any more things.'

Miss Pepper was also very annoyed, and stared in horror as Snubby presented himself to her and asked her advice about the oil.

'To think I scrubbed you from head to toe this morning – and you look exactly like a ragamuffin again!' she said. 'Well, you'll have to stay in bed tomorrow while I wash your own dirty clothes, the ones you took off this morning.'

'Oh *no!*' said Snubby in horror. 'Stay in *bed*? I couldn't!'

But Miss Pepper was quite firm about that and the next day Snubby found himself compelled to have his breakfast in the caravan, sitting in his bunk. He was very angry indeed, and Loony simply *couldn't* understand what all the fuss was about.

'I simply daren't borrow anything else of Barney's or Roger's,' groaned Snubby to a sympathetic Loony. 'And as I've only got his old vest to wear, or my pyjamas, I don't see *how* I can go out of the caravan till Miss Pepper cleans up those torn dirty things of mine.'

He lay and thought angry thoughts for a time, and then an idea came into his head. 'That ice-cream shop!' he said. 'I believe it sells second-hand clothes. I'm sure I saw some hanging up. Loony, what about us slipping out and buying some before the others come back? I'm NOT going to lie here all day! I'll turn my pyjama trousers up to my knees so that they are more like shorts – and keep this vest on.'

And, very soon, a rather peculiar figure slipped out of the caravan, and ran down to the little village. Snubby grinned as he looked down at himself, and wondered if the old lady in the shop would notice his peculiar attire.

Old Mrs Jones, her snow-white hair tucked under the black net cap, didn't seem at all surprised to see a small boy in vest and turned-up pyjama-legs.

'You'll be one of the children up at the inn?' she said in her sing-song voice, with a twinkle in her eye. 'Is it an ice-cream you are wanting to buy?'

'Well, yes – among other things,' said Snubby, giving her the grin that always made old ladies love him. 'Look – I've got into trouble over my clothes, and I want to buy some more. Have you got any that would fit me – second-hand ones, I mean?'

'Well, now, there's that pair of long trousers,' said old Mrs Jones, pointing to a most dilapidated pair, hanging on a hook, 'Clean they are, though dirty they look, for I washed them myself. And there's this jersey, red and yellow, gay it is, and not badly worn.'

'Long trousers would be fine,' said Snubby, pleased, and put them on over his pyjama legs. 'Hey, Loony, how do I look?'

Loony barked sharply and wagged his tail. 'He says I look about sixteen, instead of twelve,' said Snubby with a grin. 'Now for the jersey – my word, I've gone gay, haven't I! Is it clean, because if it isn't, Miss Pepper will rip it off me at once?'

'It is clean,' said Mrs Jones. 'And you shall have a cap too – a good one. See the big peak!'

Snubby put it on and fancied himself very much in it. 'Thanks awfully,' he said, 'How much do I owe you?'

'That will be two shillings for the cap, four shillings for the trousers, and three shillings for the jersey – nine shillings – and an ice-cream thrown in for nothing,' said Mrs Jones, laughing at Snubby's peculiar appearance.

'Oh, I say – that's jolly kind of you,' said Snubby, and paid up at once. He took the ice-cream wafer, gratefully.

'It is my son who has the inn where you are staying,' said Mrs Jones. 'So good he is at cooking! He went to London to learn. Ah, to think that a poor boy like my Llewellyn, with never two pairs of trousers to his name, should have gone to London and learnt to cook! And now that inn is his! Always, all his life, he has said to me, "Ah, if only that inn was mine!" How I laughed! "I have

221

five pounds on my old stocking," I said, "and that has taken me eighteen years to save – and you want to own that inn"!'

'Gosh – how did he get it, then?' asked Snubby, licking the last of the ice-cream.

'He made friends in London,' said the old lady proudly. 'Important friends. And they lent him the money to buy the inn he so much wanted. How happy my Llewellyn is now!'

Snubby thought of the cross-looking, dour man he had seen the night before. 'Goodness – he doesn't *look* very happy!' he said. 'I say! I must go! Miss Pepper will be sending out a search party for me or something. Good-bye and many thanks!'

And away he rushed, really a very peculiar figure indeed. What in the world would the others say!

Chapter Eleven

A Very Strange Happening

Snubby had a few moments of doubt as he walked up the steep slope to the inn. 'If they jeer at me I shall run away!' he said to Loony, who wagged his tail sympathetically.

The first person he met was the boy Dafydd, with his faithful goose. Dafydd gave a loud shriek when he saw him and tore off with Waddle behind him – though whether the shriek was because Snubby looked so peculiar, or because he was scared of Loony was not clear! Snubby stared after him, frowning. If that was the effect he was going to have, things were not going to be easy!

Roger, Diana and Barney came out of the inn at that moment. They had been looking everywhere for Snubby, having missed him from the caravan. They looked at him, not recognising him in the least, and wondered why Loony was following this peculiar-looking lad.

Snubby had pulled the big peaked cap down over his face, and he grinned when he saw that the others did not recognise him. He swaggered up to them, hands in pocket, and pretended to speak in Welsh, in a peculiar-sounding hoarse voice.

'Collq-inna-dooly-hector-sonkin-poppyll?' he said, his cap still pulled down over his face.

'What on earth is this fellow saying?' asked Roger, astonished. 'And why is Loony with him?'

Diana gave a sudden shriek, and pulled at Snubby's cap. 'It's Snubby! SNUBBY! Where have you been? Where did you get those *awful* clothes?'

'They're not awful. They're fine – *and* clean,' said

Snubby, turning himself round and round so that they could admire him. 'I bought them at the ice-cream shop – second-hand.'

'Snubby! How *could* you buy clothes like that – you don't know *who's* worn them before!' said Roger.

'What does that matter? I tell you, they're *clean*!' roared Snubby. 'Oh gracious goodness – here comes Miss Pepper!'

What the others had said was nothing to what Miss Pepper said! She insisted that he should go straight back to the caravan and take off 'those TERRIBLE clothes, ESPECIALLY that cap,' and wait till she came with clean ones.

'I'm not going to,' said Snubby obstinately. 'Fancy expecting me to waste a lovely morning like this in that caravan, when I've gone and got myself clothes to wear. It's no *good*, Miss Pepper, I'm going to wear these clothes till my others are clean – and if you all think I'm not fit company for you, all right, Loony and I will keep away from you! Come on, Loony – they're looking at us as if we were a couple of bad smells!'

And with that Snubby marched quickly off down the hill, his peaked cap at a very cheeky angle indeed. Diana called crossly after him. 'Well – you *do* smell in those clothes! You smell dreadful!'

Snubby took no notice at all, and soon disappeared round a bend. Miss Pepper suddenly began to laugh.

'Oh dear!' she said. 'What a *sight* he looks – and yet I really do believe he's quite proud of those awful clothes. I only hope to goodness he won't want to go on wearing them when his own are ready. Well – what are you three going to do today?'

'Bathe – have a walk, perhaps fish if we can get a boat,' said Barney. 'It's a pity Snubby's behaving like this. Why didn't he think of putting on his bathing things – it's warm

224

enough for him to wear them all day on the beach. I'll take them down with me, shall I – in case he does join us, and then I can tell him to wear them, and stay with us.'

So, when the others went down to the beach, they took Snubby's bathing things with them. But there was no sign of him, or of Loony either!

Snubby was angry and hurt. Fancy calling him a bad smell! He caught sight of himself in the glass window of the ice-cream shop as he went by, and stopped. H'm! He did look a bit odd, perhaps. Pity the trousers were so big and sloppy – and the jersey certainly *was* a bit loud. But the cap was fine!

'I suppose we look a bit ragamuffinish again, Loony,' he said sorrowfully. 'Now – what shall we do? I know – we'll find a nice quiet place, and read that code-letter from old Bruce. I'll tell you what he says.'

Loony wagged his tail. He knew who Bruce was – a very close school friend of Snubby's, a rascal almost as bad as Snubby, the bane of their form-master. The two of them had invented a most involved secret code, using both figures and letters. It took Snubby about two hours to write a letter in their secret code – and even longer to decipher any he got from Bruce! Still, it made them both feel very important indeed, and they enjoyed that.

'We'll go somewhere out of sight of the others,' said Snubby to Loony. 'Look – what about going down to that broken bit of cliff over there – see? We could hide among the fallen rocks nicely, and see what old Bruce has got to say in his letter.'

So down they went together and were soon ensconced among the warm rocks, the sea not very far away. Snubby took out Bruce's letter. It was on a squared piece of paper, neatly torn out of his maths book.

Snubby looked at it and gave a small groan. 'It's rather

a long one,' he said to Loony, gazing at the mass of neat little figures, interspersed with letters. 'It'll take us ages to decode. Still, it's all good practice, Loony. You never know when you might have to use a code. Now – let's see – 12 – 6 – J – 567 – P – gosh, what does P stand for now? I wish I had my code-book with me. Hallo – who's this?'

A man was coming over the rocks towards them. He was short and wore a black beard, and dark sunglasses. Snubby glanced up at him, expecting him to pass by. But he didn't.

He came towards Snubby, and stood beside him. 'Give that to me!' he said in an angry voice.

Snubby was extremely startled. He hastily stuffed his precious code-letter in to his pocket. 'What's up?' he said. 'What do you want?'

'That letter!' said the man savagely. 'How dare you open and read it?'

'Well, why shouldn't I? It was sent to me, not to you,' said Snubby, beginning to feel that the man must be crazy. 'Don't be daft!'

'You know you had to meet me here and give me that letter,' said the man, his voice shaking with rage. 'And I find you have opened it and are trying to decipher it! How dare you! I shall see that your uncle beats you well!'

'What on EARTH are you talking about?' said Snubby, absolutely at sea. 'This is NOT your letter. It's mine, and I'm certainly not going to give it to you. It's in a very secret code that my friend and I know.'

'Your friend? Your *friend* knows the code – and you too? You lie!' said the man. 'You are a foolish boy who hopes to make me give you money for handing over my letter.'

'Oh, don't be an ass,' said Snubby, getting up. 'If this is a joke, it's pretty silly. I'm going!'

226

But to his enormous surprise the man threw him roughly back on the rocks, dug his hand into Snubby's pocket and tore out the letter. He slapped Snubby hard across the face and turned to go. But this was too much for Loony! He began to growl angrily.

What! This man dared to knock Snubby over and slap him! With a very fierce snarl indeed Loony flung himself on the surprised man, who shook him off with great force. He picked up a piece of rock and flung it at Loony, who only just dodged it in time.

'Loony! Come here! He'll kill you!' shouted Snubby. 'He's absolutely mad. Let him go.'

Reluctantly Loony sat down and watched the bearded man clamber up the cliff and on to the roadway. The little spaniel growled angrily till he was out of sight, sad that he could not chase him. He turned to Snubby and whimpered, pawing him as if to say, 'Are you hurt, master? Is everything all right?'

'I'm not hurt, only angry,' said Snubby, 'and jolly puzzled too. Why did he come here to me? Did he think I was someone else? And what on earth was he gassing about – a letter in code, he said – and took my letter from old Bruce! I suppose he saw it was in code. Look here, Loony, there's something peculiar about this. let's go and find the others.'

And off they went along the beach. They soon saw the others sitting on the sands, sunning themselves after a bathe. Snubby went up to them and sat down,

'Got something to tell you all,' he said in a low mysterious voice. 'Listen!'

At once they sat up, grinning at Snubby's peculiar appearance, but eager to hear him. He began to relate what had happened.

They all listened, most astonished. Barney whistled. 'You're not making this up by any chance, are you?'

he said, for Snubby had at times invented some curious stories.

'No! No, of course I'm not,' said Snubby indignantly. 'It's true, every word of it – and here's the bruise I got on my elbow when that fellow flung me down on the rocks.'

He showed them quite a massive bruise. Barney looked at it and frowned.

'Either that fellow was quite mad – or there's something extraordinary going on,' he said. 'Why did he mistake you for someone else, though? You must have looked like the person he was to meet – a real tramp, if you don't mind my saying so, Snubby. A proper ragamuffin! The kind of person who *might* be a go-between, if something dirty was going on.'

'I'll take these things off at once then,' said Snubby hastily. 'Got my bathing things? I'll just pop behind that rock. A go-between! Phew – just wait till I see the real one, if ever I do!' He went behind a rock and hastily flung off his awful clothes, putting on a pair of bathing trunks. And then, *just* as he joined the others, someone passed them, dressed in clothes very like Snubby's – long dirty-looking trousers, a bright woollen jersey, a peaked cap – and behind him ran a small black dog!

'There you are!' whispered Barney, nudging Snubby very hard indeed. 'See! I bet that's the fellow *you* were mistaken for – a regular ragamuffin! He's even got a little black dog – a mongrel poodle – and he's making for the rocks over there where *you* were sitting. Now what do we do?'

Chapter Twelve

Snubby And The Ragamuffin

They all watched the little ragamuffin go to the patch of fallen rocks where Snubby had sat. The small dog leapt about at his heels, and then sat down by him, as he settled himself on one of the rocks.

'See? He's waiting for someone,' said Roger. 'I bet he's got the *real* secret code-letter all right – the one that mad fellow thought *you* had!'

'I expect that man was told to look out for a ragamuffin of a boy, sitting on those rocks, with a black dog,' said Barney. 'And the boy would hand him a letter – secret instructions about something or other, I should think – and . . .'

'And old Snubby happened to go to that very spot, looking like a ragamuffin himself – with Loony who's as black as any dog can be expected to be!' said Roger. 'And what was more, Snubby happened to be reading a letter in code – his code and Bruce's – but how was the man to know that? He must have been certain it was his own code-letter!'

'Gosh – no wonder he was furious with me then!' said Snubby. 'He must have thought I was actually trying to decipher his secret instructions or whatever they were! You know, he might have killed old Loony, if that rock he threw had hit him!'

'I think this is pretty serious,' said Barney. 'Do we tell Miss Pepper, or not?'

'We *don't*!' said Diana at once. 'She might want to leave immediately! And it *is* so nice here! I don't expect anything horrid will happen now, especially as Snubby has taken off those frightful clothes. You're *not* to wear them again, Snubby.'

'Not even the cap?' said Snubby, disappointed. 'I rather fancied myself in that.'

'*Certainly* not the cap,' said Barney. He stared round at the boy still sitting patiently on the fallen rocks some way along the beach. 'That kid will have to sit there a long time! The bearded fellow won't be back, that's certain. He's probably going slowly mad trying to decipher Snubby's code, and making it fit in with his!'

'I'm going to talk to that boy,' said Snubby, getting up. 'I might find out something.'

'Better not,' said Roger.

'Why?' said Snubby, walking off in his bathing things. 'We're sure that horrible fellow with the beard won't come back again – he thinks he's got the letter he wanted. The boy will just think I'm some tripper or other.'

And off he went with Loony, whistling a dance tune, jigging along in time to it. When he came near to the waiting boy, he suddenly remembered his Christy minstrel pretence, and began to make a noise like a banjo, pretending to strum with his fingers.

It was a very very peculiar noise and the boy looked up at once, thinking he was hearing a real banjo. He was astonished to see Snubby's pretence, and laughed.

'Twang – a – twang – a – twang – a – twang – a – twang – a – twang-a-twang-twang!' The sounds that Snubby made between his teeth were exactly like a cheap banjo!

'Hallo!' he said, sitting down grinning, 'I like your little dog. What's his name?'

'Woolly,' said the boy, running his hand over the poodle's woolly back. 'What's your dog's name?'

'Loony,' said Snubby. 'Short for lunatic. You waiting for someone?'

'Yes. A man with a beard,' said the boy. 'Got to give him a letter from my uncle.'

'Who's your uncle?' said Snubby, strumming his pretend banjo again.

'Morgan the Cripple,' said the boy, beginning to imitate Snubby. 'Twang-a-twang-a-twang! He was a fisherman, but he broke his leg – and he lets out fishing boats now instead of fishing.'

'Why didn't he *post* the letter?' said Snubby. 'Lazy fellow!'

'How do I know?' said the boy. 'I say, look at your dog and mine making friends! I do wish that man would come for his letter. I thought I was late – but he's later still. And I did want to go out in a boat with my Pa this morning.'

'All right. You give me the letter and I'll wait here for him,' said Snubby. 'And if he comes I'll give it to him, see? He won't know I'm not you, will he – we've both got a black dog!'

'Well – I'd get a fine thrashing if anyone found out,' said the boy. 'But I'm not waiting here all morning. Here – take the letter – and wait till he comes. Don't say a word about me, though!'

'Right. You go off,' said Snubby, feeling suddenly very excited. 'I'll wait about on these rocks with Loony, my own black dog!'

The boy thrust a letter into Snubby's hands and went off quickly, his poodle at his heels. Snubby sat there on the rocks, and waited, his heart beating. The man wouldn't come back, of course – but he must stay here on the rocks till the boy was out of sight!

It seemed ages till the boy disappeared. Snubby looked along the beach, to where he had left the others. They were all there, watching intently.

Snubby stood up as soon as the boy was out of sight,

and then he and Loony raced over the sands to the other three. He flung himself down beside them, panting.

'The boy *was* waiting for the man with a beard,' he said. 'His uncle – a man called Morgan, who hires out boats – gave the letter to him to deliver. The boy didn't say why – I don't think he knew. He's a bit simple, I think. He said he was late, and he hoped the man would come soon, because he wanted to go out in a boat with his father.'

'And so you offered to wait in his place and deliver the letter?' said Barney. 'We wondered what was happening when the boy suddenly went off.'

'Yes. And he gave me the letter!' said Snubby, triumphantly slapping his bathing trunks where he had hidden it. 'What do you think of that?'

Everyone stared at Snubby, and nobody really knew *what* to think. Snubby always did such surprising things!

'Let's go back home and examine the letter,' said Barney. 'I don't know whether we ought to or not – but it does seem as if something peculiar must be going on. Why should Morgan, whoever he is, send a letter in code to a man like the one who knocked you about so roughly? Why *in code*? If Morgan is only a fisherman, presumably *he* didn't write it – so someone else must have given it to him to hand to someone else – it was too secret and precious to be trusted to the post!'

'*Do* let's go and examine it,' said Diana. 'We might have to take it to the police, you know. But what could be going on in a dear little place like this – full of country folk and fishermen?'

'Smuggling perhaps?' said Roger hopefully.

'What kind of smuggling could go on here!' said Barney. 'No, I don't think it's that. In fact I can't *imagine* what it is. Come on – let's get back. Anyway, it's getting on for lunch time.'

Snubby smacked his lips at once. 'Ha – good cooking – very good cooking!' he said. 'Oh, by the way, I learnt something from old Mrs Jones at the ice-cream shop this morning, when I went to buy these smashing clothes. She told me that Mr Jones, who keeps our inn, is her son – and she said it's always been his dearest wish to own it, and now he does, because some rich friends he met when he was learning to be a chef in London, lent him the money to buy it.'

'And I suppose those rich friends are Sir Somebody This and Sir Somebody That, whom she told us so often came down to stay,' said Roger. 'I bet they don't have to pay a penny when they come.'

They were nearly at the inn now, and Barney gave Snubby a nudge. 'We'll go to the caravan and see your letter there,' he said. 'We've plenty of time.'

Soon all four, with Loony and Miranda, were shut in the caravan. Snubby was just about to show them the letter, when Loony barked sharply.

'I bet that's Dafydd again, with that Waddle of a goose,' said Diana, crossly, and opened the door. Yes, it was! He was up on the wheel, peering in at the window.

'Go away, you little snooper,' said Diana, half amused, half cross.

'Soon be dinner,' said Dafydd solemnly, his arm round the goose's neck.

'Well, we'll be in good time,' said Diana. 'Run away, now!'

She shut the door and they peered at the envelope Snubby took from his bathing trunks. 'It's a bit squashed, because I've sat on it,' he said, and slit the envelope. He drew out a one page sheet of paper, folded in four, and opened it out flat.

'There! It's in code, as we thought! said Barney,

233

excited. 'We'll never decipher it, of course. Look at all the little figures and letters!'

'No wonder he thought that Bruce's letter which I was trying to read, was *this* one,' said Snubby, staring at it. 'All this mess-up of figures and letters! Gosh – I wish we could decipher them.'

'Well, we can't,' said Barney, folding up the sheet. 'What are we to do with it? Shall we just wait and see if anything happens? The man who took *your* letter, Snubby, will soon find out that it's not the right one, because he won't be able to decode it – and if he could, he'd only read a lot of rubbish!'

'Well, I like *that*!' said Snubby indignantly. 'Bruce and I don't write rubbish, let me tell you.'

Nobody took any notice of his indignant remark. Diana spoke to Barney.

'And when the bearded man finds out that he's got the wrong letter – from a boy who wasn't the messenger after all – and that therefore someone else took the *right* letter from the fisher-boy and went off with it, what will he do?'

'Ah – what *will* he do?' said Barney, tickling Miranda under her chin. 'I think we'd better wait and see – and in the meantime, we'll keep this letter very very carefully!'

Chapter Thirteen

Two More Visitors At The Inn

Miss Pepper came to the caravan, just as the four children were getting up to go. She looked sharply at Snubby, fearing that he might be wearing his dreadful clothes – but he was still in his bathing trunks. The old clothes were on one of the bunks.

'You can throw those away, Snubby,' she said. 'See here are your own things, washed and cleaned up. Please put them on.'

'Can't I come in to lunch like this?' said Snubby, looking down at himself.

'No,' said Miss Pepper definitely. 'Diana, how brown you are getting! Did you have a nice morning?'

They went off together talking. Barney had been thinking deeply, and now he turned to Snubby and Roger. 'I think it wouldn't be a bad idea to take a walk over to the fishing jetty this afternoon and see if we can spot Morgan the Cripple, and perhaps talk to him,' he said. 'I'd like to see what kind of a fellow he is – and wouldn't I like to know what he's mixed up in!'

'Good idea!' said Snubby at once. 'Do you hear that, Loony? Walkie-walk this afternoon!'

Loony promptly went mad, and raced round the little caravan at top speed, jumping from bunk to bunk, barking.

'Er – Loony,' said Barney, 'sorry to disappoint you, old fellow – but you're *not* coming with us this afternoon!'

'Why ever not?' demanded Snubby, astonished.

'Use your brains!' said Barney. 'If that boy who gave

you the letter is there, he'd recognise Loony at once, and, even though you wouldn't be in bathing things this time, he'd perhaps recognise you if you had Loony with you. But without Loony, and wearing ordinary clothes, I don't see how he *could* recognise you.'

'Loony won't like not coming,' said Snubby gloomily. 'And he'll bark the place down if we leave him in the caravan.'

'Well – we'll get Di to stay with Miss Pepper this afternoon, and keep Loony with her,' said Barney. 'It's either that, or we leave *you* behind with Loony, Snubby.'

'Oh, Diana will have Loony all right,' said Snubby. 'Stop showing off, Loony please – we know all about your wonderful jumping – look what you've done to my bedclothes, you ass!'

They went off to the dining-room of the inn, and found Diana at the table, and Miss Pepper at the sideboard, putting slices of cold ham on to plates. Snubby went to help her, and Loony at once sat himself exactly below Miss Pepper's right arm, hoping she might perhaps drop a slice of ham!

Barney told Diana in a low voice what he proposed to do that afternoon, and she was quite willing to stay behind with Miss Pepper and Loony. 'We could all three go for a little walk,' she said. 'Miss Pepper would like that. By the way – there are two more visitors at the inn!'

'Who?' asked Barney, looking round the table, pleased to see an enormous salad, and mounds of new potatoes. 'My word – what a fine spread!'

'I don't know their names,' said Diana, 'but look – here they come now!'

Two men walked into the room, one tall and commanding, with a monocle in his eye, and a smart, upturned moustache. The other was a short man, with a black beard and sunglasses.

Snubby turned at that moment to take two plates of ham to the table, and at once saw the two men. He jumped violently and a piece of ham leapt off one plate, and was at once snapped up by a delighted Loony. Snubby went quickly to the table and hissed at the surprised Barney and Roger, nudging them, and nodding over towards the table by the window where the two men sat with their backs to them.

The boys knew immediately what he meant! The man with the beard and the sunglasses was the one who had snatched Snubby's letter from him! Good gracious – and he was staying in the hotel!

'Has he seen Loony, do you think?' whispered Snubby. 'He might recognise him. He can't recognise me, I'm sure, now I'm properly dressed.'

'Take Loony out at once,' ordered Barney. 'Quick – before they see him. Here, stick a bit of my ham into his mouth, then he won't mind what you do with him! Lock him into the caravan.'

Snubby snatched a piece of ham off Barney's plate, picked up Loony, and put it into his mouth. Loony was so amazed at this extraordinary generosity that he didn't even bark. Snubby was able to streak out of the room with him at top speed, certain that the men hadn't seen him.

Miss Pepper was astonished to see him carrying Loony out of the room. 'Was he sick or something?' she asked, sitting down at the table. 'Poor Loony! Perhaps he swallowed too much sea water this morning.'

'You never know,' said Barney, and changed the subject at once. 'This must be home-cured ham, mustn't it, Miss Pepper. It's got a wonderful flavour!'

'It probably is,' said Miss Pepper. 'Diana, pass me the salad cream, please.'

Snubby came back, grinning. 'I'm sorry that Loony felt sick,' said Miss Pepper.

'He'd better stay behind this afternoon,' said Barney solemnly, 'and perhaps go for a walk with you, Miss Pepper – and Diana, too?'

'Yes. That's a good idea,' said Diana. 'Would you like me to go for a walk with you, Miss Pepper?'

Miss Pepper was really delighted. 'We'll go up into the hills,' she said. 'And you could take your field-glasses with you, Diana, and your bird book, and we could try to spot some interesting birds for your school essay.'

Roger winked at Barney. Everything was going along very nicely!

Snubby kept on staring at the two men, and Barney kicked him to make him stop. Who were these men? It should be easy to find out from Mrs Jones. He grinned secretly to himself to think that one of them probably had Snubby's code letter from his friend Bruce in his pocket – and had probably tried a dozen times to decode it, and failed!

Barney had a chance of finding out who the men were immediately after the meal. the two of them walked out of the room and went upstairs, and Mrs Jones came in to clear away, with Dafydd and Waddle hovering about outside in the hall as usual.

'Two more visitors, I see, Mrs Jones,' said Barney as she stopped to stroke Miranda, and give her a titbit.

'Oh, yes – they come often,' said Mrs Jones proudly. 'They are Sir Richard Ballinor, and Professor Hallinan – he's the great bird expert, you know. They are friends of my husband, he met them in London, and they know his cooking is good, very good, so they come here often, and they love the place, they love the mountains and the hills and the sea, and . . .'

238

The boys waited patiently till she had run on for some time, and then Barney interrupted.

'I expect they were pleased when your husband bought this place,' he said, 'it makes a nice holiday spot for them, doesn't it?'

'Ah, the good kind men, they lent my husband the money to buy the inn he so much wanted,' said Mrs Jones, in her lilting Welsh voice. 'So always I welcome them and give them my very best.'

I expect they've got that Best Room of yours then!' said Diana at once. Mrs Jones nodded.

'But that is not the room they *like* best,' she said. 'The room they always have is the room you have – with the two windows. But there – that Miss Pepper of yours is not one to change her mind, is she?'

'No, she's not,' said Roger and Diana together, remembering how many times in the past they had tried to make Miss Pepper change her mind about something! And then they heard Miss Pepper's voice at the door.

'Aren't you coming, children? Loony is barking his head off in the caravan!'

'Right,' said Barney, and they left Mrs Jones, who would certainly have chattered for an hour if they had stayed!

Miss Pepper and Diana and Loony set off for their walk in the hills, Diana with the field glasses slung over her back. Loony was rather puzzled that Snubby didn't come with them, and was inclined to stay with him – but when Snubby artfully rolled into his bunk and pretended to go to sleep, Loony at once decided that a walk with Diana was better than an afternoon in a boring caravan, with everyone shushing him.

'Now let's take our bathing things, and go all the way along the beach to the fishing jetty,' said Roger. 'We can

239

bathe whenever we like – either before we look for Morgan the Cripple, or afterwards.'

'Better be afterwards,' said Barney. 'It's idiotic to bathe too soon after lunch.'

They set off with Miranda scampering in front of them, only leaping on to Barney's shoulder when they met a dog or a shouting child. The sun shone out of a cloudless sky, and became very hot indeed as they walked over the white sand, past the caves.

They came near the little stone fishing-boat jetty. Not many people were there. A few old boatmen sat on the low sun-warmed wall, and a woman sat knitting on a wooden seat. Barney and the others lay down on the sand nearby.

A dirty, unkempt boy in a bright woollen jersey came running on to the jetty with a mongrel poodle, and Barney sat up at once, nudging the others. 'That's the boy who gave Snubby the letter,' he said. 'There can only be *one* mongrel poodle in this little place, surely!'

They all sat up and watched the boy. He went to where a boat was being untied, and helped to push it off. It was a pretty sight to see its sails unfurling and filling with wind.

A man came on to the jetty at that moment, dressed in fisherman's clothes – a man who limped badly and walked with a stick.

'Morgan the Cripple, do you think?' said Roger, as the fisherman went to talk to some old cronies on the wall. 'Come on – let's go up on the jetty. We might be able to get into talk with him.'

But before they had got up from the sands someone else strode on to the jetty – a man with a dark beard, wearing sunglasses. He called sharply to Morgan, who got up at once. 'Here, Morgan – I want a word with you!'

'I bet there's going to be a quarrel!' said Barney excitedly. 'Let's hope we hear it. Come on – we'll get nearer to the wall!'

Chapter Fourteen

An Exciting Afternoon

'Come over here,' said Morgan to the bearded man, and took him to one side of the jetty, out of hearing of the other fishermen there. Barney and the others crawled over the sand as near as they dared, and lay down hidden by the stone jetty wall.

'Morgan – that letter you gave your nephew to deliver to me,' began the man. 'That wasn't the one you were given for me, you know it wasn't.'

'What are you talking about, Sir Richard,' said Morgan in a deep puzzled voice. 'That letter never left my pocket, and that I swear, from the time it came to me till the time I gave it to Dai this very morning. Didn't he go to the pile of rocks we arranged?'

'Yes. He was there – dressed as you said, and the little black dog too, so I knew it was the right boy,' said the beared man. 'But I tell you *he gave me the wrong letter. I can't make head or tail of any of it!*'

'That were the letter given to me for you,' said Morgan obstinately. 'Jim give to me as usual, straight from his pocket to mine it went, and all he said was, 'We'll be back Friday. Be ready,' and off he sailed again. That letter was what he give me, I tell you.'

'I don't understand it,' said the bearded man, staring at Morgan. 'Where's that nephew of yours? I'll have to question him – though how *he* could have changed the letter beats me. Morgan, if you're double-crossing me I'll pay you out in a way you won't like!'

'I'm not double-crossing anyone!' said Morgan, raising

his voice angrily. 'Do I want to double-cross myself? I'm in this as much as you are, aren't I?'

'Don't shout like that,' said the other man, looking round anxiously, afraid of the other fishermen hearing.

'I'll call Dai,' said Morgan surlily. 'He's there, watching that boat. He'll tell you it was the letter all right. Dai! DAI! Here a minute!'

The small boy and the poodle came running up. 'Yes, Uncle Morgan?' said Dai, glancing at the bearded man, and looking scared.

'Did you give this gentleman the letter I gave you for him this morning?' said his uncle sternly.

'Yes,' lied the boy. 'Yes, of course I did.'

The bearded man suddenly caught hold of the small boy, and held him in such a fierce grip that he began to howl. 'You didn't give me any letter! You're not the boy I saw! He was bigger – and his dog was a black spaniel – not a poodle.'

'Let go the boy,' said Morgan sternly, seeing that Dai was scared almost to death. 'You said you had a letter given to you by a boy – who *was* the boy then, if it wasn't Dai?'

'I don't know – I tell you, it was a boy with a spaniel – a real ragamuffin, like your nephew,' said the man, glaring at the terrified boy. 'And when I came up to him, I saw he was actually *reading* the letter! It was in code. I immediately thought it was the letter he should have delivered to me and took it, though he tried to stop me.'

Morgan laughed harshly, and turned away. 'Then you are a fool, Sir Richard. The boy wasn't the right ragamuffin, and the letter was his, not yours.'

Sir Richard grasped Morgan's arm and swung him round. 'Man, this is urgent, you know that. I've not got the right letter, I tell you – the letter you gave to Dai. Where's *that* letter? You, boy, answer me at once!'

'I – I gave it to a boy who came to talk to me,' wept poor Dai, terrified out of his life. 'I waited and waited for you, and this boy said he'd give it to you for me. I didn't know you'd already been – and gone off with the wrong letter.'

Sir Richard pushed the boy away from his with such force that he almost toppled over into the water. Morgan scowled. 'Leave the boy alone. What harm's been done? You got a letter you couldn't read – and someone else has got a letter *he* can't read. I'll get in touch with Jim and he'll send another.'

Sir Richard took out a handkerchief and mopped his forehead. he came close to Morgan and spoke in his ear, so that the three boys listening down on the sand below the jetty could only just hear his words.

'You deliver the next letter to me yourself, Morgan. If anything goes wrong, it'll be laid on *your* shoulders for thinking that idiotic nephew of yours was trustable. If Jim's letter hadn't been in code, there'd be someone else now who would know enough to spoil all our plans for Friday – yes, and for always!'

'Aw – shut up,' said Morgan rudely, and turned away.

'And if I find that boy whose letter I took – and who got *my* letter from Dai – I'll wring his neck!' said Sir Richard in such a bloodthirsty tone that Snubby, who could hear every word, felt suddenly scared. What had seemed rather a peculiar joke, was turning into something that wasn't a joke at all! Why on earth had he gone and talked to Dai and persuaded him to hand over the letter?

'I'd know the boy anywhere,' went on Sir Richard, still in the same angry voice. 'Awful ragamuffin – a tramp of a fellow in long, dirty-looking trousers, a horrible jersey, and a peaked cap too big for him – and a black spaniel. Dai is dressed much the same, but he isn't as big as this other fellow – and the black dog misled me, of course.'

Snubby was feeling distinctly uncomfortable now, and so were Barney and Roger. How maddening that this bearded fellow was staying at the inn! Would he recognise Loony? And then Snubby?

Morgan strode off, leaving the other man by himself. The fishermen on the wall looked at Morgan curiously as he passed. They had been too far away to hear anything that was said – but they knew there had been a quarrel.

'Your grand friend upset, Morgan?' called one old fellow. 'Wasn't your last catch of fish good enough for his lordship?'

Morgan didn't answer. The fisherman nudged one another and grinned as the bearded man walked after Morgan, but nobody dared to call out to him. Dai had disappeared entirely, hidden somewhere out of sight.

The three boys on the sand lay there silently for some time, and then, hearing no more voices, rolled over and looked at one another. 'Let's go and bathe,' said Barney, in case anyone was listening. He added in a low voice, 'We'll talk later. Come on.'

'Yes – a bathe would be fine, it's so jolly hot,' said Roger loudly. Snubby said nothing. He was still very shaken by what he had overheard. He hoped the letter was safe in the caravan. Had he better destroy it?

They said no more till they were well away from the jetty. Then Barney mopped his head and said 'Whew! What on earth do we do next? You've landed us into something now, Snubby – all through that idiotic code-letter from Bruce.'

'It wasn't idiotic,' said Snubby in a rather meeker voice than usual. 'Anyway, that fellow – fancy him being the Sir Richard Mrs Jones told us about – that fellow couldn't puzzle out our code. It's a jolly good one, and not idiotic as you seem to think.'

'Let's bathe,' said Barney, 'and perhaps when we feel

a bit cooler, we can think this business out. Good thing we didn't bring Loony, Snubby – that fellow might have spotted him – and us.'

'I say – what on earth are we going to do with Loony now?' said Snubby in sudden dismay. 'We mustn't let that fellow, Sir Richard, see him at all – but you know what Loony is – rushing about all over the place!'

They all splashed into the cool sea, and when they came out they felt decidedly better. They sat on the sand and talked.

'Today's Wednesday – and whatever is going to happen is planned for Friday. *I* think it's smuggling,' said Roger. 'There are only two more days to go. Do we go to the police, do you think?'

'No. No, I don't think so. If we do, they will question that bearded fellow, and whatever's planned won't happen,' said Barney, frowning. 'I'm just thinking of something we heard one of the fishermen yell out to Morgan. He said "Wasn't your last catch of fish good enough for his lordship?" Well now, what did that mean? It means that Morgan hires out a boat to Sir Richard, presumably for catching fish – but perhaps brings in *something else* – either instead of fish, or hidden in the catch.'

'Something that he wants brought here to be hidden, do you think?' asked Roger.

'Yes. Perhaps something he wants to hide for some considerable time,' said Barney thoughtfully. 'I wonder who this Sir Richard really is – and his friend Professor Hallinan, the bird expert. I think they are just *posing* as Sir Richard and the Professor – using their names instead of their own. I think I'll walk into Dilcarmock and telephone my father after tea, and ask him if he can find out.'

'They must be rich, to lend Mr Jones the money to buy the inn,' said Snubby, screwing his toes into the sand.

'I can't think *why* anyone should lend a few thousand

246

pounds to a fellow like Mr Jones, just because they liked his cooking so much,' said Barney. 'I mean – when you lend money, you expect to get some good return from it – the profits made on the visitors that come to the inn, for instance. But very little profit can be made on *that* inn, I'm sure. Beside ourselves there are only those two men there!'

'Well – what *does* he give them in return then?' said Snubby. 'Do you imagine he lets them use his inn as a kind of headquarters for whatever they are really up to?'

Barney sat us straight and smacked his knee. 'Of *course*! You've hit it! What other reason could there be? There's a little gang here – Morgan and Jim, whoever he is – and Mr Jones – all in some game together, and this inn is somehow the heart of it. Gosh – we *have* tumbled on to something!'

'But what have we tumbled on?' asked Snubby, excited. 'How can we find out what it is? I SAY – this is pretty exciting, isn't it? I simply can't wait till Friday!'

Chapter Fifteen

Oh, Loony

Loony was extremely glad to see the boys when they came back, and rather astonished to be shut up immediately in the caravan, when everyone went to have tea. He barked dismally, and Miss Pepper was surprised at Snubby's seeming hard-heartedness.

'I really can't see why he can't come in to tea,' she said. 'He was as good as gold with us this afternoon. We had a wonderful walk – and Diana spotted some most unusual birds with the field-glasses.'

'There was one bird I couldn't make out,' said Diana. 'A green bird with a red top-knot.'

Mrs Jones tells me that there is a Professor Hallinan staying here,' said Miss Pepper. 'A famous ornithologist, and . . .'

'A *what*?' said Snubby, astonished.

'Bird expert,' said Miss Pepper. 'So I suggested that Diana should ask him about the bird. He'd be sure to be able to identify it.'

The three boys felt extremely doubtful about this, as none of them believed that the Professor was a real bird-man, any more than Sir Richard was really a Sir Anybody! But Barney winked at the boys, and said cheerfully, 'Yes, Di – good idea. I'll come with you and listen to what he says. Might learn something – you never know!'

Snubby gave a sudden chuckle. 'No – you never know!' he said. 'Miss Pepper, we're going to walk in to Dilcar-mock after tea – coming?'

'Good gracious no! I've had enough walking today,'

said Miss Pepper. 'You'd better catch a bus part of the way, it's quite a distance.'

The two men came in to tea at that moment and nodded to Miss Pepper. Diana determined to catch Professor Hallinan when he went out of the room. So she hovered about with Barney, while Snubby and Roger went to comfort poor Loony in the van.

At last the men came walking out, and made for the stairs. Diana darted to the tall moustached one, with a monacle in his eye.

'Oh please do excuse me, Professor Hallinan,' she said breathlessly. 'But I know you are a famous ornith – ornith – whatever it is, and know all about birds – so *do* you think you could help me to name a bird I saw today?'

'Er – surely! I'd be pleased to try,' said the Professor. 'Where did you see it?'

'Flying over the hills,' said Diana. 'Green, with a red top-knot.'

'Ah well, I fear I couldn't identify a bird on so little description,' said the Professor, courteously. 'It *sounds* as if might be a rare immigrant, which is sometimes seen here – Latin name *Lateus Hillimus*. Yes, it might be that.'

'Oh – thank you,' said Diana. 'I hope I remember such a peculiar name!'

Barney now entered the conversation, very politely. 'I saw a Short-Necked Curlikew,' he said, 'just outside the inn, it was. Surely that was unusual sir?'

'Very unusual,' said the Professor.

'And would you say that the Dotty Shade Warblers could be found in these hills?' asked Barney. 'I have heard they nest at times.'

'Er – well, yes, I believe they *have* been known to nest here,' said the Professor. 'Excuse me – I must join my friend.' And away he went up the stairs.

Diana stared at Barney in the utmost amazement.

'Short-Necked Curlikews! I've never heard of them in my *life*,' she said, 'and I know the names of *most* of our birds now. And who ever heard of the Dotty Shade Warblers?'

'Nobody,' said Barney, taking her arm. 'Your Professor is a fraud, dear Diana. What did he say that green bird of yours was – a *Lateus Hillimus*? Poppycock! You won't find *that* bird in any of your bird books! He's no more a bird expert than I am. I only wish I'd asked him if he had ever seen the curious nest of a Poppy Cockbird.'

Diana giggled. 'Gracious – I've a good mind to put the Poppy Cockbird into my school essay, just for a joke – and draw one too. But I say, Barney – do you really think the Professor is a fraud? He was so polite and knowledgeable too.'

'All tricksters are,' said Barney. 'And I bet that his friend, Sir Richard as he calls himself, is no more a botanist than the Professor is a bird expert! They're frauds both of them – using other people's names – pretending to be what they're not. My father knew their names – but I bet if he met them here, he would have spotted that they were bogus. Anyway, I'm going to phone him and ask him to make some inquiries, so that we can be certain.'

'Well, let's go and break the news to the others,' said Diana. 'Come on. Goodness – to think that the bogus Professor said that he thought your equally bogus Dotty Shade Warblers could be found in these hills! How do you *think* of names like that, Barney?'

'It's easy!' said Barney. 'Come on, Di. I want to be off to Dilcarmock to telephone my father. And we *must* keep Loony out of Sir Richard's sight, there's no doubt about that. He'd recognise him at once!'

They went halfway to Dilcarmock by bus, and then walked the rest of the way. Loony was delighted. Two long walks in a day – he was truly in luck!

Barney telephoned his father. 'Dad? It's Barney here. Can you hear me?'

'Yes – speak up a little though,' said his father. 'Are you all right?'

'Fine,' said Barney. 'But there's a bit of a mystery on about two men here – the famous experts that old Mrs Jones at the ice-cream shop told us about . . . Sir Richard Ballinor, and Professor Hallinan – they've arrived at the inn, and I've a feeling they're *frauds* – no more experts that I am! The Professor doesn't know one bird from another. What are they like, Dad? The real men, I mean?'

'One is tall, with an upturned moustache, and wears a monacle,' said his father. 'And the other, Sir Richard, is rather short, and has a beard.'

'Gosh,' said Barney, surprised to hear his father give such a close description of the two men at the inn. 'That pretty well describes the two fellows here, Dad – the ones I think are frauds. I say – could you possibly find out if the real Sir Richard and the real Professor are at their homes? If they are, I'll know for certain these two fellows are frauds, and we'll watch them to see what they are up to. But if you hear they're away in Wales – well – I suppose they won't be frauds after all. I think they are, though, in fact, I'm sure of it!'

His father chuckled. 'Quite a mystery!' he said. 'I'll certainly find out where the real Sir Richard and Professor are – they're both members of my Club and I can easily enquire there. I'll let you know at once whether your two men are false – or genuine.'

'Thanks,' said Barney. 'Don't telephone though, Dad – in case one of the men answers. Send me a telegram – and put just one word – "False" if the real experts are not the ones here – and "Genuine" if they are. Then I'll know what to do.'

'Right. But don't get mixed up in anything unpleasant,

Barney,' said his father. 'Let me know if there's any more I can do to help. I'll find out what you want at once, and you'll get a telegram tonight. I'll put the inn's telephone number, so that the post office will phone it through to you personally. Now don't get into any trouble – if these men aren't what they seem, they may be most unpleasant if they think any snooping is going on.'

'Right, Dad. Thanks and goodbye,' said Barney and put down the receiver. He went out of the box and told the others what his father had said. 'We'll know for certain tonight if what we think is correct,' he said. 'I *bet* we're on the right track!'

The four walked halfway back, and caught the bus the rest of the way, feeling quite tired. Even Loony decided that it was possible to overdo this walking habit! Miranda, of course, loved it all, for she sat on Barney's shoulder most of the time – and was thoroughly spoilt by all the passengers in the bus!

'You'll be sick down my neck if you accept any more sweets from people,' said Barney at last. 'Stop nibbling my ear, Miranda, you tickle!'

At a few minutes before eight, the telephone bell rang, and Mrs Jones came hurrying into the room where everyone was sitting. 'For you, Master Barney, please.'

Barney shot out, and a voice over the phone said, 'I have a telegram for you, sir. It has only one word though, and that is – "*False*".'

'Thanks,' said Barney, and put down the receiver. 'False! Well, we guessed right. Mr Jones's rich and important friends are no more than rogues who are making money in some dishonest way with his help! Rogues who are working in disguise and using other men's names! Now we can go right ahead, and try and find out what's happening. Friday night is apparently *the* night. If only we knew what to look for!' He went to tell the

252

others. Diana wanted to tell Miss Pepper, but nobody agreed.

'But all this sounds as if it might be dangerous,' said Diana. 'And surely the *police* ought to be told those men are frauds.'

'We'll wait till Friday comes, and see if we can find out what is happening,' said Barney. 'And for goodness' sake, let's keep Loony out of sight. If one of those men spots him, and guesses that he belongs to one of us, there will be danger – because they'll know Loony's owner has got the real letter, and they'll go for Snubby at once to get the precious letter!'

'All right. Let's destroy it then!' said Snubby promptly.

'No,' said Barney. 'We might have to produce it, to show we really did get hold of it – when the police come in on the job – as they'll have to sooner or later. I'll take it and hide it somewhere safe. I'll get it now.'

He went out of the room, and down to the caravan. The letter had been put into Snubby's pillow-case, on his bunk. Barney slipped in his hand and took it out. Then he found some drawing-pins and took them and the code-letter outside the van. He crawled underneath it and pinned the letter on the under-part of the caravan, very firmly indeed.

He crept out, grinning. If anyone found it there he would be very very clever!

Loony was sitting sadly by himself in the van, wondering why he wasn't allowed in the inn. Barney felt sorry for him and left Miranda there for company. The little monkey sat close to Loony, chattering in his ear, but he took no notice at all. He was waiting for his beloved Snubby to come for him!

Everyone went to bed early that night, for they were very tired.

'What with bathing and walking, and all the rest of the

excitement we've had, I can't keep awake another minute!' said Snubby with a tremendous yawn that set all the others off too, Miss Pepper as well.

'Come along, Diana,' she said, getting up. 'You go off to your caravan, boys. Sleep well!'

They all slept very well indeed, and Diana didn't want to get up when the hot water arrived next morning, brought as usual by Mrs Jones, followed by Dafydd and the goose!

'Oh, Mrs Jones – I don't think we need have the goose in here,' protested Miss Pepper, and Mrs Jones shooed both the little boy and Waddle away.

'I didn't even know they were behind me,' she said. 'That Dafydd – he puts his nose everywhere, and that goose, he is just as bad – in my larder he was yesterday, Miss, as sure as I stand here, pecking at the scones I had made for tea. Sir Richard and the Professor, they make such a fuss of my Dafydd, Miss, he follows them all day long, they spoil him, I say, and . . .'

'Well, thank you, Mrs Jones, we'll be down in half an hour,' said Miss Pepper firmly, knowing quite well that if she didn't interrupt Mrs Jones, she would be standing there talking till breakfast time!

Everyone was punctual for breakfast for once, and Sir Richard and the Professor were at their table too. Nobody knew that Dafydd and his goose were once more peeping in at the window of the caravan – and that Dafydd was feeling very very sorry for poor lonely Loony, left there to wait for Snubby to return.

'Poor dog Loony,' said Dafydd softly, and tapped on the window. 'Poor dog!'

Loony saw Dafydd's small face peering in at the window and barked hopefully, pawing at the window-pane as he stood on his hind paws on one of the bunks.

'Dafydd will undo the door for poor dog Loony,' said the small boy pityingly. 'Wait, dog Loony.'

He scrambled down from the wheel he was standing on, and with his goose behind him, went to the door. It was shut, not locked, and he opened it easily.

Loony shot out at top speed, barking, and the goose fled for its life, cackling as if had laid a hundred eggs. Dafydd was cross. He had at least expected a word of thanks from Loony!

Loony tore across the slope of the hill and into the hall of the inn, the door of which was always left open. Where was Snubby? He flung himself against the door of the dining-room and scampered in, barking delightedly.

'LOONY!' said Snubby in horror. 'You bad dog! How did you get out?'

Loony threw himself on Snubby and licked him, whining as if he hadn't seen Snubby for a month. Barney glanced quickly round at the two men at the window table, with their bacon and eggs in front of them. Sir Richard was staring at Loony in amazement, and he nudged the Professor. 'That's the dog!' he said. 'I'd know him anywhere. He belongs to that boy, see?'

Barney couldn't hear what was said, but he could guess. Blow! Now the men would know that Snubby was the boy who had their letter. 'Quick, Snubby!' he said, 'let's get out of here with Loony. Buck up! Those men have spotted him – and you too!'

Chapter Sixteen

A Day Out For Snubby!

Snubby was really scared. He got up at once, and followed by Barney, left the table and went quickly out of the door. Loony went too, barking in delight. Miss Pepper was most astonished, and stared after them indignantly.

'Where have they gone – and why did they leave the breakfast table without a word to me?' she said. 'Is one of them feeling ill, Diana?'

Roger gave Diana a little kick under the table, afraid she might say something that would make trouble. 'Er – didn't you think Snubby looked a little pale?' he said.

'Perhaps it's a bit of the sun. He may have said a word to Barney about it.'

'I'd better go and find out,' said Miss Pepper.

'Oh, wait till Barney comes back,' said Roger. 'Don't leave your hot bacon and eggs! I expect old Berney will be back in a minute.'

He shot a glance at the two men sitting at the window table. They were talking earnestly, and the bearded man looked angry and troubled. Roger wished he could hear what they were saying.

Snubby was now safely in the caravan with Barney. Loony at his feet, and Miranda cuddled in Barney's arms. They were talking earnestly.

'How did Loony get out? He can't open the door himself!' said Snubby. 'I bet it was that little nuisance of a Dafydd – always snooping round! Well, *now* the fat's in the fire! Those men spotted Loony all right – and know

I'm the boy who took the code-letter from that fraud Sir Richard.'

'Yes – and they're certain to try and get it now,' said Barney. 'How, I don't know – but it might be jolly unpleasant for you, Snubby, if they catch you! I think the best thing for you to do is to hide.'

'All right. But where?' asked Snubby dismally. 'In the caravan? They'd soon find me here.'

'No, certainly not in the caravan,' said Barney. 'I almost think the best thing to do would be to catch the next bus to Dilcarmock and spend the day there. Unless the men happened to see you getting on the bus they's never guess you'd gone there. I'd better come with you.'

'Yes, do,' said Snubby, still looking dismal: 'But what on EARTH are we going to tell Miss Pepper?'

'The truth!' said Barney, getting up. 'I'll see if I can catch Roger's ear and tell him what we're going to do – and he can tell Miss Pepper we decided to go to Dilcarmock, and rushed out to catch the bus – and apologise for us.'

'I never finished my bacon and eggs,' groaned Snubby. 'Oh, why did I ever get mixed up with that idiotic letter?'

'I'll see if I can catch Roger,' said Barney, and ran up to the inn. He was careful not to be seen from the dining-room window, for he knew the men sat there. He went to the dining-room door and peeped in. Miss Pepper had her back to him, and he was able to signal to Roger unseen.

'Excuse me a moment, Miss Pepper,' said Roger, and slipped out of the room before she could ask him any questions. She was puzzled and annoyed.

'What *is* everyone doing this morning?' she said. 'I hope *you* feel all right Diana. I think I'd better go and see what is happening.'

'Well, have some hot toast first,' said Diana, trying to

give the boys as much time as she could. 'Take this nice brown piece.'

Barney told Roger their plans in a few words. 'We think Snubby had better clear off for the day – so we're going to Dilcarmock by bus and won't be back till supper time. Then I'll lock Snubby into the caravan, and we'll say he's tired – and I'll take him something to eat there – and perhaps have it with him, in case those men try to get him. Got it?'

'Yes,' said Roger. 'But Miss Pepper is getting very suspicious. For goodness' sake go now – she'll be out in half a minute, I know she will.'

'Right. We'll go at once,' said Barney, and went to fetch Snubby from the van. Roger watched them go racing down the slope to the village below. Would they catch the bus? It was about due now, and if they missed it they would have to wait a whole hour. He went back to the inn and met Miss Pepper hurrying out, having eaten bacon and eggs and toast very quickly indeed.

'Oh, Roger! What *is* happening?' she asked. 'Really! Leaving the table like that, one after the other, without a word of explanation! Where are Snubby and Barney?'

Roger looked round carefully before he answered, in case the man might be within hearing. 'Well, it's all quite simple,' he said, smiling brightly. 'Apparently they made up their minds to go to Dilcarmock for the day, and had to rush off very suddenly to catch the bus. They asked me to apologise to you.'

'Well – why in the world couldn't they have said just one word to me about their plans,' said Miss Pepper, still puzzled. 'Aren't you and Diana going?'

'Er – no – we thought we'd stay and keep you company,' said Roger. 'What about going out in a boat, Miss Pepper, just us three?'

'Well, that would be very nice,' said Miss Pepper. 'Very

nice indeed. But I shall have a few words to say to Barney and Snubby when they come back this evening – tearing out of the room like that in the middle of breakfast!'

The two men came out of the inn at that moment, talking in low tones, looking all round. Roger was sure they were looking for Snubby. They looked at him, and Sir Richard took a step forward as if he were going to say something. Then the other man pulled him by the arm, to stop him. Obviously nothing was going to be said in front of Miss Pepper!

'I bet they know she'd call the police if they began to make a rumpus about Snubby and secret letters!' thought Roger. He was glad to see Diana coming out behind the men.

'Di! We're going boating!' he shouted. 'Just the right morning for it – hot sun and a wind off the shore.'

'Oh *good*!' said Diana, longing to know what had happened to Snubby and Barney, but not daring to ask in front of Miss Pepper. Roger took Diana's arm and hurried her off to the caravan. 'Just going to tidy up the bunks!' he called. 'We'll be ready in ten minutes' time.'

Diana thought it was a very good idea of Barney's to go to Dilcarmock for the day. 'If only we can get Friday over, with whatever's supposed to happen then, I'll feel safer!' she said. 'Oh dear – why does Snubby *always* get into trouble? And us with him! And he never seems to mind, does he? I bet he's sitting happily in the bus now, pretending to play banjo or something, and keeping everyone in fits of laughter.

Diana was almost right in her guess! Snubby *was* in the bus – but he wasn't playing a pretend banjo, he was playing a mouth-organ – or rather, pretending to, his hand up to his mouth, making a most realistic zz-zz-zz noise, exactly as if he were playing a jiggy tune! And as Diana had surmised, everyone was delighted, laughing and egging him on. No – Snubby wasn't feeling nearly as worried as the others!

When Miranda slid down to the floor and began to dance in time to Snubby's horrible noises, even the bus driver had to look round – and the bus almost went into a ditch!

'Shut up now, Snubby,' said Barney, alarmed. 'You'll cause an accident.'

Back at the inn the others were preparing for a morning's boating. Miss Pepper insisted on large sunhats being taken, for the sun would beat down on the boat and there would be no shelter at all. They had to go and buy some at old Mrs Jones's shop, which meant an ice-cream each, of course.

While they were eating them, the two men from the inn passed slowly by, and peered in. They said nothing, much to Roger's relief, and walked on.

'I don't somehow like those men,' said Miss Pepper. 'I can't imagine why they're down here – they don't seem to fish or bathe – and look, they're in their city suits even on a day like this! If they weren't who they are I'd think they were up to no good!'

'I wouldn't be surprised if you're right, Miss Pepper,' said Roger solemnly, and Diana gave a sudden giggle.

They had a glorious morning quite far out in a boat. They took turns at rowing and steering and lying flat with a hand over the side dragging through the water. The two children bathed from the boat as well, and slowly their faces, arms and legs turned a bright red-brown. Miss Pepper was extremely glad of her enormous sunhat!

Barney and Snubby also had quite an amusing time in Dilcarmock. It was a big seaside town, full of trippers, and had a tremendous lot of side-shows. Barney, who had once been a circus-boy, used to going round with fairs, enjoyed joining in the amusements he had known so well

– hoopla stalls – dodgem cars – swings – roundabouts and so on. He even met someone he had once known at Rilloby Fair, and they had a wonderful talk which poor Snubby couldn't even share.

Miranda loved it all, of course, and Loony met so many stray dogs tearing about that he had the time of his life. He thought Dilcarmock was much more interesting than Penrhyndendraith!

'Time to get the bus back,' said Barney at last. 'We shall miss supper at the inn if we don't – even though you must have had at least a dozen ice-creams, Snubby, and goodness knows how many shrimps, and some of that awful gingerbread, and three meat-pies, and – let me see – how many cheese sandwiches was it?'

'Well, I'm beginning to feel hungry for my supper, all the same,' said Snubby. 'So don't let's miss the bus, Barney. Loony, keep to heel. I don't want to lose you just as the bus is due.'

They went to the bus stop, and the bus came rumbling along in about two minutes. They settled into the front seats, Miranda on Barney's shoulder, eager to see everything as usual. Loony lay at Snubby's feet.

'I do hope those two men won't try to get me this evening,' said Snubby suddenly. 'I'd forgotten all about them, I was enjoying myself so. Do you think I dare go in to supper?'

'Yes – you'll be all right if we're all with you,' said Barney. 'But we *must* go about together, all four of us *and* Loony, till bedtime. We can say we're jolly tired and go off early, see?'

They were glad to walk up the slope to the caravan, for they really *were* tired. Roger was there, waiting for them with an anxious face.

'I say!' he said, as soon as he saw them. 'Something's happened – the code-letter's gone from under the caravan where Barney pinned it. I think that silly, snooping little Dafydd found it. I can't find the little wretch anywhere, or I'd take it from him – and I only hope the men don't see him with it! Isn't he a *pest*?'

Chapter Seventeen

Where Is The Code-Letter?

Barney and Snubby looked at Roger in horror. The code-letter had gone? Who would have thought anyone could possibly find it, pinned so neatly to the underside of the caravan?

'Not only that – but our caravan lock was broken when I went to it after tea – and the whole place was upside down!'

'*That* must have been the two men searching it for the letter,' said Barney at once. 'Dafydd wouldn't dare to do that. He wouldn't be able to break the lock for one thing.'

'Why do you think Dafydd has the letter?' asked Snubby.

'Well, I'll tell you.' said Roger. 'You see, Miss Pepper, Di and I came back for lunch, and I went to get something out of the caravan – and I saw Waddle the goose standing by it. The lock wasn't broken then. I was surprised to see Waddle all by himself, because he's like a dog, always at Dafydd's heels . . .'

'Where was Dafydd then – under the caravan?' asked Barney.

'Yes! I looked all round for him, and couldn't see him – and then the goose stuck its head under the caravan and cackled as if to say "Buck up, Dafydd!" And *I* looked under and there was the little pest, as quiet as a mouse!'

'Did you see if he had the letter?' asked Snubby.

'No. I didn't think about the letter then!' said Roger. 'I just shouted at Dafydd and told him to come out, and said he wasn't to go near the caravan. He's too light-

fingered – takes anything he fancies, like a monkey. Oh
– sorry, Miranda. I forgot you were present!'

Miranda chattered as if she understood, and Roger
went on with his tale. 'Well, Dafydd shot off with Waddle
– and then I suddenly remembered the letter and crawled
under the van to have a look. And the letter wasn't
there – but the drawing-pins were scattered on the ground
below so *somebody* must have taken them out to get the
letter. And I'm dead certain it *was* Dafydd, because if it
had been the two men they wouldn't have come in the
afternoon and searched the caravan for it, would they?'

'Not if they'd taken the letter in the morning,' said
Barney. 'Well now, the thing is – has that little pest got
the letter still? We'd find it out as soon as we can.'

But Dafydd had gone to bed! 'He is fast asleep,' said
Mrs Jones. 'Such a boy he has been today, and that goose
of his! Into my larder they were, and up the stairs, and
into mischief everywhere, and . . .'

'Er – would he like this little clock we won at hoopla
in Dilcarmock?' said Barney, bringing a gay little clock
out of his pocket.

'Indeed and he would, oh indeed to goodness!' said
Mrs Jones. 'But not tonight, sir, he is asleep! Tomorrow
I will give it to him myself.'

'No, *I'd* like to give it to him,' said Barney, putting the
clock firmly back into his pocket, and went off before
Mrs Jones could say any more.

'We'll make him give up the letter in return for the
clock,' said Barney. 'The little wretch! He's everywhere!
Fancy crawling under the caravan!'

'Well, kids do silly things like that when they're as small
as he is,' said Snubby. 'I remember thinking it was grand
fun to crawl under my uncle's car when I was his age,
and let oil drip on me.'

'You *would*!' said Diana. 'Ugh! Thank goodness I didn't want to do things like that.'

They had a pleasant supper, and, much to their surprise, the two men were not there.

'Have they gone, Mrs Jones?' asked Barney, nodding his head towards the window-table. She shook her head.

'Oh no, young sir. They had an early meal and have gone to see some friends. Busy men they are, sir, even when they are down in quiet Penrhyndendraith – rich men, important men, sir, and proud I am to think they like our inn – but it's the cooking, and very good cooking! You too like my husband's cooking, I know! You . . .'

'Yes, yes, Mrs Jones,' said Miss Pepper, and the cheery little woman took the hint and scuttled out of the room.

'She's absolutely non-stop!' said Snubby. 'Honestly, I never know why you stop her, Miss Pepper. I could listen to her for ages.'

'I dare say,' said Miss Pepper. 'But you and I have slightly different ideas, Snubby.'

'Don't squash me like that,' said Snubby crossly. 'Anyone would think I was an orange.'

Miss Pepper simply couldn't stop laughing, and the other chuckled. 'You *can't* squash old Snubby,' said Roger. 'We've all tried – but he's made of rubber. He bounces up again immediately.'

They all went off to bed early again, really tired with their long day. The three boys held a conference in their caravan.

'I'll nab Dafydd first thing tomorrow morning if I can, and get that letter from him,' said Barney. 'And Snubby must be very very careful not to go near the two men, in case they think he's got it on him – they know it's not hidden in the caravan, because they've searched for it – what a mess they made, the wretches!'

'How am I to stay away from the fellows tomorrow?' demanded Snubby. 'I can't *keep* going off to Dilcarmock.'

'We'll think of something,' said Barney. He yawned. 'I'm going to sleep – and woe betide Dafydd tomorrow if he doesn't give me that letter!'

The next morning they looked for Dafydd and Waddle as soon as they got up, but they were nowhere to be seen. Barney went along to the kitchen, where Mr Jones was cooking breakfast that smelt too delicious for words.

'Er – good morning. Do you know where Dafydd is?' asked Barney politely.

Mr Jones turned, scowling, holding a frying-pan in his hand. 'No, I do not. I will not have him here when I cook.'

The boys went out of the kitchen hurriedly, feeling that Mr Jones did not want them there either when he 'cooked.'

'What a dour, surly fellow,' said Roger. 'You'd think he'd be jolly cheerful, having this inn for his own.'

They kept a sharp eye out for the two men, but did not see them. Barney went cautiously into the dining-room to see if they were there – and found Mrs Jones clearing dirty plates away from the men's table.

'Oh – have they had their breakfast already?' asked Barney.

'Yes – early they were today!' said Mrs Jones. 'Sir Richard, he said they had much business to do today, and . . .'

'Oh, he did, did he?' said Barney. 'I wonder what kind of business he does in a little place like this.'

'Sir Richard owns two fishing vessels,' said Mrs Jones, 'and many other things. He . . .'

But just then Miss Pepper came in with Diana, and Mrs Jones hurried out of the kitchen to tell Mr Jones they were down.

The boys went hunting for Dafydd again after breakfast, keeping a sharp lookout for the two men, who, however, were not to be seen,. It wasn't until nearly lunch-time that they found Dafydd, wandering along with Waddle as usual. He came up to them at once.

'Mum says there is a clock you have,' he said. 'A clock for me.'

'Oh, she told you, did she?' said Barney, taking the gay little clock out of his pocket.

Dafydd gazed at the clock in delight, and rattled something off in Welsh. He reached out for it – but Barney held it away.

'Dafydd,' he said, 'if I give you this – *you* must give *me* something.'

'My knife!' said Dafydd, and dug his hand into his pocket.

'No, Dafydd – I want that paper you found under our caravan,' said Barney. 'You were bad to take it. But if you give it to me now, you shall have the clock.'

'Paper gone,' said Dafydd solemnly.

'Gone? Where's it gone?' demanded Roger.

'Men took it,' said Dafydd, pointing in the direction of the inn.

'When?' said Barney sharply.

Dafydd did not seen to know. He suddenly began to cry. 'They shout at Dafydd,' he said. 'Dafydd sit there, to make a boat with the paper,' and he pointed to a little wooden seat in the inn garden. 'And man come and say 'You give me that!' and he take it – like this' And Dafydd made a grab at the clock Barney was holding.

'Good gracious!' said Roger. 'That's a blow, isn't it! Dafydd, when was this?'

'Man hit Waddle,' said Dafydd, aiming a blow in the air. 'Bad man. Steal from Dafydd. You give me clock now?'

'No. You haven't got the letter to give me,' said Barney sternly. 'You were a bad boy to take the paper away and make a boat.'

'He probably didn't think it was ours,' said Roger, as the little boy began to cry bitterly. 'After all, you don't usually find a paper sheet stuck under a caravan! He couldn't have guessed it was so important.'

'I suppose he couldn't,' said Barney, looking at the sobbing child. He suddenly put his arm round him. 'Stop crying. We forgive you. See, here is the clock – you wind it up like this – it says tick-a-tock, tick-a-tock!'

Dafydd was overjoyed. He stopped crying at once and took the clock. He held it to Waddle's ear. 'Listen!' he said. 'Tick-a-tock, tick-a-tock.'

The goose backed away, not at all sure about the clock.

'And this is how you set the alarm bell going,' said Barney, hoping the child would understand. 'See – you wind *this* little handle – and now listen!'

The alarm bell shrilled out and the goose raced off in fright,, cackling loudly. Dafydd was entranced. He suddenly put his arms round Barney and gave him a great hug.

'You nice boy,' he said, 'Dafydd get back paper for you. Yes, Dafydd give it to you.'

'I wish you could, old chap,' said Barney. 'But it's too late now! Run along.'

Dafydd went to find his goose, and the others looked at one another hopelessly.

'No good,' said Barney. 'Those two men have the letter – and know all they want to, whatever it is – they know what "Jim" had told them to do tonight, and everything. Well, it's about lunch time. Where's Miss Pepper?'

I'll go and get her. She's upstairs,' said Snubby. 'Come on, Loony, let's go and tell Miss Pepper she's VERY late!'

And away he went at top speed with Loony, racing up

the stairs. But Miss Pepper was not in her room, and Snubby turned to go down again, Loony running in front of him.

He stopped dead as he saw Sir Richard coming along the landing, out of the Best Room. The man saw him and rushed at him, catching him by the collar.

'You! You pest! How dare you take that letter from that boy Dai! How much do you know? You tell me, or I'll throw you down the stairs.'

He swung Snubby over the stairway as if he really meant to keep his word. Snubby, half choked, was terrified out of his life.

He gasped out something, but the man could not understand, and shook him as if he were a rat. 'Answer me! I'll get the truth out of you if I choke you!'

Loony heard the angry voice and came tearing up at top speed. The little spaniel gave an angry snarl and flung himself on the man, nipping him sharply in the calf of the leg. Sir Richard let Snubby go, and yelled with pain, and the boy at once fled into Miss Pepper's room, and locked the door behind him.

He listened, gasping and choking and heard the man rush down the stairs, pursued by a very angry Loony Gosh – now what was he to do? He simply DARE not slip out of Miss Pepper's room – that fellow might get him again!

Chapter Eighteen

Dafydd's Discovery

Roger, Barney and Diana waited patiently for Snubby and Loony to come down with Miss Pepper. In a short while Miss Pepper appeared from the garden of the inn, where she had been sitting, reading a paper.

'Oh – are you ready for lunch?' she said. 'Where's Snubby?'

The others looked at one another. Where *was* Snubby – and why hadn't he come down when he found that Miss Pepper wasn't in her room? Barney felt suddenly alarmed.

'I'll fetch him,' he said, and went into the inn. He tore up the stairs, and came to Miss Pepper's room. It was shut and locked. Loony was there scratching at the door whining. Barney knocked. 'Snubby! Are you there?'

Snubby's voice answered him, sounding rather weak. 'Yes. Oh, Barney, is it you? I'll unlock the door.'

He unlocked it and Barney went in at once. 'What have you done to your head?' he said. 'My word, you look awfully pale, Snubby. Has something happened?'

'Yes,' said Snubby, lying on Miss Pepper's bed again. 'That bearded man attacked me – half choked me, and almost flung me down the stairs. I must have hit my head somehow – against the wall, I suppose, when he shook me till my teeth rattled! Loony went for him and bit him – good old Loony!'

'Grrrrr,' said Loony, fiercely, remembering.

'Gosh!' said Barney in horror. 'What a brute the fellow must be! You'd better stay out of his way, Snubby. He's furious with you for getting his letter from the little fisher-boy, Dai, of course. Pity we couldn't read it!'

'I'm staying up here,' said Snubby. 'I don't know what you can tell Miss Pepper, but today I'm quite definitely keeping out of Sir Richard's way.'

'I'll tell her you hit your head and hurt yourself,' said Barney, troubled. 'I'll suggest to her that you stay up here as it's much quieter than downstairs. Perhaps after to-night those men will go. Do you want any lunch? I could bring a tray up for you.'

'No thanks,' said Snubby. 'I couldn't eat a thing. My tummy feels all of a wobble.'

'Bad luck, old son,' said Barney, thinking that Snubby must indeed feel terrible not to want his lunch. 'Try to get a bit of sleep.'

'My head's begun to ache,' complained Snubby. 'Oooh, Loony, I *am* glad you went for that spiteful wretch!'

Loony leapt on the bed, and Snubby pushed him down. 'Sorry – this is Miss Pepper's bed, not mine,' he said. 'Though I dare say if I went to lie on Diana's bed, *she* wouldn't mind you coming beside me.'

Barney went downstairs and told Miss Pepper that Snubby had somehow hurt his head, and wanted to lie down quietly, and that he didn't want any lunch. Miss Pepper was quite alarmed to hear this and ran up the stairs at once. Barney quickly told the others what had happened, and they listened in dismay. Poor old Snubby.

Miss Pepper came down at last and they began their dinner. Miss Pepper was quite worried. 'I cannot *imagine* what Snubby was doing to bang his head like that,' she said. 'How very sensible of him to want to lie quiet this afternoon – of course my bedroom is just the place! Nobody will disturb him there. I'll pop up after lunch to see if he's all right, and then leave him in peace till tea-time. He says he has a most terrible headache, poor boy.'

271

'I bet he'll be all right by tea time,' said Roger, eating an enormous chunk of home-cooked meat-pie. 'I say, wasn't that little monkey of a Dafydd pleased with his clock! He must have set that alarm off about twenty times since we gave it to him. I keep hearing it trilling away somewhere or other.'

Miss Pepper went up to see Snubby after lunch, and was glad to find him fast asleep, with Loony on guard. She tiptoes out of the room, hoping that he would sleep till tea-time and then feel quite recovered.

'Wouldn't you like to bathe this afternoon?' Miss Pepper asked the three children. 'And lie out in the sun?'

'Sounds fine,' said Roger. Let's go a good way along the beach this afternoon, where there are those rock-pools. I bet some of them would be as warm as toast to wallow in.'

So they all went over the white sands, and settled down by the rock-pools. The rocks were quite high there, and the tide was going out, leaving warm, shallow pools in which swam grey shrimps.

They bathed, and then lay either in the deliciously warm pools, or on the hot sand. Miss Pepper put up a huge sun umbrella, lay down under it and fell asleep.

Barney lay in one of the pools, amused to feel a shoal of little shrimps trying to nibble his leg. He sat up to tell the others – and caught sight of two people coming along the sands, deep in talk together.

'Hist!' he said in a low voice. 'I spy Sir Richard and the other fellow coming along. Keep your heads down. I wonder where they're going?'

The two men walked quickly past on the sand, talking in low voices. 'Gone to chat to Morgan and Jim, I suppose,' said Barney. 'About the Doings tonight, whatever they are! What do you bet that one of Morgan's boats is coming in at dead of night with some mysterious "catch" that they don't want anyone else to see unloaded?'

'Look – isn't that Dafydd and his goose?' said Roger, in surprise. 'Following some way behind the men?' I wonder what he's up to? See how close he's keeping to the cliff – as if he doesn't want them to see him?'

'Doing a bit of shopping again, I suppose,' said Diana. 'You just never know where that child will pop up next!'

They all lay down again in the pool, their heads propped against convenient rocks. Diana yawned. 'I think I'd better get out and lie in the sun. I'm almost asleep, and I don't want to wake up choking in the water!'

It was a truly lazy afternoon, and the four, with Miranda too, thoroughly enjoyed it, though they missed Snubby and Loony very much. Miranda sat near Barney on a rock just above his head, sad because she could not sit on his shoulder as usual. But nothing would persuade her to lie in the pool too!

After about an hour Miranda began to chatter quietly, and Barney sat up in the pool. 'What's up?' he said. 'Someone coming?'

A small brown face, with a shock of untidy hair above it, peered round the rock at him. It was Dafydd! A long curving neck peering round as well, and Barney saw that Waddle was there too.

'Shhhhhh!' said Dafydd mysteriously, and then began to point with his finger some way up the beach, jabbing the air with it.

'What is it? What do you want to tell me?' said Barney in a low voice.

'Men,' said Dafydd. 'Two men. Dafydd see where they go. Dafydd want paper back, and follow men. Up long hole.'

'What on earth does he mean?' said Barney to Roger, who was listening. 'Do you suppose he went after the men with some wild idea of getting back that letter for us?'

'Up long hole,' said Dafydd, nodding. 'Dafydd take you.'

'This sounds interesting,' said Barney. 'Let's go with him and see what he means. Wait a bit, though – is that voices? Maybe it's the men coming back. Dafydd, come down here.'

Dafydd and the goose scrambled over the rocks and sat beside Barney, Dafydd's bare feet in the water, and the goose paddling solemnly round the pool.

'Men come back,' said Dafydd, peering over the rock. Barney pulled him down.

'Keep still,' he said, and Dafydd understood and sat quite still, swinging his feet to and fro in the warm pool.

The men passed by once more, on their way back, and were soon out of sight. Dafydd stood up. 'Up long hole?' he said, pointing over the sands. Barney and Roger scrambled out of the pool, shook themselves like dogs, and followed the small boy and goose back along the way the men had come.

They came at last to the caves that led into the cliffs, and Dafydd disappeared into one of the two marked 'DANGEROUS'. Barney pulled him back.

'No! This cave is dangerous,' he said.

Dafydd obviously didn't understand. He ran right into the cave, and the two boys followed him, feeling rather scared in case part of the roof fell.

'I suppose if the men *did* go into the cave, it can't be very dangerous!' said Roger.

'Or maybe they labelled it "Dangerous" themselves,' said Barney grimly. 'Perhaps they've got a convenient hiding-place up here!'

'Well – it's not much of a cave!' said Roger, as they came to the end of it. 'Nowhere to hide anything here!'

'Look at Dafydd,' said Barney. 'He's climbing up that rock – now he's running along a ridge – he's gone!'

So he had! He disappeared halfway along the ridge of rock, and Waddle the goose, left behind on the sandy floor of the cave, sent a sorrowful cackle after him.

Dafydd appeared again, beckoning. They could only just see him, outlined agaist the dark cave-wall, standing on the ridge.

'Up long hole!' said the small boy. 'You come too. Up long hole.'

Barney and Roger began to feel excited. They climbed part of the rock at the back of the cave, come to the ridge, and walked along it. Halfway along there was a hole in the wall of the rock, and it was through this that Dafydd had disappeared. He had now slipped through it again, and the two boys peered after him in the dim light, for the cave was almost dark.

'You come too?' asked Dafydd, and added something in Welsh that they didn't understand.

'Rather!' said Roger, and scrambled through with Miranda at his feet. 'Where in the world does this lead to? What a pity we haven't a torch. I say – it really *is* a long hole, isn't it – as far as we can see, anyway! Come back, Dafydd – we can't go scrambling about in pitch darkness!'

Chapter Nineteen

Very Exciting!

The two boys and Miranda climbed back into the cave where Waddle greeted them with loud cackles. Dafydd leapt down and joined them.

'Long, long hole,' he said. 'Men go up long hole. Dafydd too. Long, long, long.'

'All very mysterious indeed,' said Barney. 'Thanks, Dafydd. Did the men see you?'

'Not see Dafydd. Dafydd not get letter,' said the small boy, looking doleful. 'Dafydd make clock go Tr-r-r-r-r-ring, and men call out quick!'

Barney laughed. 'You little monkey! You crept behind the men, and set off the alarm! My word, they must have been scared. Good for you, Dafydd. Now you must go home.'

Dafydd set off across the sands, and the boys went to tell Diana where they had been. She was intensely interested.

'The men *must* be smuggling something,' she said, 'and hiding it up Dafydd's long, long hole.' I bet to-night there will be fresh goods to take up there.'

'Yes, quite probably,' said Barney. 'I wonder why they went there to-day, though. Perhaps to make room for the new goods? I wish we'd had a torch – we'd have gone right up the the very end of the hole. It's a steep passage really, of course, but Dafydd kept calling it a long, long hole! Funny little chap – he went up the rocky cave-wall like a monkey – well, like Miranda did, actually – with a spring and a leap and a jump! He must have eyes like a cat – I believe he would even be able to see in the darkness of that passage! It seemed to go up pretty steeply, as far as we could tell.'

'Barney – let's watch to see if those men go out to-night,' said Roger eagerly. 'They'd have to pass fairly near our caravan if they did, and old Loony would be sure to bark. We could creep after them, and see what they take into the cave, if they do go there.'

'Yes. I don't see why we shouldn't,' said Barney, suddenly excited. 'Snubby can come too if he's feeling better – but not you, Di. Miss Pepper would hear you slipping out of your room.'

'I do hope old Snubby *is* better,' said Diana. 'Fancy that man attacking him like that! The sooner I hear those two men are in prison, the better I'll be pleased. Passing themselves off as a Sir Somebody and and Professor!'

Miss Pepper suddenly woke up with a jump and looked at her watch. 'Good gracious! It's tea-time!' she said 'You run on ahead, children, and tell Mrs Jones to get tea. I'll follow at my own pace.'

'Good,' said Barney, as they ran off over the sand, 'now we can slip upstairs and tell Snubby what we've discovered, without Miss Pepper overhearing.'

They found Snubby feeling much better, and began to tell him of their afternoon's excitement – but Snubby interrupted.

'Listen!' he said, 'something awfully peculiar happened this afternoon, when I was lying here, half asleep. Loony heard a noise first, and barked. I sat up, thinking those men might be coming into the room – but I hardly thought they would, with Loony barking like mad! But the noise didn't come from *outside* the room – it seemed to come form *inside*.'

'What noise?' asked Barney, puzzled.

'I don't exactly know how to describe it,' said Snubby.

277

'It was a – a sort of bumping and banging – and it came from that side of the room near the fireplace, but – well, as if it was *under* the room, sort of muffled.'

'Oh, Snubby!' said Diana, looking suddenly scared, 'it must have been the Noises that Mr Jones warned us about, when he said we'd better not have this room, we'd far better have the Best Room. He said that Noises sometimes came in the night – but I've not heard any so far. Miss Pepper and I thought it was just nonsense, of course. And now *you've* heard them!'

'Yes. I certainly heard them,' said Snubby. 'I didn't dare to get off the bed – and Loony began to bark his head off, and ran all round the floor, trying to find out what was making the noises.'

'What on earth *were* they, do you suppose?' said Barney puzzled. 'Is there a door behind the chest – a cupboard, or something?'

'Look and see,' said Snubby, and the three children peered round the back of the great chest. But no door was there, only the stone wall.

'It's a mystery,' said Barney. 'But I say, we'd better not stay up here discussing it. Miss Pepper will wonder what's up again. Are you coming down to tea, Snubby?'

'Rather. I feel jolly hungry – and I don't particularly want to stay alone in this room of noises any longer,' said Snubby. So down they all went, to find Miss Pepper patiently awaiting them, and a very fine tea on the table.

The four children, with Miranda and Loony, went to have another talk after tea, in the caravan. They shut the door and spoke in low voices. Barney told Snubby of their idea to follow the men, if they went out that night, and see if they went up the 'long, long hole.'

'I'd like to come – but I don't think I will,' said Snubby. 'I feel a bit shaky now I'm up. I'll tell you what I will do, though – when you have left the caravan to follow the

278

men, I'll nip upstairs and lie on the couch in the room next to Diana's and wait till I hear them come back – and report to you as soon as you reach the caravan.'

'Righto, if you want to,' said Barney, understanding quite well that Snubby wasn't particularly anxious to stay all by himself in the caravan that evening!

'Better find our torches,' said Roger. 'We shall certainly need them. Do you mind if we take Loony with us, Snubby?'

'Er – no,' said Snubby, wishing he could say yes, he did mind! He knew he would feel much safer with Loony somewhere near him!

They found their torches, and then put on warm jerseys, for the wind had changed and now blew cold. They went to join Miss Pepper, and set off for a short walk in the hills behind the inn. A bird flew up as they walked over the heather, and Barney pointed to it solemnly.

'Is that a Crazy Corn-Crake, or a Yellow Black Bird?' he said. 'We'd better ask the Proffessor when we get back!'

They all began to feel excited when they were back from their walk, and had had supper.

'It's not dark till about ten,' said Barney, 'so we'll have a game of cards, shall we? Anyway the men are still here, so we needn't worry about them slipping off without us seeing them!'

The two men were walking up and down outside the window well in sight. At about ten they came indoors and went upstairs.

'Getting ready to go, I expect,' said Barney. 'Come on, we'll be off to the caravan and keep watch. We'll say good night to Miss Pepper now.'

Miss Pepper and Diana went upstairs to bed. 'Good luck!' Diana whispered to the boys, as she left. Snubby went off to the caravan with Roger and Barney, who slipped on their warm jerseys again and put their torches into their pockets. Snubby began to wish he was going too, but they wouldn't let him.

'You still look groggy,' said Barney.'We don't want you fainting, just as we go up the long, long hole, and watch for the men. They won't guess we're watching, so they'll probably come straight out of the front door.'

The caravan was in darkness, and the three boys peered out of the window, Miranda too. At about half past ten they heard footsteps, and by the light of the half moon saw the two men coming down the slope.

But wait – there were *three* men, not two! Barney nudged Roger sharply. 'See who the third man is – Mr Jones! I *thought* he was in this, didn't you?'

'Wait till they've gone round the bend, then we'll follow,' said Roger excited. 'Gosh! Fancy Mr Jones going too!'

They slipped out of the caravan with Loony as soon as the men were round the bend, leaving poor Snubby alone. He didn't like being on his own and shot up to the house, creeping up the stairs and going to the room next to Diana's as he planned. He lay down on the couch there wishing heartily that he had Loony with him.

Meanwhile Roger, Barney, Miranda and Loony were stalking the three men. They were now down on the beach, making their way to Merlin Cove, where the caves ran back into the cliffs. The moon gave enough light for the men to be clearly seen in front of them, and the boys were careful to keep out of sight by walking close to the cliffs.

'Tide's coming in,' said Roger, 'and its going to be pretty high tonight, with that strong wind blowing off the sea. Hallo – look! Is that a boat coming ashore?'

They stopped, keeping close to the cliffs, and watched a boat being rowed ashore. Two men were in it, and the boys felt sure that the man rowing was Morgan. Who was the other?

'Jim, probably, whoever he is,' said Barney. 'I can't see that they have much in the boat – if they are bringing in goods they have smuggled in a fishing catch.'

The three men did not go down to the boat when it grounded on the sands but waited while it was pulled up on the beach by Morgan and the second man. Then Morgan and his friend began to lift what seemed to be big packets out of the boat, and went up to the caves with them.

The men took them and disappeared into the cave marked 'Dangerous.'

'The one we were in this afternoon, of course!' said Barney.

Then Morgan and his friend went back to the boat and staggered up the beach with more packets, evidently the last ones for they, too, disappeared into the cave. One of them came back and pulled the boat right up to the cave entrance, making it fast.

Then he too went into the cave, and it seemed as if all of them had gone to some hiding-place where the packets were to be placed.

The two boys and Loony went right up to the cave and stood outside, listening. Not a sound was to be heard except the little waves breaking on the sand as the sea came in.

'Come on,' said Barney. 'Into the cave we go, and up the wall at the back on to that ridge. Maybe we can hear the men if we listen at that hole that goes up and up,'

They went in quietly, not switching on their torches at first, for the moon shone into the cave and lighted it.

'Up we go!' said Barney, leaping up the wall on to the ridge, and pulling up a most surprised Loony. 'And don't let's make any noise, for goodness' sake. Loony, not a growl or a bark from you, or you may put us in danger. Here's the hole, Roger. I'll lead the way!'

Chapter Twenty

The 'Long, Long Hole'

The two boys shone their torches up the hole.

'It goes up and up and up!' said Barney. 'It's rather like a shaft, only not so steep, of course. I can't hear a thing, can you?'

'No,' said Roger. 'The men must be a good way up – come on!'

They began to clamber up the long, steep passage, switching on their torches every now and again to show them their footing. Not a sound could they hear until at last Loony gave a little growl of warning. They snapped off their torches at once.

'Voices!' whispered Barney. 'Voices some way in front. We'd better be careful now. Shade your torch with your hand, Roger, when you switch it on. Come on – they're a long way ahead yet. Quiet now, Loony!'

They went on again, listening for any sound from above, but could hear nothing. Either the men had now gone beyond hearing, or were being very quiet. The boys came to a very steep part indeed, and discovered that rough steps had been cut there. They climbed up them, and came to what seemed to be a small cave in the very heart of the cliff. They sat down to rest for a moment, panting with the long, steep climb. Loony ran round, sniffing here and there.

'Loony! Miranda? Where have you gone?' whispered Barney, switching on his torch and shining it round the little cave. '*Now* where are they, Roger? I can hear them, but can't see them!'

283

He got up cautiously, and went farther into the cave. He found the two scraping about behind a big rock, unearthing the bones of some small animal. 'Leave that alone!' whispered Barney. 'Come with us. We're going on up the hole.'

Miranda leapt on to his shoulder and Loony reluctantly left his find. Once more they all scrambled up the steep passage, which was, in truth, more like a 'long, long hole,' as Dafydd had said.

'Have you any idea of the direction we're going in?' asked Roger.

'No – except that we seem to slant to the left all the time,' said Barney. 'We must have got beyond the cliffs by now and be burrowing up the hills at the back of them.'

They heard noises again a little later, and stopped to listen. The noises went on and on, and sounded as if goods were being moved or stacked.

'I bet they're opening those packets and stacking the contents somewhere,' said Roger. 'Shall we go any nearer?'

'Yes – but I think perhaps only one of us,' said Barney. 'You stay here with Loony and Miranda, and I'll go as near as I dare. Keep your hand on Loony's collar.'

Barney went on up the steep passage, and soon the sound of voices was quite loud. Counting was going on – '100 – 200 – 300' Barney heard. He looked up the passage, which was not so steep here, and saw a bright circle of light not far ahead.

'That's where the passage stops and the hiding-place is,' thought Barney. 'They're all up there together. I can hear Morgan's deep voice now – I wish I could hear what he's saying – but I hardly dare creep any closer.'

He stayed for about ten minutes, listening to the sound

of goods shifted about and stacked, and voices arguing. Then suddenly he got a shock.

The men were coming back, and the lamp or whatever it was that he could see shining some way up the passage, in the hiding-place, was suddenly switched off. The beams from torches appeared instead! Barney scrambled back to Roger quickly, finding it much easier to go down than it had been to climb up!

'Roger – they're coming down!' he whispered. 'Pretty quickly, too. Come on. Where's Miranda?'

'She slipped off,' said Roger. 'I didn't see her go. She's probably gone down again.'

They went down farther, hoping to see Miranda waiting for them, but she was nowhere to be seen. Loony didn't like slithering down any better than he liked scrambling up! They came to the little round cave where Loony and Miranda had unearthed bones. 'There she is!' said Barney, exasperated, shining his torch on the little monkey.

She leapt up to a jutting piece of rock and chattered at him. 'Come here at once,' ordered Barney in a low voice, but Miranda chose to be annoying, and sat up on the rock, swaying about and chattering all kinds of nonsense.

'We'll have to go on, Barney,' said Roger. 'I can hear the men getting quite near.'

'Well, I'm not leaving Miranda,' said Barney. 'Come on – let's hide behind that rock where Loony unearthed those bones. The men will never guess anyone is here – they don't know they were followed.'

'All right,' said Roger, feeling uneasy as the men's voices became louder and louder. He and Loony went quickly to the big rock and stood silently behind it, Loony pressing against his legs. Miranda at once dropped on to Barney's shoulder and put her tiny paws down his neck.

The voices came very near, and the sound of the men's

feet was almost deafening as they slipped and slithered down the steep rocky passage. Loony couldn't help giving little growls as they passed the entrance of the small cave in which the boys were hiding.

Roger tapped him sharply, afraid that the men would hear, and stop to investigate. But mercifully they didn't, and soon the sound of their voices and feet grew less and less, until finally the boys could hear no sound at all.

'It's all right now – we can go,' said Barney, relieved, and switched on his torch. 'Miranda, take your hands out of my neck, you tickle terribly. And stay on my shoulder, or I'll never bring you out on an adventure again!'

The boys went down the hole, slithering over very steep parts, making far more noise than when they went up! They came at last to the end of the hole, and stood on the ridge of rock on the wall of the big cave. The moon shone into the cave – and what a shock the boys had!

The moon now shone, not on white sand, but on heaving water! Water that was already as high as the ridge they stood on! It caught the moonlight at the entrance, and then shimmered in the light of the boys' torches, at the dark rear end of the cave.

'The tide's come in to the cave – *right* in – and it's still coming!' said Barney in horror. 'I never thought of that. It's swept into this cave – and all the caves, of course – and the wind is piling up the waves high enough to swamp the lot. What shall we do?'

'I reckon the men only just got away in time,' said Roger. 'But, of course, they had a boat. Look out – that wave will sweep us off the ridge!'

They leapt back a little way up the hole just in time to avoid being swept away as an enormous wave splashed right over the ridge. They retreated back up the hole, scared.

'Well,' said Barney, 'it certainly looks as if we're going

to be penned up here for some time, because the tide isn't full for an hour or two. It's that strong wind that's making it so high. Blow! Snubby will be waiting and waiting for us to get back – and he'll be worried stiff.'

'I say – let's go back up the hole and see what the men have hidden in that hidey-hole, or whatever it is, right at the top of the passage,' said Roger, excited. 'Come on – it's a fine chance for us, Barney! We know the men can't come back, because they wouldn't be able to get through the water in the cave.'

'You know – that's an idea!' said Barney, delighted. 'A really good idea! If we find out what's hidden there, we can go to the police tomorrow, and tell them, not only about the men, but about what they've hidden, and where it is! If only we hadn't to make that wearisome climb all over again!'

'Oh, come on – it won't seem so bad this time, because we don't need to be afraid of the men hearing us,' said Roger, and Loony barked all the excitement in his voice.

So back they all went again, up the long, shaft-like passage – and certainly this time it did not seem so long, for they could go as carelessly as they liked, and not be afraid of making even the slightest noise! They let Loony bark, and allowed Miranda to scamper ahead as much as she liked.

They came to the last part of the passage, which was steeper than ever.

'There's a rope-ladder here, at the very end,' panted Barney, shining his torch in front of him.

Roger saw a strong rope-ladder stretching up from the end of the rocky passage to the entrance of the hiding-place. He held Loony while Barney went up the rope with Miranda. Then he went up too, leaving Loony below.

The boys stared round at the hiding-place. It was about eight feet square, a natural hole in the rock that someone had made into a kind of cell by chipping the walls smooth, and the floor level. It was stacked with oblong packets, marked with numbers. Except for a few empty bottles which had held drink of some kind, and a couple of old rugs, there was nothing else to be seen.

'Gosh – what a wonderful hidey-hole!' said Roger, looking round. 'I wonder who first discovered it. Barney, what do you suppose is in those packets?'

'I think I know all right!' said Barney. 'They're packets of stolen bank-notes! Bank-notes that can't be passed for some considerable time, because the numbers are known – but which could be shipped across to Ireland easily enough, perhaps from this Welsh coast – or stored till the hoo-ha and excitement has died down, and then used some time in the future!'

'I *say*! But there must be millions here!' said Roger, amazed. He patted a big packet. This will be about the only time in my life that I shall ever be able to say I have laid my hands on hundreds of thousands of pounds! Barney – *now* I can see why those men got Mr Jones into their power – they badly wanted some good headquarters down here on this coast – where they could bring their goods by boat and hide them, and take them away again by boat – over to Ireland, perhaps, as you say!'

'Yes. Or help themselves to a packet or two when they knew they knew they could get rid of the notes undetected in London, or some other big town!' said Barney. 'Do you remember the last bank raid, Roger – where the thieves ambushed the driver of a bank van – and drove off in the van with hundreds of thousands of pounds? Not one note has been traced so far – and I wouldn't mind betting it's all here!'

Roger's heart began to beat fast as he glanced round at the stacked packets again.

'Could we open one just to see?' he said.

'Better not,' said Barney. 'We'll tell Miss Pepper tomorrow – and I'll telephone my father. He'll get on to the London police. The village policeman here couldn't possibly deal with it.'

Roger sat down on a pile of the packets. 'To think I may be sitting on half a million pounds!' he said. 'Oh, Barney – I *wish* we could get out of here and tell everyone! To think we're penned up here for hours because of that high tide.'

Barney glanced all round the little room, and then happened to look upwards. What he saw so astounded him that he stood as if turned into a statue, staring, staring. Roger was quite alarmed.

'What's the matter?' he said, and looked upwards too. He was as amazed as Barney at what he saw.

'A *trap-door*! A wooden trap-door! Set in the roof of this funny round hole. BARNEY! Let's open it and get out and see where we are. Quick, Barney!'

Barney was as excited as he was, but more cautious. 'Wait a bit, wait a bit! We don't know where the trap-door leads to, ass. We might walk straight into trouble! Shut up, Loony, shut up barking! Gosh, we've excited him now, too, and he'll bark the place down. I'd better go down the ladder and drag him up here. Perhaps he'll be quiet then.'

They stacked up the packets high enough to reach the trap-door, and then mounted them. Both boys raised their arms, and pushed at the wooden trap-door, which fitted closely into a square of the roof. But it would not budge.

'Must be fastened the other side!' panted Barney. 'Oh, *blow*! Try again, Roger!'

They tried again, banging at the trap-door in their impatience, making a tremendous noise.

'I expect it opens into some deserted cellar or pit,' said

Roger. 'Probably nobody will hear us, Barney. Try again! Oh, Loony, DO be quiet!'

'I suppose the men prefer to use the cave way when they bring the money in,' said Barney, taking a rest, 'because it's so easy to bring it by boat. Nobody would suspect a boat going out by night, and Merlin's Cove would be quite deserted then. But the men don't need to help themselves to the money by way of the cave and the hole. When they want it, they've only to open the trap-door and drop neatly down, collect what they want, and go back through the trap-door again. Very clever!'

'Let's try the trap-door again,' said Roger. 'We might use one of the packages as a battering-ram – they're solid enough! Do stop barking, Loony – it's quite deafening in here!'

The two boys stood on the packages – and then they suddenly leapt down in fright. Loony growled fiercely, making Miranda jump in fear on to Barney's shoulder.

'Someone's opening the trap-door!' said Roger. 'I can hear noises up above. Oh, gosh, Barney it's not those men, is it? We're trapped if it is. We've no getaway at all!'

Chapter Twenty-One

The Trap-Door Opens!

And now how was Snubby getting on, lying alone in the little room next to Miss Pepper's, missing Loony very much – listening anxiously for the two men to return to their room nearby?

He was quite determined to creep behind the big couch he was on, if he heard so much as a footstep! But he heard nothing at all for what seemed like hours, and at last fell asleep very suddenly indeed.

Diana too, in the next room was fast asleep, but Miss Pepper was still reading a book. At last she yawned, shut her book and blew out her candle. She was just going to sleep when she thought she heard a little noise. She opened her eyes and listened – no – it must have been an owl outside.

She fell asleep, and then awoke again some time later. She sat up. What had awakened her? she listened intently. There – a noise – it came again and again. It almost sounded as if it was in the room!

Miss Pepper was not easily scared, but her hand was trembling a little as she lighted her candle again. Diana woke up, as the light flickered in the room.

'Are you all right, Miss Pepper?' she asked, sleepily, thinking it was the middle of the night, although she hadn't really been asleep very long. 'Ooooh – what's that?'

'I don't know,' said Miss Pepper, puzzled. 'I heard noises – but there doesn't seem anything to cause them.'

'Oh, Miss Pepper – they must be the noises Mr Jones

told us about!' said Diana. 'He didn't want us to have this room because of them – nor did Mrs Jones.'

'Oh yes,' said Miss Pepper. 'But I really thought that was only a bit of nonsense. There – did you hear that? A deep-down sort of noise – bump!'

'Yes,' said Diana, scared. 'I don't much like it. Where's it coming from, Miss Pepper?'

'I don't know,' said Miss Pepper, getting out of bed, and holding the candle into every corner. Diana thought she was very, very brave! Bump! Boomp! Bump!

'It's coming from the old chest!' said Diana, with a little scream.

'No, dear, no,' said Miss Pepper. 'Don't be silly. There's nothing in the chest but our clothes. You know that.'

Miss Pepper went to the door of their room and opened it, looking out, holding her candle up to make sure that the three boys were not playing some sort of a silly joke in the middle of the night to scare her and Diana. They could be very annoying at times!

But no – no one was there. She noticed that the door of the next room was a little open, and went to it. Was anyone hiding in there?

She had the surprise of her life when she saw Snubby fast asleep there, sprawled on the big sofa, still in his day clothes! What on *earth* was he doing there? She went over and shook him. He awoke in a hurry, scared stiff, thinking the men had got hold of him!

'Why are you here, Snubby? Did you hear any noises?' asked Miss Pepper, wondering if by any chance she could be dreaming it all.

'Ooh – you *did* frighten me,' said Snubby. 'What noises? No, I've heard none – but I did hear some when I was resting in your room today – bump – boomp – bump!'

'Yes – that's what *we've* been hearing, Diana and I,' said Miss Pepper. 'Come and listen, Snubby.'

So Snubby joined Diana in the next room, and they all listened. But they could hear absolutely nothing at all now.

'Funny!' said Snubby. 'Not a sound to be heard. Can I sleep on your couch at the foot of the bed, Miss Pepper – to – to see that you're safe, you know.'

Miss Pepper smiled a little. 'Of course, Snubby – but now tell me why you were sleeping in the next room, instead of in the caravan with the others? What's happened? Have you quarrelled?'

'I can't tell you just yet, Miss Pepper,' said Snubby awkwardly. 'Tell you tomorrow, perhaps.'

He snuggled down on the sofa, with a blanket thrown over him, and Diana and Miss Pepper got into bed again. The candle was blown out, and they all lay in darkness, hoping to goodness that there would be no more disturbing noises. None came, and one by one the three fell asleep once more.

Some time later Snubby woke again, and sat up, astonished. He heard a MOST surprising noise – so surprising that he thought he must have been dreaming. But no – there it was again – wuff-wuff-wuff! It was Loony barking!

'Miss Pepper! I can hear Loony barking!' he cried, shaking her awake. 'But it can't be! Di, wake up! Can you hear Loony?'

Now they were all awake and listening. Wuff-wuff-wuff! Yes, that was Loony all right. But where was he? The barking sounded near, and yet muffled.

'This is really mysterious,' said Miss Pepper, worried. 'Where in the world can Loony be?'

Then loud noises came – bang! Bang-bang-bang. They sounded almost as if someone was knocking at a door somewhere, very fiercely indeed.

'The noises *are* coming from the chest,' said Diana, almost in tears.

'Let's move it out,' said Snubby. 'I thought the same myself this afternoon, when I heard them. Come on – help me, both of you – it's most FRIGHTFULLY heavy!'

It certainly was – but they managed to shift it at last – and there, where it had stood, was a wooden trap-door, shut tightly down!

'Gosh – look at that! No wonder they didn't want you to have this room!' said Snubby. 'This trap-door must be used for something secret – for whatever dirty work those two men are doing! There – I can hear Loony again! AND Barney's voice – listen!'

'But – but who put them down there and shut the trap-door on them?' said Miss Pepper, overcome with amazement. 'I never heard of such a thing in my life! Can we lift up the trap-door, Snubby? Oh dear – I feel as if this *must* be a dream!'

'Can't be,' said Snubby. 'It's much too noisy. Gosh, they're banging at the trap-door again. They couldn't open it while the chest was standing on it, of course. Hey, wait a bit – I'll pull this handle – ah – UP she comes!'

And the trap-door gradually lifted as Snubby and Diana pulled at the iron handle!

Down below, there was great consternation of course. Barney and Roger were absolutely horrified to see the trap-door being raised from the other side! They at once thought that somehow the two men were there, and that now they would be discovered – and properly trapped. They ran to the rope-ladder and began to climb down it. But Loony wouldn't come. He began to bark excitedly as the trap-door opened, and he heard Snubby's beloved voice.

'Hey!' called Snubby, taking the candle from Miss

Pepper, and sticking it down the hole. 'Loony! What on earth are you doing there! LOONY!'

Loony nearly went mad, trying to jump as high as the trap-door and failing miserably. Barney and Roger and Miranda paused when they heard Loony's happy barking, and heard Snubby's voice.

'That *can't* be Snubby opening the trap-door!' said Barney amazed. 'But it's his voice! Quick, let's get back into the little room and see.' So back up the rope-ladder they went – and saw Snubby peering through the open trap-door, waving a candle, and Loony almost mad with joy.

'SNUBBY! How did you get there?' yelled Roger. 'Where are you?'

'In Miss Pepper's room. Under the old chest,' said Snubby, getting muddled in his excitement. 'But I say – how did YOU get down there? Gosh, this really MUST be a dream. Hand Loony up, will you, before he goes stark raving mad!'

Loony was handed up, and promptly did go completely mad, tearing round and round the room, leaping on the beds, and barking at the top of his voice. Miranda leapt through the trap-door too, and poor Miss Pepper's bedroom became a complete madhouse, as the two animals chased round and round.

Barney and Roger climbed through the trap-door, helped by Snubby, and were soon sitting on the beds, laughing and most relieved at their extraordinary escape.

'*Well*! To think that passage from the cave led right up to Miss Pepper's bedroom!' said Barney. 'I never even dreamed it would go to the inn – but of course, now I think of it, it went so very steeply up a slope and veered this way all the time right to the hill that rises up against the back walls. So easy to make a secret entrance! Everything fits in beautifully now – the men staying here – and wanting this bedroom – because it's the entrance to their hidey-hole – and . . .'

'I simply cannot *imagine* what you are talking about,' said poor Miss Pepper. 'Will you kindly enlighten me?'

'Oh, don't go all starchy, Miss Pepper darling,' said Snubby hugging her. 'We've had a secret from you – listen.'

And he and the others poured out their strange story to the amazed Miss Pepper. She could hardly believe it.

'Why didn't you tell me anything of this?' she demanded. 'I would have taken you all away from here AT ONCE.'

'That's just why we didn't tell you!' said Roger. 'We couldn't bear to leave in the middle of something mysterious like this. Isn't it *exciting*, Miss Pepper?'

'It's certainly *exciting*,' said poor Miss Pepper, quite overcome. 'I wonder why it is that I can never go away with you children without getting mixed up in something really undesirable!'

'But Miss Pepper – don't you think it's *desirable* to catch thieves?' said Barney. 'Those two men must be two of the cleverest rogues in the country – and we've found out! Oughtn't we do something about it at once?'

'Oh dear – in the middle of the night?' said Miss Pepper. 'Well, perhaps we ought.'

'Roger, you and Snubby see if you can get some of those packages up into the bedroom,' said Barney. 'And I'll go down quietly to the telephone, and wake up my poor father – and tell him to inform Scotland Yard – or his local police if he thinks it's best – of our discoveries.'

So, while Snubby fetched a rope from the caravan to fix to the strong handle of the trap-door, and then slid down it to pass up packages to Roger, Barney went quietly down to the telephone, woke up his astounded father and told him the news. He kept an ear open for the two men to come back, but not until he had put down the receiver and gone upstairs again did he hear quiet footsteps.

He slipped into Miss Pepper's room, shushing the others, and listened until he heard the men's door quietly shut. Then he slipped out again, and came back looking so triumphant that Miss Pepper was astonished.

'What have you been up to now, Barney?' she said. 'Nothing much,' said Barney. 'The men left the key of their room outside in the lock, so I just slipped out, and locked them in. They will have to wait there till the police come and let them out – because I've got the key in my pocket!'

It was very late when at last the three boys, with Loony and Miranda, went down to the caravan to get a little sleep. Diana and Miss Pepper crawled into bed, but could not go to sleep for a long time, because they had to talk and talk and talk!

'It will be an exciting day tomorrow!' said Diana – and it certainly was! Two cars arrived about nine o'clock, full of plain-clothes police, and poor Mr Jones had the shock of his life when they appeared in his kitchen!

The two men also had a terrible shock when they found their door well and truly locked on the outside – and were faced by four sturdy policemen when at last it *was* opened!

'What's the meaning of this!' blustered Sir Richard angrily – but he calmed down at once when an inspector reached out and tugged off his beard!

'Ah – George Higgins,' said the inspector. 'I thought so. You look more like yourself now, George. You and your friend took some fine-sounding names, didn't you! Would you please come with us – and your friend too. Don't worry about the bank-notes – we'll take care of those!'

And within twenty minutes the police cars had gone,

taking with them the false Sir Richard and the equally bogus Professor, both of whom they had been looking for for some considerable time. Alas – Mr Jones went with them!

Poor Mr Jones! As Mrs Jones said. 'He's not bad is my Llewellyn, not wicked at all. It was those men, with their lies and their promises. They tempted my poor Llewellyn, they lent him money to buy the inn. How was he to know they were bad men – a Sir and a Professor! And his cooking, it was so good, so very good cooking!'

Morgan and Jim were also paid visits by the police, and disappeared from the little village of Penrhydendraith for a long time.

Mrs Jones, in tears, begged Miss Pepper not to leave. 'I have no money!' she wept. 'Stay here with the children, and let me have your payment. What else shall I do? My cooking is fair, not very good cooking like Mr Jones's, but it is not bad. Have pity on me, Miss Pepper.'

'Well, we don't *really* want to leave,' said Miss Pepper. 'We can none of us go home at the moment – and I'm very very sorry about all this, Mrs Jones. We'll stay for another two weeks at least. And let's hope it will be a *holiday*, not a peculiar mystery to be solved, with noises in the night and all the rest of it!'

And a holiday it is, with sunny days, blue seas, white sands – boating, fishing, bathing, walking! All the four are as brown as berries – and they have been joined by another boy, small and just as brown. Dafydd has tagged on to them, with his faithful goose Waddle – and his precious alarm clock!

Everyone knows when the five are coming down to the beach. Wuff-wuff-wuff! Chatter-chatter! Cackle-cackle-hiss! R-r-r-r-r-ring! R-r-r-r-r-ring! R-r-r-r-r-ring!

'Somebody ought to write a book about those children and their doings!' said old Mrs Jones, as they go by.

Well, Mrs Jones – somebody has!